Fallible

HIS PERFECT CLANDESTINE LIFE
RIPPED APART BY LOVE, SEX, AND LIES

Paul Howard Surridge

Fisher King Publishing

Fallible

Published by
Fisher King Publishing
fisherkingpublishing.co.uk

Trade Paperback ISBN: 978-1-916776-35-7
Ebook ISBN 978-1-916776-36-4

A CIP catalogue record for this book is available from the British Library.

Printed and bound by CPI Group (UK) Ltd. Croydon, CR0 4YY

MIX
Paper | Supporting responsible forestry
FSC® C013604
FSC www.fsc.org

"Very few of us are what we seem."

Agatha Christie

CHAPTER 1 – A GOOD LIFE

Lucy Padstowe, twenty-nine and a woman of steely confidence, was shaking as she put down the phone. Melancholy visited her from time to time; but genuine alarm, the kind that penetrated to the core, was rare. Here habitual calm had been strengthened by two years in charge of the private office, riding the excitements and ploughing through the weary troughs… so, the cabinet secretary's words had brought on a tremor of unease that was unfamiliar to her.

"So, what do you think, Tom? Should I read more of this manuscript?" Susie said in a raised voice, having read a paragraph from an unsolicited novel sent to Tom Taylor's publishing company.

Tom stopped what he was doing. "Who on earth submitted that? They must think we are foolish."

Susie wandered into Tom's office clutching the script. "Why? I thought it was quite good." Tom frowned at Susie.

"James Naughtie. Those are his words from his novel The Madness of July; clearly our budding author believes plagiarism is the only way to get noticed."

Susie shook her head and smiled. "You amaze me. How can you remember text from an arbitrary novel?" She pouted her cherry red lips, lent forward, and kissed him on the cheek.

Tom smiled.

"I love you, boss." Susie was Tom's personal assistant. They had been having an affair for almost two years. It was not the first time he had strayed from his marriage. A succession of attractive assistants came and went over the years, some he seduced, others avoided his overtures. None remained in the job as long as Susie.

It was a warm Saturday morning. A breeze drifted across the manicured gardens of Tom and Penny's home, a substantial eight-bedroom Edwardian country house nestled in two acres of woodland, Lakewood, eight miles south of Guildford. Tom had inherited the property from an aunt he barely knew.

Inheritance aside, they had earned a good living in the book business, Taylor Publishing. Previously, Tom had worked for a major publishing house. His forte was identifying talented writers some of whom would go on to produce best sellers.

To those who knew them, they were the perfect couple. Attractive, intelligent, charismatic, and full of life. They were social magnets.

Tom and Penny had a mutual love for sailing and had invested in a yacht they had ceremoniously named The Storyteller. Moored at Hamble on the south coast of England, they often sailed across to the Isle of Wight to see friends, staying over in a cottage they had purchased on the island a few years earlier.

There were no children in the marriage. Penny had an older sister who lived in Australia, whom she saw infrequently, and Tom had an older brother, Rod, who lived in the same county, who was married to Mary, a part-time librarian. Rod drifted in and out of unsuitable work earning only a meagre living. At the time, he had resented Tom's inheritance from his aunt; he was left out of her will entirely.

While Tom had offered a sizeable amount of the spoils to his brother, Rod's pride prevented him from accepting it. It would be an understatement to say the brothers did not get on. They were very different characters. Rod lacked personal motivation to do anything worthwhile and considered himself a failure, and that frustrated Tom.

Of course, Rod would never admit to being envious of Tom and Penny's lifestyle, arguing that wealth and possessions were not for him. He preferred the simple life. Truth be known, he envied Tom's abilities and success, but to save face, knowing he was incapable of competing with his younger brother, chose instead to condemn him as exploitative, money grabbing, and right wing. Tom was a self-confessed capitalist and mocked Rod's left-wing leanings. They were, as brothers, at opposite ends of the spectrum.

Rod and his wife lived frugally; they had no choice. She came from a well-off family. Her father had built his own engineering business, so she was used to living a comfortable lifestyle, quite different from the hand to mouth existence she shared with Rod. Her father had never liked Rod and begged her not to marry him, believing the marriage would end in tears. She had ignored that advice.

After breakfast, Tom's phone rang. He looked to see who was calling but chose not to answer it.

"Who was that darling?"

"Oh, just work. It can wait."

The phone rang again. This time, he answered it.

"Hello. Tom Taylor. Yes. Good morning, Oscar… Can I get back to you later?" He ended the call. Penny frowned. She had begged Tom not to take business calls at weekends.

"Sorry, just work stuff ahead of next week's trip to Copenhagen."

Tom was attending a book fair and was also meeting with his distributor. It was Penny's birthday in a week's time, and knowing he would be away most of the week he had arranged to take her shopping in Guildford where he had bought a surprise birthday gift for her, and they were to collect it from a local independent jeweller.

Having parked, they sauntered around the city hand in hand and eventually arrived at the jewellers where they were accompanied to a private viewing room. Penny was curious.

"What's all this about?"

She was used to Tom surprising her with gifts and flowers, but this seemed special. Tom's phone pinged – it was a text message. He ignored it. A moment later, it pinged three more times. Again, he took no notice, saying he would look at them later.

Tom was always confident he could purchase items of jewellery, knowing they would be to Penny's taste. Thomas Braithwaite, the owner of the shop introduced himself to Penny. He was a man in his seventy's and sported a handlebar moustache; impeccably dressed in a black suit, white starched shirt with detachable collar, bow tie and waistcoat. He placed before them a red leather display box, delicately opening it to reveal three exquisite items. A platinum and gold necklace encrusted with large diamonds, matching earrings, and a bracelet. Penny was overwhelmed; Tom could do no wrong.

The following morning, they were drinking coffee on the veranda when the house phone rang. "Hello, Tom Taylor… Sorry, who is this? Detective Inspector Gale? How may I help you?"

After a short exchange, Tom put down the phone and returned ashen faced to Penny. She immediately got up from her chair.

"What has happened, Tom?" Tom motioned for her to sit down.

"That was a Detective Inspector from Guildford police station... Mary has been found dead at home and Rod has gone missing."

"Mary's dead?"

"I am as shocked as you are, darling." Penny was motionless, stunned by the news.

"Did he, you know, the inspector, say anything else?" It had only been a short conversation; Tom had little to tell her.

"Not much. A neighbour called to take the dog for a walk and found Mary lying in the hallway, dead. Rod is nowhere to be found. The police came across our number in their kitchen. The inspector wondered if we knew of his whereabouts, of course I said we had no idea. They have a search party out looking for him.

"But I don't understand, had she fallen or something?"

"Darling, I know no more than I have told you. I want you to relax and be patient. I am sure they will find him."

"For God's sake, Tom! How can I relax and be patient? You said it yourself; Mary is dead. She's dead!" Penny was tearful. Tom followed her into the sitting room.

"When did we see them last, Tom?" He sat next to her on the sofa.

"The last time they were here, November, I think. We had the dinner party that Ginny and George came to, do you remember?" Ginny and George were close friends and neighbours living in a house up the lane. Penny and Ginny lived in each other's pockets and met often. Tom was unsure where Penny's question was leading.

"I saw Rod a few weeks ago in the village and he looked a bit rough. Unshaven and scruffily dressed." Tom was not surprised by the revelation. Rod was always scruffy.

"You said nothing at the time."

"I forgot. It was odd though, because I waved to him, and I was convinced he had seen me. Isn't there anything we can do, Tom? We could phone him?" Then she remembered Rod did not possess a mobile phone. It was against his 'eco' credentials.

The very mention of Rod's name frustrated Tom. For a moment, he forgot Mary was dead and chose to have a rant about his brother.

"He is a bloody idiot. Why the hell has he gone missing,

especially now? I am sorry but I have had it with my brother. The moods, the way he tries to foist his misguided views on me. Do you remember at the dinner party when they were here, he spouted off about the government's green agenda and accused me of not caring about the environment. He said I should get rid of the Porsche and the Range Rover and go electric?" Penny shared that view but was reluctant to say so.

"I know he irritates you, but he is your brother." Realising she touched a nerve she quickly changed the subject. They returned to the veranda and continued talking.

"Now I think about it, I have seen Rod since the dinner party. I went to a car accessory and repair store to get the windscreen wipers replaced on the Range Rover. There was a pet store adjacent and as I got out of the car, I saw Rod holding a bag of dog food. It was a bit awkward, to be honest. He seemed very keen to talk and insisted we went for a drink in the café opposite. I forgot to tell you."

Penny was eager to find out more. "So, what did he want to talk about?"

"He had been offered an opportunity, along with several other people, to become an investor in a second-hand car business by a chap he met in a pub." This surprised Penny.

"Second-hand car business? What does Rod know about cars?! I thought he was anti vehicles because they pollute the environment?"

"That is my brother, a contradiction in terms!"

"And where would he get the money to invest in such a business? They always complained about being poor?"

"I will tell you how. He asked me if I would lend him one hundred and fifty thousand pounds, just like that. Said he would repay me with interest once the business got off the ground."

"What did you say?"

"At first, I was cool, calm, and collected. I asked him on what basis he planned to invest, who the other investors were, had they prepared business plans and a budget, was it a new or existing business, where they planned to acquire stock, what he knew about the trade, what part he would play in the business, and whether he would have an income to repay any loans he took out. I also asked him what Mary thought of the idea. By the time I had got through the immediate questions that came to mind, he exploded."

"What do you mean, exploded?"

"He accused me of belittling him. Undermining his attempt to get his life back on track - not that it was ever on track - and of course, my condescending attitude! He asked me for a second time if I would lend him the money. I said no, I would not, and he stormed off."

"Why am I only finding out about this now?"

Tom felt mildly uncomfortable. "Sorry, but if you remember, you and Ginny were in the West End at a show and I did not see you until late that evening. You were eager to tell me how much you enjoyed the day when you returned, I completely forgot to tell you about Rod. Penny shook her head.

"It does not matter now, what does matter is that Mary is dead, and Rod has gone missing… Is there a link?"

Tom paused for a moment. "God, I hope not? Just thinking back, it is possible he ignored you in the village because he thought you knew about my conversation with him regarding the loan and felt embarrassed."

Penny was agitated. "Tom, I am not concerned that he ignored me, I am worried about his whereabouts and poor Mary. I cannot believe she is dead. Are we really going to just sit here waiting for the inspector to call back?" Tom thought it best they waited for an update.

For the next couple of hours, they pottered about the garden. The telephone rang. Tom rushed into the kitchen to answer it. It was the inspector. They had found Rod in a drunken, comatose state at the rear of a supermarket. The police thought he had spent the night there. They had taken him to the police station and were to question him once they deemed he was in a fit state to respond.

There was a certain amount of relief on both Tom and Penny's faces after hearing the news, but they were concerned how well he would react to the news of Mary's death assuming he wasn't already aware. The inspector agreed to call back after they had spoken to him but thought it would not be until the following morning. They both wondered whether Rod was in some way involved in Mary's death.

Later that morning, the inspector phoned again. Rod would be held in custody for further questioning. Early forensics indicated Mary had been strangled, and Rod was their prime suspect. Later, Tom discovered Rod had failed to tell the police of his investment in the car business, for fear that might complicate things. He had also told them a pack of lies about his movements prior to Mary's death. He claimed he had visited the golf club before going on a pub crawl but could not remember which pubs he had visited or name anyone he had met. The police conducted their own investigation at the golf club discovering that Rod had borrowed from members a substantial amount of cash. The inspector agreed Tom could visit Rod at the police station the following morning.

Tom postponed his business trip to Denmark and, the following morning, went to the police station with Penny. Having been told the news about Mary, Rod was in a state of shock.

"They are accusing me of murdering Mary. Why would I murder her, I love… loved her!" He broke down in tears.

Penny tried to comfort him.

"Tom. I did not kill her you do believe me?" Tom knew it was essential they found him a lawyer.

It mattered little what Tom and Penny said to him, over and over he repeated that he had nothing to do with Mary's murder. Tom attempted to calm him down.

"Look, Rod. What we think is irrelevant, it is pointless trying to convince us, what the police think is what matters right now. We need to get you a lawyer!" Rod was insistent he had no need of a lawyer, he was innocent. Tom was already irritated by his brother's outburst.

"You are a bloody fool. I cannot understand why you think that by pleading your innocence, the police or indeed prosecutors will take your word for it. You are their prime suspect. They do not have any evidence, yet, but before you know it, you will be serving time. Is that what you bloody well want?" Tom could not contain his frustration.

Rod became angry. "So, there you have it, Penny. My brother believes I am guilty of murdering my wife. What do you think?" Penny was not about to enter the fray.

"Look Rod, you are both emotional. Tom knows you did not kill Mary, but he has a point. By refusing to speak with a lawyer, you reduce the chances of being released any time soon. Please, please let us help you.

"So, you agree with Tom, do you? I am guilty?"

Tom had heard enough. "Whether you like it or not, I am going to call my lawyer, Peter Stone. He is a close friend; I will ask him to represent you. I have had it for today. Come on Penny, we should go." With that, they left Rod sitting forlornly at the table. On their way out, Tom asked to see the inspector and informed him that Tom's lawyer would be in contact to represent Rod.

Tom and Penny were silent most of the journey home. The

moment they entered the house, Penny headed to the drinks cabinet pouring them both a large whisky. Tom phoned Peter, his lawyer and friend, and explained the situation.

The following afternoon, Tuesday, Peter went to see Rod. He had an hour-long meeting to establish the facts. The police had not charged Rod with Mary's murder, but Peter knew they would if they gathered enough evidence. After leaving Rod, he phoned Tom suggesting he paid them a call at their home to update them.

He arrived forty minutes later and told them about the conversation he had with Rod, Tom's phone pinged several times during the discussion, but he chose to ignore the messages.

"Well, Rod is certainly struggling mentally, Tom. He was agitated throughout the meeting; In fact, I battled to get a word in edgeways. He told me what he remembered which conflicted with the statement he made to the police.

Tom and Penny listened attentively. "Thanks Peter. Candidly, what do you think? Did he kill Mary?" Penny was shocked that Tom would be so blunt.

"Look, Tom. You have asked me to represent Rod, and of course I am happy to do so, but I cannot answer your question. Rod repeated over and over that he did not do it. Mary left home to go to work, at the library he said, and that was the last time he saw her. He told me about the investment in the second-hand car business and there is little doubt he was duped. You can imagine someone going on a pub crawl under those circumstances. But did he kill his wife? Well, there appears to be no motive. It is what the police think and any evidence they can find to help with a prosecution we need to be concerned about. To be honest, his immediate prospects are not looking good, but the police need evidence that he strangled his wife, and that is the missing link. They are conducting a forensic search of the house as we speak." Tom's phone rang but he chose to ignore it. This time, though, he reached for the handset and turned it off. "We are grateful, Peter. Thank you."

Peter departed. Just as his car left the driveway to join the main road, Penny spotted a red sports car coming toward the house.

"Who is that?" Tom went to the window and stood staring for a moment, quickly turning and heading to the front door. Penny followed. The car pulled up outside and Susie, Tom's assistant, got out holding a file. Penny was intrigued.

"Well, well, that is a very smart car, Susie is it new?" They went inside.

"Hello, Mrs Taylor. Yes. I got it a couple of weeks ago." Penny was surprised that she could afford such a car, she knew what Tom paid her.

"It must have been expensive did you treat yourself?"

Susie was keen to explain. "No. My boyfriend bought it for me."

"Gosh, that is generous! But then, I have to say you are a beautiful woman, what man could refuse you? How long have you been seeing him?" Tom thought Penny was asking too many questions and wanted to change the subject, but Susie was insistent she answered the question.

"I have known him for about five years, but we have been seeing each other for about two years on and off."

"Did you know Susie had a boyfriend, Tom?" He said nothing and led Susie into the hallway.

"Well, if he is that generous you will want to keep him." Penny smiled.

"I am trying to, but he is anything but dependable. He tells me he loves me but fails to answer my phone calls or text messages."

"I am so sorry dear; men can be so thoughtless. Well. I hope it works out for you. I assume you have come to see Tom, so can I make you some tea or coffee?"

"No, thank you."

Penny headed for the kitchen to make a coffee for herself. Meanwhile, Tom led Susie into his study and closed the door.

As soon as they were out of earshot, he confronted her.

"Why have you come here, to my home?"

She was surprised by his tone. "Why have you not returned my texts and voicemail messages, Tom?" Despite the tension Susie went to kiss him, but he stepped back.

"For God's sake, what is the matter with you. We agreed you would not come to the house, ever!"

Susie was angry. "I had no option! You failed to return my calls and messages, what was I to think?" Tom opened the door a touch to check that Penny was not in earshot.

"For your information, my brother is in police custody and his wife Mary is dead! That is why I have been preoccupied!"

Susie showed no sign of real concern. "You could have called and told me; it only takes a second. Why ignore my calls? I fail to understand you, Tom. You say you love me and want to be with me. I should be the first person you would want to speak to, not her, Penelope," she almost spat the name… "the woman you are married to but cannot wait to escape from!"

Tom was uncomfortable. She was right; he had told her on more than one occasion that he would divorce Penny and they would be together.

"Look, I have told you several times it is not that simple, the time must be right."

"But you have been saying that for over a year. When will the time be right, Tom? Why not go into the kitchen right now and tell your wife you are leaving her? Tell her you want to be with me, the woman you love enough to buy her the red Porsche parked on your driveway."

Tom was angry, but also mindful that Penny was not far away. "I repeat, it is not that simple. Please, can we meet this evening to discuss this at your apartment, but not now. I have things to do with regard to my brother. I will come over, I promise." That was music to Susie's ears.

"Okay. What time, and will you stay the night?"

"Seven thirty, now please, you must go."

She was excited by the prospect of Tom spending the night with her. "Tom… I love you. You do know that?"

"Of course, I do." With that, they kissed. Tom led her out of his study to the front door as Penny appeared from the kitchen.

"Are you off, Susie?"

"Yes, Mrs. Taylor."

"You can call me Penny, you know. After all this time, you still insist on calling me Mrs. Taylor, but she does not have to, does she Tom?" Tom just wanted to avoid a scene, so he hurried Susie out onto the driveway without answering. Penny followed.

"Thanks for bringing the file, Susie."

"My pleasure, Tom."

Penny had her final say. "And look after that chap of yours, Susie. They can be challenging at times, men, that is, but persistence pays off, you know." Susie took a long look at Tom.

"I hope so, I have no intention of putting up with any more of his nonsense. I shall insist that he pays me more attention or else…" She drove off as Penny and Tom returned to the sitting room.

"She is such a nice girl. Her relationship sounds quite fragile. Do you know her boyfriend, Tom?" He felt distinctly uncomfortable and wanted to change the subject.

"No, I have never met him. Shall we have a drink?"

"Not for me, thanks. Did you tell Susie about Rod and Mary?"

"Only briefly. Look, with all that has been going on, I will have to go to the office for a few hours this evening. I have cancelled my trip to Denmark, but I have a few loose ends I need to sort out. Is that okay?"

"Of course, darling. I fear we will both be consumed by the Rod and Mary situation for some time to come."

After an early supper, Tom left for the office, or at least that is what Penny believed.

CHAPTER 2 – INFIDELITY

Tom headed straight for Susie's apartment in a desirable part of central Guildford. Tom was still agitated that she had driven to the house unannounced which worried him and he needed to clear the air. They had an understanding that she was never to go to his house unless invited, but she had broken that pledge.

Susie was dressed provocatively in a revealing nightie, Tom was hesitant.

"What is the matter, Tom?" They stood apart looking at each other.

"Susie. You must not come to the house again, promise me?" Susie's mood changed.

"It is all your fault. If you had answered my text and voice messages, there would be no need." Tom retaliated.

"For God's sake! I told you my brother's wife is dead, and my brother has gone missing. Dealing with that is far more important than answering your messages?" Susie stormed into the bedroom, and Tom followed.

"You must understand…" before he had a chance to finish, she snapped back at him.

"I am sorry, Tom. It is you that fails to understand… I gave up my boyfriend two years ago because you wanted me to yourself. You said over and over that you wanted to be with me and would divorce your wife…"

"But I do, I do… but it is not that simple." He knew he had made idle promises he could not keep.

"And you have said those very same words over and over, but that is all they are, words!"

Tom retreated to the sitting room and looked out of the window. Susie came up behind him and hugged him.

"Darling, I want you, and you want me, so why do we have to wait for the right time, and what does that even mean?"

Tom knew he had made endless promises to her. He had manipulated her to maintain the relationship. He bought the Porsche and the apartment for her, but it was clearly not enough. She wanted him to leave his wife and marry her. It was inevitable he would need to deal with the situation one way or another. He thought for a moment before responding.

"Susie, you know I love you. You know I want to be with you, but please understand it makes no sense to rush into something we will regret unless the time is right." Susie sat on the sofa.

"Tell me, what would constitute the right time, Tom?" He had to produce a compelling answer that would satisfy her, at least for now.

"If I did as you ask and literally told Penny today that I was leaving her for you, how do you think she would react?"

"Why would I care how she reacted. You love me not her. You keep saying you want to be with me and that your marriage is stale and boring. I imagine from what you have told me, she would be pleased to be rid of you anyway."

Tom swallowed hard. He had told her a pack of lies over the preceding two years to win her affection. Of course, the reverse was true. He did love Penny, but he also wanted to maintain the affair with Susie, and assumed he could continue lying to her and would get away with it.

"Look. I have the business to think about, the house, and the rest of the assets. Penny owns half of everything. If I do as you ask, can you imagine how difficult it would be to obtain a divorce without losing everything I have worked for over the past twenty years?" This was not going to quell Susie's demands.

"You, see? Another excuse. I do not care about any of those things. I am not after your money, or your assets, Tom. I love you and you are all I want! We could get by; I know we could.

We could live here in the apartment." Tom knew he was not going to win her over with anything he said.

"You are so sweet. If only life were that simple. I promise you I will find a way of sorting this out, but please, you must give me more time… please just let me get through this family drama with Rod and Mary and I will do as you ask. When this is all over, I will tell Penny I want a divorce." Susie grabbed him and led him into the bedroom. He switched off his phone.

It was close to 11.00 pm and they were still in bed. Tom looked at his watch, shocked at the time.

"Look, darling, I cannot stay the night I am sorry. I need to go to the police station first thing in the morning to try and get my brother released."

"Oh, do you have to go?" Tom got out of bed and got dressed. "Will I see you tomorrow, Tom?"

"Not sure I will be able to see you, but I will call you as soon as I can. Love you!"

Tom left for home. He switched on his phone and immediately received three ping's. Text messages from Penny. He read them. 'Tom, where are you? I'm worried. I called the office expecting you to be there?' The second message read, 'Tom, I can't get you on your mobile or the office phone. Please get back to me ASAP.' The third message sent a shiver down his spine. 'Tom. I am going to the office. I am worried something has happened to you.'

For two years, he had enjoyed a mistress readily available in the office or at her apartment. It was perfect. He also had a loving wife, a successful business, and a degree of wealth. As he drove away from the apartment bought for Susie to live in, he knew he was in danger of his world collapsing around him. Previously, he fobbed her off with lies and promises about bringing his marriage to an end. A wife he claimed he had no affection for, but now, with Susie arriving on his doorstep, she had turned up the heat. Susie loved him and would not be mollified. He had successfully kept Penny in the dark about his mistress, she was blissfully unaware that her husband was cheating on her. There was no reason for his relationship with Penny to suffer, he genuinely loved her. Tom was an expert in covering his tracks. It was easy. He had a business that demanded he was flexible and able to be away from home or at the office at the drop of a hat. The perfect cover.

Penny's third text complicated things. It would take her twenty minutes to get to the office. Once there, she would instinctively know he had not been there himself. The likelihood was that she would call or text him again and he would need a plausible excuse. He was right. His phone rang and he answered it.

"I am sorry I have not responded to your messages. The car broke down and I had to call the relay service."

"Thank goodness, I was really worried about you! I went to the office, but I could see you had not been there. Where are you now?" There was relief in Penny's tone.

"The car is fixed. Nothing serious. I am on my way home. Should be about twenty minutes, see you back at the house."

It was almost 11.55 pm when he arrived home. Just as he parked in the driveway, Penny too arrived and parked next to him. They got out of their cars and embraced.

"Sorry. It has been a nightmare trying to get someone to come out to fix the car."

"When you broke down did you not think to let me know?"

"I did not want to worry you and believed the relay people would be there in no time."

Penny offered to make some coffee. Tom declined wanting to avoid an inquisition. "Gosh, I am tired I think I will go to bed."

Within the hour, Penny was asleep next to him as he

remained wide awake, thinking about how best to deal with the increasingly complex relationship with Susie. It was now evident he could only manage her demands for a limited period before she did something that would undermine the secrecy of their relationship. Despite the danger, he was reluctant to give her up. That too had challenges. Susie would not go lightly, and their relationship would come out into the open. Then what? Tom needed to discover a way of keeping Susie happy whilst maintaining his marriage. But how?

The following morning, they woke early. Tom made tea and took it up to Penny. Overnight, he had slept little, trying to fathom a way forward.

"Thanks for the tea, darling. So, what was the matter with the car yesterday? It was only serviced a few weeks ago?"

"Alternator." Tom knew little about car mechanics and Penny even less, so that one word sufficed.

"I wonder how Rod is today. He must be feeling wretched. Can you imagine what he must be going through?" With all that was going on in his life with Susie, Tom had quite forgotten about his brother's predicament.

"Yes, I will find out. I will call Peter when I get to the office." Penny looked at him quizzically.

"Why are you going back to the office today? Tom understood why she was asking but was mildly irritated by the question.

"The fact that I have postponed my trip to Denmark does not mean I am on holiday. There is always plenty to do." Penny was surprised by his tone of voice.

"Why are you barking at me, Tom. I was just asking."

Tom took a deep breath. "I am sorry, I have so much on with work and Rod… I am a little on edge." He kissed her on the cheek and gave her a cuddle.

After breakfast, he left for the office. Penny took the

opportunity to call her neighbour and friend Ginny and invited her around for coffee. Ten minutes later the doorbell rang. Ginny was usually full of fun, but today, she looked worried. Penny was concerned.

"Did you speak to George?" The last time they had met, Ginny told her she discovered George was having an affair. Penny advised her to confront her husband.

"Yes, I did. I kept remembering what you said about living with George knowing there was no trust. I knew it would be impossible to put aside seeing them in the restaurant together, so I plucked up the courage to tackle him when he returned home from work yesterday. He came in and barely acknowledged me. I asked him how his day had been, but he ignored me. I was really angry. I followed him into the study and told him I had seen him in a restaurant with a young woman. I asked who she was. I was expecting him to panic, but he was cool, calm, and collected. He just said, 'What woman, which restaurant?' I was shaking, a bundle of nerves. I said he had lied to me that he had a meeting in Birmingham and would stay overnight in a hotel because I saw him having dinner with a young girl in Epsom."

Penny was keen to know what happened next.

"So, did he deny the relationship?" Ginny was tearful as Penny tried to comfort her.

"It was surreal, not at all what I expected. I thought he would be nervous and deny everything, but no. He just looked me in the eye quite coldly and said, 'I am sorry, Ginny. I am having an affair, and I should have told you sooner. It is best if I pack a bag and leave. We can discuss a divorce once the dust has settled.' As you can imagine, I was devastated. I could not believe what I was hearing.

After twenty-seven years of marriage, it was all over in just one short statement. I was dumbfounded. I did not know what to do or say. I wanted to scream. I wanted him to tell me it was over, but I just kept silent. He simply went upstairs, packed a bag, and left."

"I am so sorry. I cannot believe George would do this to you. Surely, he cannot believe a relationship with a young woman would last. Men are such fools. They seem incapable of seeing beyond the next sexual encounter and are prepared to sacrifice everything, and for what?" Ginny was inconsolable. "Added to that, Jack died suddenly. I know he was old, but it was a shock." Jack was Ginny's terrier and very much a part of the family. Penny knew she doted on him.

"Goodness me, I am so sorry. So much to contend with. Why did you not call me?"

"Oh, I did not want to trouble you, I know you and Tom have enough on your plate with Mary's death and Rod in custody."

Penny was concerned, wanting to know what Ginny planned to do next.

"Have you heard anything from George since he left? How are you going to deal with all this?"

"I struggle to sleep. I really am in a tizz. I don't know whether I should beg him to come back and forgive him, or just accept the marriage is over and get on with my life." Penny felt guilty for suggesting Ginny confront George in the first place. She had no idea this would be the outcome.

They spent the rest of the morning talking about the options Ginny had and concluded that it was worth trying to reconcile with George.

CHAPTER 3 – THE INVESTIGATION

Tom spent an hour in the office unravelling arrangements for his business trip to Denmark, knowing he would be embroiled in his brother's detention. His phone rang. It was his solicitor.

"Tom. Sorry to call you this early but I thought I should let you know that the police have decided to detain your brother for another seventy-two hours. I have arranged to see him later this morning." Tom was not surprised.

"So, he is their key suspect?"

"Certainly, but they will not charge him unless they have enough evidence. I need to find out more. I rarely express a view in such matters but on this occasion, I do not believe your brother murdered his wife."

"Well, that is a relief." Peter was quick to respond.

"That is only a personal take on things, Tom. I will call you again with an update later."

"Thanks Peter. I will await your call."

As Tom put the phone down, Susie arrived. She immediately threw her arms around him. He withdrew awkwardly. "Is something the matter, darling?"

"Oh, I am sorry. I have just been told that my brother has been detained for another seventy-two hours. At least my solicitor, you know, Peter, who is representing him, thinks my brother is innocent."

Susie responded without thinking, "Perhaps your wife murdered her?" Tom glared at her. He was outraged she would suggest such a thing.

"I cannot believe you just said that! What is the matter with you?"

Realising her blunder, Susie backtracked. "Tom, I am sorry. Forget what I said. Of course, I did not…" But Tom was not about to listen to an apology.

"Bloody stupid. Do you honestly think making a remark like that brings me closer to you? Well?"

"What can I say, but you must understand my frustration. You constantly tell me you love me and want to spend the rest of your life with me but do absolutely nothing about it. You said a year ago that you would get a divorce…"

Tom had to remind himself that it was his fault. He could no longer assume his lies would suffice. The relationship was at a crossroads where he could lose everything if he acted irrationally. She loved him, and wanted to be with him, and believed from what he told her, it was just a matter of time before they would be together as a couple.

"Look, I am sorry. I have so much on my plate to deal with. I need you to be supportive and by that, I mean giving me space to sort things out with my brother. I cannot focus on anything else right now." Of course, that was perfectly acceptable to Susie. He was telling her that he still wanted her and would, in time, deal with matters so they could be together. Yet another compromise, a promise that she would agree to, at least for the time being.

"Susie. Take the day off? Do you remember that dress we saw in town a couple of weeks ago? I know you wanted it. Go and buy it and l will settle up with you."

"You are such a lovely man, and so generous too. Just how I expect my boyfriends to be! So, will I see you later in the week? Please, please call me, Tom, and let me know how things are going with your brother and pop round to the apartment if you can. And remember you have some people to call about the cancelled trip." Tom grabbed her, and they kissed. Susie left with a smile on her face.

As she closed the door, his phone rang. It was Penny.

"Darling, I have the police inspector here at the house. He said he wants to question me about Mary's death. Can you come home. I want you here?" Tom was alarmed.

"Can you put the inspector on the phone, darling?" A pause, then Tom heard a man's voice on the other end of the line.

"Mr. Taylor."

"Hello, inspector. What is all this about? You want to question my wife about Mary's murder?"

The inspector insisted it would not be necessary for Tom to return, but Tom insisted he would. The journey would take twenty minutes.

As he arrived at the house he was greeted by Penny, the inspector, and a policewoman.

"What is this all about, inspector? Why do you need to question Penny? Shall we go into the drawing room."

"I need to ask Mrs. Taylor a few questions if I may."

"Of course, inspector," replied Penny, "but I am puzzled… why me?"

"We completed a forensic search of your brother-in-law's house and found a letter addressed to Mrs. Mary Taylor apparently from you, warning that unless she stopped seeing your husband, Tom, you would kill her." Penny was visibly shocked and paused before she responded.

"From me…? From me, about Tom? No, I think you have made a mistake, inspector."

"The content is explicit. The letter refers to your husband's affair with Mrs. Mary Taylor and is signed, 'Penelope'." Penny and Tom looked at each other.

"I am at a loss for what to say. Can I see the letter."

"I have a copy; the original is with forensics." He handed the letter to Penny. She read it aloud.

"'Bitch! How could you treat me like this, Mary? Please leave Tom alone. I have seen you together. How do you think I feel seeing the two of you together like this?'"

Penny shook her head in disbelief.

"Inspector, I do not know what to say, but I certainly have no knowledge of the letter, despite the fact it seems to have been typed on our personal home stationery. But I am not the author, Inspector! Someone else has typed it. It could be anyone, but why?" The inspector looked at Tom.

"We also found a locket in her personal belongings engraved 'To Mary, love T.' Tom was keen to defend Penny.

"This is bizarre, Inspector." The inspector ignored him.

"So, you deny any knowledge of the letter, Mrs. Taylor?"

"Emphatically! I cannot begin to tell you how ridiculous this is! Of course, I did not type it!"

He turned to Tom.

"Mr. Taylor, did you have an affair with Mrs. Mary Taylor?" Tom looked at him eyes wide open.

"Inspector. No, of course not, and I have no knowledge of any locket either. Perhaps 'T' was a past boyfriend before she met Rod? Who knows, but I can assure you 'T' is not me!" Penny spoke.

"Why on earth would anyone want to implicate us in this way? Surely Rod must be able to shed some light on this?" The inspector was unconvinced.

"I am afraid I must ask you both to accompany me to the police station for further questioning." Tom was taken aback.

"What, you are arresting us?"

"I am not arresting you, just asking you to come to the station for further questioning. If it is not convenient right now, in a couple of hours." Tom and Penny agreed to the latter and the inspector and the policewoman left.

"Can you believe what is happening, Tom? Why did Mary have that letter authored in my name? Can you think of any reason why we are being dragged into this?" Tom was equally surprised by the revelations.

"None of this makes any sense. I must call Peter and ask

him if he will join us at the police station later. I know this may sound odd, darling, but you really have no idea about the letter and the locket?" Penny looked stonily at Tom.

"Are you serious? Do you really think I am hiding something, Tom?"

"No, of course not. I asked in case there is something we can relate to that makes any sense."

"And what about you? Were you having an affair with Mary?" Tom frowned.

"Fair enough. I am sorry, it was stupid of me to ask." Tom went into his study to call Peter. It was made clear in the conversation that Peter could not function as their legal representative as he had already been appointed to manage Rod's defence. Penny joined him in the study.

"I have tried over and over Tom to understand why someone would type that letter as if it were from me. And the locket. I am worried, Tom."

"Look. We know we are innocent, so there has to be an explanation. The letter was either typed by Mary herself, but then, why would she do it, or a third party has tried to implicate us to conceal their identity. One way or another, I am confident the police will find the truth."

To relieve stress Penny was keen to talk about something else.

"By the way, have you heard the news about George?" Tom wondered why she had changed the subject.

"George has left Ginny."

"Left Ginny, why?"

"He has been having an affair with a young woman. Ginny went through his diary and found the letter 'A' appearing in his notes. He was due to have dinner with 'A' on a particular Tuesday evening in a local restaurant, but he told Ginny he would in Birmingham on business and would stay overnight.

She went to the restaurant and waited to see if they would arrive, and they did. Who would have thought that George of all people would have an affair?" Tom felt uncomfortable.

"Goodness me! Had George mentioned anything to you, Tom?"

"No. Nothing." Penny continued.

"Ginny confronted him about it, and he readily admitted he was having an affair and wanted a divorce. He packed a bag and left that evening. As a matter of interest when did you see him last?" Tom was decidedly ill at ease.

"When we played golf a couple of weeks ago."

"And he said nothing, not even a hint?"

"Darling, I would have told you if he had." Penny shrugged.

"I know what you men are like, you stick together." Tom wanted to move onto something else.

"Do you have any plans before we head off for the police station?"

"No, not really. Life's odd. I mean, one minute we are happy, and everything just runs its course, then Mary's dead, Rod's in custody, and we are accused of being involved. George leaves Ginny… and I forgot to mention Ginny's dog died. All in the space of a few days."

"Cheer up darling, we will sort this out. Shall we go? I don't want to get held up in traffic."

As they entered the police station, the inspector was there to meet them. Tom waited in a holding room while Penny was led to an interview room for questioning.

The interview lasted for thirty-five minutes. The inspector wanted to know more about the relationship Tom and Penny had with Mary and Rod. Penny was honest and forthcoming. She explained that the two brothers had a distant relationship, and when they were together their views clashed on almost every subject. At the heart of the problem was Rod's envy of his younger brother's business success and the lifestyle Tom and Penny's enjoyed. By comparison, Rod was unable to hold down a job for any length of time and he and Mary struggled to make ends meet financially.

Penny went on to explain that Mary had come from a well-off family who witnessed Rod's character flaws and wanted nothing to do with him. Mary's parents had tried to dissuade their daughter from marry him, believing the marriage would end in failure.

She explained about the arguments the brothers had, Rod's attempt to invest in the second-hand car business, the fact that Rod had extended their home mortgage without Mary knowing, by forging her signature on bank documents, and the money Rod borrowed from friends at the golf club etc… She didn't hold back.

The inspectors first interview with Rod after his arrest had not revealed the investment in a second-hand car business nor Rod forging Mary's signature, although Rod was unlikely to admit to that even when intoxicated. He saw both revelations as significant. The inspector then turned his attention to the letter, allegedly from Penny to Mary when she threatened to kill her. Once again, Penny denied any knowledge of the letter or its content.

Tom's interview raised some suspicions in the inspector's mind. When asked about the relationship he had with Rod and Mary, he admitted a difficult relationship with his brother and broadly repeated what Penny had told him earlier but when questioned made no mention of Rod attempting to raise cash for an investment. Tom emphatically denied he had ever had an affair with Mary. When the inspector asked Tom directly if Rod had any money worries, again he denied any knowledge.

Of course, Tom did not want to raise the matter believing

it would further implicate Road in Mary's murder whether he had committed the crime or not. And anyway, he believed it was for the police to conduct their own enquiries. The inspector had a different view and referred to his interview with Penny. Caught out, Tom attempted to justify his reasons for not mentioning the matter but found himself floundering. The inspector reminded Tom he was obliged to tell the truth and be forthcoming with any information relevant to the police enquiries. The inspector moved on to the locket found in Mary's bedroom and suggested that Tom had bought it for Mary as a token of his affection. He pressed Tom on his relationship with Mary several times which failed to gain traction. Tom again flatly denied any knowledge of the locket and the alleged relationship. The interview concluded and like Penny, he was told he might be called again for questioning.

Later, Tom expressed his frustration that Penny had gone into so much detail about Rod and Mary's life and problems and especially the business investment, the loans, and Rod forging Mary's signature. He had told Penny about the latter, never expecting her to tell anyone let alone the police. "Why on earth did you tell the inspector about Rod's investment in the car business and why, oh why, did you tell him that he had forged Mary's signature? It gives the police additional evidence that Rod had a motive for killing her!" Penny was not used to Tom lashing out at her in such an aggressive manner.

"I am sorry, Tom, but I just answered the inspector's questions. What was I supposed to do?" Tom gritted his teeth.

"I too am sorry, I did not mean to come across in such a harsh way, but you can see by saying what you did, you have given the inspector further evidence of Rod's guilt? Penny paused for a moment.

"No. I have done nothing wrong. I just told the truth. Did you expect me to lie?" Despite Tom's frustration, in a roundabout way, he could see her point of view. They remained silent for the remainder of the journey home. Tom's phoned pinged several times. Only after they entered the house did he look to see who had sent the messages. It was Susie, but it was clear he first needed to mend fences with Penny before responding.

"Look, I am sorry, really. I should not have said what I did in the car. Of course, you just told the truth. I know that. I was just frustrated that the inspector cornered me over the situation, and I had to backtrack and made a hash of it. Penny accepted his apology. Tom's phone rang. He went into the study to answer it. It was Susie, who else?

"Hello Gorgeous. How are you today?" Tom was not in a flirtatious mood.

"I am fine, but in the middle of something right now, can I call you later?"

"Why not come to the apartment this evening, I could make supper?"

What irritated Tom most was Susie's lack of tact, her selfishness. She must know by now he was unable to drop everything at the drop of a hat. Susie, however, had no interest in his marriage to Penny. As far as she was concerned, he had committed himself to her and it was only a matter of time before they would be together. Tom, again, had to remind himself that the situation he found himself in was of his own making.

"That would be lovely, but not possible. As I told you yesterday, I have a lot on with my brother. We were at the police station earlier being questioned." Susie was intrigued.

"Questioned? What… you and your wife?" She was not prepared to utter Penny's name.

"Yes, the police found letters at Rod's home allegedly written by Penny to Mary, threatening to kill her for having an affair with me… Me! They also found an engraved locket, which I supposedly gave her." Susie found this amusing. Tom instantly regretted confiding in her, it was none of her business.

"So, when did you give Mary the locket, you naughty boy?" Tom was taken aback.

"That is not funny. Why would you say that?"

"Oh, come on Tom, you take everything so seriously…! Were you having an affair with her as well as me?" Tom abruptly ended the call and banged his fist on his desk in frustration. Penny heard the noise and went to see what happened.

"Is everything okay?" His phone rang. It was Susie, again. He chose not to answer it.

"Should you get that?" Penny was eager to know who the caller was.

"No, just Susie. I said I would go to the office to sort out some queries she has with the accounts, and I forgot. I will phone her back shortly.

"Would you like a cup of tea, darling?"

"Yes, that would be good, thanks."

Penny went to the kitchen and Tom phoned Susie back. She answered immediately but Tom paused before speaking, trying to think what to say to her. He knew it was pointless getting into a row. It would only create an atmosphere, and he was increasingly concerned that his relationship with her was unravelling, and Penny would find out. Of course, that was the last thing he wanted.

"Tom, are you there?"

"Yes, I had to end the call abruptly, I am sorry."

"Are we okay? I was only teasing earlier. I know you did not give Mary the locket, of course not.

"Susie. I know my detachment is tough on you right now.

I am unable to give you the time you want with me…" Susie stopped him in his tracks.

"That suggests that I am the only one who wants this relationship, is that true?" Tom paused. He wanted to say: 'For God's sake, give me a break,' but he knew it would only inflame the situation. "Of course, not, darling. Just give me time to get through all this police stuff and I will make it up to you. Did you buy the dress?" Anything to distract her.

"I did. A perfect fit, thank you. I also bought a handbag to match… I hope that is, okay?" Of course, Tom was not about to complain, so long as it kept her happy, at least for the time being. Penny wandered into the study with Tom's tea.

"Tea, darling." Tom nodded. Susie heard her in the background.

"She has made you, tea? You must be in her good books." It was awkward. Tom did not want to brush Susie aside by saying something so obviously contrived as, 'Okay, thanks for calling, I will get back to you,' as it would annoy her and indicate to Penny that he was trying to hide something, so he continued the conversation quite normally.

"Yes, Penny has just made some tea."

"Who is it darling?" Penny was keen to know.

"Susie."

"Oh, do give her my love and ask her how she is getting on with her boyfriend?" The tactic had failed. Now he had to contend with Susie suggesting he put Penny on the line, and Penny waiting for a response to her question.

"You can update me when I am in the office next, Susie. Thanks for making those calls for me. See you tomorrow." He put the 'phone down.

"Spoilsport! I wanted to know how she is getting on with her man!" Penny left the study and Tom sat and drank his tea, once again reminded that the relationship with Susie was becoming too much to handle. It would be impossible to contain her for much longer. Eventually, everything would come out and he risked losing everything, including the woman he really loved, Penny. It was time to put aside the affair, and indeed the notion that he might find another mistress who would be equally appealing but less demanding. An unlikely scenario.

The unanswered question, of course, was what he would to say to Susie to end the relationship, without her going berserk and telling Penny what they had been up to. Perhaps the best option was to pay her off. The apartment she lived in rent free was in Tom's name. Penny was unaware of the asset. He could gift it to her on the proviso that she stayed quiet. It was an expensive option, but it would take a gesture of that magnitude to have any chance of succeeding. He finished his tea and took the empty mug to the kitchen.

"I asked Ginny over for a coffee, is that okay?"

"Oh right, so you want me to disappear into the study." Penny was quite happy for Tom to be around but knew the study would be his preferred choice.

"Whatever you choose, darling. Join us if you wish." The doorbell rang.

"Oh, that must be Ginny now. She is very early!" Tom went to the door.

"Hi Ginny, how are you today?" She was tearful.

"Oh, dear, are you okay?"

"No, I am not, Tom. I have no idea what to do. I guess Penny has told you that George has left me?"

The last thing Tom wanted was to get embroiled in a conversation about George's affair with a young woman and for obvious reasons, but that is precisely what Ginny wanted to do; pour her heart out.

"Penny did tell me. I am so sorry."

"George is there at the house moving out more of his things. What should I do or say?" Penny stepped in to console her. Ginny turned to Tom.

"Did you know anything about George's girlfriend?"

"No. I knew absolutely nothing."

"I thought he would confide in you if he were to confide in anyone. Not even when you last played golf together?" Tom did not want to have this conversation.

"No. He said nothing." He stood motionless as Penny and Ginny walked into the drawing room. The doorbell rang, saving him from the interrogation. To his surprise it was George.

"Hi Tom. I knew Ginny was coming across and thought I would come to say hello. It has been a while. I am sure you've heard the news?" Tom was in a quandary, wondering if he should invite George in or step outside with him. In a split-second, Ginny appeared saving him from having to make the decision.

"Yes, George, why not come in, I have told them you have left me for a younger woman!" She burst into tears as Penny led her back into the drawing room.

Tom ushered George into his study. Ordinarily, a close friend would show surprise and mount an inquisition, but Tom decided that it was not the best idea, especially as he was also embroiled in an illicit relationship. He decided to let George lead the conversation.

"So, how are you, Tom? I think the last time I saw you was when we played golf, what three weeks ago?"

"Yes, I think so."

"You must be shocked to hear that we are divorcing?"

"I am, George. Completely unexpected."

"Are you keen to hear all the gossip?" Tom shook his head.

"To be honest George, it is none of my business, I am sure

there is a back story. All Ginny has said is that you have taken up with a younger woman."

"In an odd way, that sums it up Tom. I have fallen in love with a young woman, and I cannot help myself. I did not plan to leave Ginny, at least, not so suddenly, but she found out that I had lied to her about my whereabouts one evening and saw me with Angelique in a restaurant… I am not proud of myself, really, I am not, but I discovered that I have a heart, and its strings are being played." Tom feared he would get sucked deeper into the conversation, but he decided that it would look odd if he failed to ask at least a few questions.

"Where did you meet?"

"I was not looking for a relationship, truly. I was in the car on my way to Guildford about six weeks ago. No sooner had I cleared the driveway and got onto the main road, when a woman flagged me down. She said her car had broken down a mile or two back and wondered if I would give her a lift to Guildford, where she would get help. I offered to go back to her car with her, but she was insistent she wanted to go the garage, so I agreed to take her…" Tom raised an eyebrow. "She was instantly flirtatious. No woman has ever been flirtatious with me, Tom, at least, not that I can remember… even Ginny when we first met. Angelique was so attractive. She suggested we had a coffee together before we arrived at the garage, and I agreed. What can I say, I fell in love with her in an instant! Having finally dropped her off, we agreed to meet again for a drink. We did and it went from there."

"Does she live locally?"

"She has an apartment in the area somewhere. She has not invited me to her place yet, truth be known, I have not been unfaithful to Ginny in the accepted sense, but Ginny does not believe that we have not slept together." Tom was surprised that George had been so frank.

"Are you sure this is what you want, George, to end your marriage?"

"I cannot answer that one, Tom. I do not want to hurt Ginny, but I cannot get this woman out of my head. Perhaps if Ginny had not discovered I was seeing her, Angelique that is, it would have fizzled out by now, I just do not know, but things have moved on so quickly that I thought I had no option but to move out. I have taken a room in a hotel for the short to medium term. I thought about buying somewhere so we could be together."

"Wow, that is certainly moving at a pace!" Tom was now intrigued and wanted to know more.

"Have you discussed that with her, Angelique?

"No. I thought it best not to discussed it just yet, but it seemed the next logical step. I am finding it difficult to concentrate at the office. Every waking minute I think about her. I feel like a teenager falling in love for the first time."

"Well, as I said earlier, it is not for me to judge, but I would be wary. You have a lot to lose if it goes wrong. In fact, you have a lot to lose even if it goes well! Divorce is never easy and can cause a lot of pain, you may find it difficult to shed the guilt for years to come."

"Thanks, Tom. You have just added to my burden, but I know it is sound advice." Tom needed clarification.

"Now you have told me your side of the story, am I under strict instructions not to speak a word to Penny? You know if I do tell her, it will get back to Ginny?"

"You can tell her if you feel you need to, but please do not lay too much emphasis on my love for Angelique. The emphasis should be on the fact that I have not been unfaithful, at least physically?"

"It sounds to me as though you are having second thoughts?"

"As I said, I am in unknown territory. For an engineer who is meant to be logical, rational; this love stuff is out of my comfort zone. Anyway, I had better go. Say goodbye to Penny for me."

"Keep in touch, George. You have my numbers. If you want someone to talk to give me a ring."

"Thanks, Tom. I will take you up on that. George left and strolled down the driveway. In an instant, Penny and Ginny came out of the drawing room to quiz Tom.

"That was a surprise, darling, George appearing at the door?" Ginny wanted to know what he had to say for himself. Tom felt compromised. Whatever he told them about the conversation, he knew he was guilty of the same misdemeanour of having an affair. How long could he keep his relationship with Susie a secret?

"Did George pour his heart out, Tom?"

"I sense he is confused."

"Not confused enough to move out and set up home with his girlfriend, and that is what she is… a girl. She must be in her late twenties or early thirties. What interest could she have in George?" Tom felt distinctively uncomfortable.

"Sorry, Ginny it is not for me to say."

"So, you are taking his side, are you?" Penny felt Tom was not to be blamed or seen as a conspirator.

"I know you are hurting Ginny, but I know Tom would not take sides." Ginny realised she was pressuring him, and it was unfair.

"Sorry, Tom, but can you at least tell me the essence of what he said, or is that a secret?" Tom had to be careful, making sure he abided by George's wish of not placing emphasis on George's love for Angelique.

"Ginny. I am genuinely sorry you are at the receiving end of all this. We, the four of us, have been good friends for years, and as Penny said I am not about to take sides. I am sure it is on no consolation but I know George did not want all this to happen…" Before he could finish his sentence, Ginny had intervened.

"…Why did he have an affair then? Why is he moving out and demanding a divorce?"

"Emotions are high and that is understandable. All I can say is that George is upset that you found out about his friendship with Angelique…" Again, Ginny interrupted,

"…I am sure he is! So her name is Angelique? That is nice to know. Is she French?"

"No idea… Look Ginny, George does not want to hurt you anymore than he already has, and he was quick to say that despite you thinking that he has slept with Angelique, he has not."

"I do not believe him. Why would he ask for a divorce and leave home if it is just a friendship?"

"Obviously, he is very fond of her…"

"…That Tom is obvious!" It was Penny's turn to try and take the heat out of the conversation. "Ginny, darling. Tom is just telling you what George has told him. It is not fair to have a go at him." Ginny started to cry again.

"Tom, I am sorry. I am in such a state! My entire world is collapsing from under me, and I have done nothing wrong!" Tom embraced her.

"Do you think he is leaving me for good, Tom?" Penny was also keen to know how the conversation ended.

"He is very confused. If I am honest, I really do not know… The reality is beginning to dawn on him."

"What do think I should do, Tom?" Ginny pulled herself together.

"If I were to speculate, I think he will want to come back, but please do not take that as gospel. It is only speculation on my part!" On hearing this, Ginny's hopes were raised.

"I think I had better get back to the house. If George is still there, I will try and have a chat with him. I want him to stay. You never know?" And with that, she was gone.

Penny drew breath as the door closed.

"This is all so sad. I do not want you having an affair!" Penny's words resonated with Tom, and he felt guilt running through his veins.

"Did he say anything that you were not prepared to tell Ginny?" Tom was on edge.

"The trouble is, if I tell you anything, you will automatically tell Ginny and that would be unfair on George."

"So, he did say something else?"

"He did say other things but did not want me to repeat what was said."

"Not even to me if I promise not to tell Ginny?" Tom sighed.

"He is in love with this woman. He has been bowled over by her and he is confused about what to do. Time will tell if it leads to anything permanent. Now, can we change the subject?"

Before Penny could probe further, the phone rang. It was Peter. He informed Tom that the police were not planning at this stage to question him or Penny further about Mary's murder. Rod was also to be released on bail as they had no substantive evidence to charge him, at least not yet. A question had been raised about where Rod would reside in the immediate term. Rod did not want to go back to the family home as there were too many memories for him there. He asked if he could stay with Tom and Penny, temporarily. Tom was pleased they were no longer suspects but uneasy about Rod living with them and suggested he called Peter back.

"Bloody hell! That is all we need!" Penny was alarmed by

Tom's reaction.

"What is the matter? What did Peter say?"

"Well, the good news is that the police have no plans to question us again, either about the letter or the locket. The not-so-good news is that they are planning to release Rod on bail, and he wants to stay here with us, temporarily!"

"Oh, that is good news, that he is being released. We can look after him. Would that be okay with you?" Penny's enthusiasm was not shared by Tom.

"Can you imagine how we would get on. It would be unbearable."

"Do we have a choice, Tom?" Tom sighed.

"I suppose not. I will call Peter back." Tom arranged for Peter to pick Rod up from the police station the following morning. Then, he left for the office so he could get some work done in peace.

Upon arriving, Susie's car was in the car park. Tom drew up beside it. As he entered the office, she greeted him.

"Anything of interest to report?" he asked her.

"I have made a couple of appointments for you for next week in London with prospective authors. Other than that, everything is running efficiently… boss!"

She followed him into his office and embraced him. He responded tentatively.

"So, what is the latest news about your brother?"

"He is being released on bail tomorrow and will stay with us, temporarily at least."

"Oh dear, you will not like that." Susie knew the brothers were at odds most of the time.

"I am not exactly relishing the prospect, but he has nowhere else to go. Understandably, he does not want to go back to his family home, knowing Mary was murdered in the hallway."

"I suppose not. You could come and stay with me if things

get tough at home?" Tom chose to ignore the offer.

"Did you sort out the issues you had with the accountants?"

"I did. They were querying the direct debit that pays for my apartment. I was unaware you were paying the mortgage through the business I assumed you were paying for it privately?"

"It makes life easier if it is paid through the business."

"You mean you do not want Penny to find out! Naughty boy!" Tom snapped.

"Obviously, I do not want Penny asking questions, and just for the record, the apartment is in my name. You are just living there and rent free." Susie recoiled.

"Why are you so touchy, Tom. Surely, the time has come for Penny to know about us. Why should we pussyfoot around hiding this and concealing that?" The last thing Tom wanted was to go through another conversation with Susie about divorcing Penny. He had enough on his plate.

"Please, not again. We have been over this repeatedly. The time is not right. I have just told you my brother is moving in tomorrow, and I have just spent the last couple of hours consoling Ginny, a neighbour, whose husband is leaving her for a younger woman. I can hardly say to Penny 'it must be the weather I also want a divorce.' I think I would rather wait for another time. You must understand, Susie. I am not going to rush into this unplanned!" Susie was intrigued.

"So, whose leaving Ginny?"

"George. You may have met them once at a lunch party at the house?"

"Oh, yes. I remember. He is quite dull, and she is very talkative about nothing and a bit frumpy."

"Whatever, Susie. Look, can we get on with some work? I have some calls to make."

"Okay boss. And please stop being so grumpy with me. I

love you and I want us to be together. Is there really anything wrong with that?" She kissed him on the cheek, left his office, and returned to her desk.

Once more he wondered if gifting her the apartment would be a feasible way out of the relationship. It would also mean she would have to leave the business and a job she loved as much as she loved him. That would also come with a heavy price tag in severance pay, well beyond what she would be legally entitled to; perhaps a price worth paying? Tom looked through his office window to where Susie was sitting. She was beautiful, how could he give her up? It was clear he could not have his cake and eat it. He was as indecisive about Susie as George was about his relationship with Angelique. What to do?

He worked for an hour and decided to leave the office. He needed time to prepare for his brother's arrival in the morning. Susie walked in as he was finishing up.

"Would you like to come back to the apartment for a quick drink?" He knew the invitation meant more than a drink. He had to say no if he had any chance of maintaining control over the relationship.

"Not possible this evening, I am sorry." She pouted her lips as she had done on so many occasions in the past. It was impossible for him to refuse her.

"Oh, please, please, just for one drink and I will let you go."

"Just one drink. You go ahead. I will meet you there." She beamed with excitement.

"Okay. Take your time, I need to get changed!" He knew what that meant. It would be anything other than a quick drink. He would be there for a couple of hours at least. His relationship with Susie was addictive. No matter what he planned or what he thought he would do to end the affair, he was lamb to the slaughter. His desire for her was unquenchable. Despite the risk that ramped up the longer the relationship continued he wanted her, he was addicted.

Susie left the office. Tom watched her make her way to the car park. She jumped into the Porsche and drove off. It was the perfect car for the perfect mistress, but for how long? Tom left the office twenty minutes later and drove slowly to the apartment. By the time he arrived, she had already changed and was waiting for him in the bedroom. He let himself in. His phone rang straight away. It was Penny.

"Hello. What time will you be home, Tom?" He half whispered.

"I have a number of overseas calls to make, so a couple of hours or so."

"Okay, see you later. Love you." He ended the call. It was a timely reminder of the dilemma he faced. He knew he should have refused to go to the apartment, but that had been the case on so many occasions. If he were a different man, he would completely ignore the perils and make the most of the affair regardless of the consequences, but he loved Penny and had no desire for his marriage to end.

Susie had poured two glasses of champagne which greeted him as he walked into the bedroom.

Sometime later, Tom's phone pinged twice in quick succession. Text messages from Penny. They had fallen asleep as they often did after sex. He looked at the clock; they had been at the apartment for almost three and a half hours. He drew breath and opened the messages. 'Let me know when you are on your way home. I will start supper.' The next message was an hour later. 'I called the office number, but someone said you had left for the day. Where are you?' This had happened on numerous occasions. His heart sank. He had to leave immediately. Susie stirred.

"Oh, please stay. Please, please stay the night."

"You said one drink and you would let me go. That was over three hours ago. I must go. I have a lot to do."

"You mean your wife wants you home?"

"Please, Susie, let us not go there. You asked me to come back, and I did. Now I must leave." Susie put on her cute pouting face; Tom smiled. He sensed that she would accept him leaving on this occasion without a tantrum and he was right. He got dressed and quickly left the apartment for his car.

Before setting off, he sent a text to Penny. 'Sorry, darling. Half an hour.' The traffic was heavy on the journey, it was almost forty minutes before he pulled into the driveway. Penny was waiting for him.

"Where on earth have you been?" He had to think of the first excuse he could produce, something he did on a regular basis.

"Overseas calls. Just went on and on.

"But someone told me you had left the office much earlier. In fact, hours earlier?"

"I went to the wine bar to drown my sorrows."

"Did you drink and drive?"

"I only had the one."

"So, what took you so long?" It was clear his excuses failed to elicit the response he expected or wanted.

"I got chatting to Mike, you know, the chap I occasionally play golf with."

"You should call or text me I have been worried." Tom felt guilty.

"Time just flew by I am truly sorry. A bad boy!" Penny smiled. She was easy to win over.

After supper, they watched TV for a while. Tom's phone pinged. A message from Susie. 'Thank you handsome. Missing you xx.' He switched off the phone.

"I think we should have a ban on mobile phones in the house. What do you think, Tom?"

Tom agreed, relieved she failed to ask who was messaging him, an answer would have required another instant fabrication.

CHAPTER 4 – ROD

It was only 9.00 am and they had been up for hours. Rod's room was ready for his arrival. Tom was concerned that given Rod's circumstances, he would end up staying longer than Tom could bare. He knew the two of them in the same house together would be challenging.

Penny, as always, was more understanding. She knew it would be difficult for the brothers to get along and told Tom she would act as arbiter if they got into a row. She was good at that. She was kind and compassionate and knew Rod would be grieving for Mary and would want to pour his heart out, as he often did with Penny. It was far better that she provided a listening ear, Tom would be hopeless.

Tom agreed she took control of the bereavement counselling, while he would keep a discreet distance. The phone rang. Penny answered it.

"Hello, Peter. You are on your way with Rod? Okay, see you soon." She called Tom who was in his study and told him they would be arriving shortly. Tom grimaced.

Twenty minutes later Penny was at the door to welcome them.

"So, how are you, Rod? Come in, come in!" Rod looked pale and drawn. He had made an attempt at shaving, but it was evident he was not up to the task. Penny took Rod into the kitchen and did her best to engage in conversation while Tom and Peter slipped into the study.

"As I mentioned on the phone, Rod is in a delicate state, Tom. The police insist as a condition of bale that he remains with you here, should they need to question him again. My current view is that the inspector knows Rod did not murder his wife, but their investigations are ongoing."

"Thanks, Peter. I am grateful for your efforts so far. Have

you any idea how long we will have to tolerate him living here?"

Peter looked at Tom inquiringly. He knew the relationship between the brothers was strained but the question seemed heartless to him.

"I have no idea the duration was not discussed. The police insist they are informed if Rod leaves the property for any reason. Rod's house remains out of bounds." Tom tried again.

"Okay. So, until the police release Rod's house, he has to remain with us?"

"Yes. If you are uncomfortable having him here, Tom, perhaps there are other family members he could go to…" Tom was beginning to see the insensitivity of his questioning. "I am sorry. I am being heartless." He forced a smile. They returned to the drawing room. Peter spoke to Rod.

"Rod, you have my number. Just to repeat what I said to you in the car on the way here, a condition of your bale is that you remain in this house until the police have concluded all enquiries. You cannot return to your home and if for any reason you do decide to reside elsewhere you must first seek police permission and inform me. If I receive any news, I will call you. Okay?" There was a hesitation before Rod responded. He was emotional.

"They think I killed Mary I know they do; I know they do." Tom was agitated.

"Rod, please, I am sure the police no longer see you as Mary's murderer, just accept it." It was Rod's turn to be agitated.

"It is fine for you. You have no idea what I have been through…" Penny intervened, fearing the first row was imminent.

"Thank you, Peter, you have been such a help."

"Yes, I must be off. Tom saw Peter out, relieved to be able

to exit the fray. Penny offered to make some tea, which Rod gratefully accepted. He was fond of Penny and appreciated her genuine concern and compassion for him. Tom returned to the drawing room.

"Look, Rod. I am not about to make a speech, but we both understand the stress you are under right now. We will do all we can to make life as comfortable for you, but we need to agree some ground rules…"

Rod was quick to retaliate. "Ground rules? You mean, I must do and say what you expect of me!"

To a casual observer Tom's tone was indelicate, but he was not about to apologise.

"Please hear me out. I am not looking for an argument, Rod. I said we are sorry you are going through all this, and we will do what we can for you, but you need to understand that you are our guest…"

Rod was riled. "Your guest! I am your bloody older brother, and I expect more respect. All you have ever done is try and undermine me!"

Penny hurried in with the tea. Tom glanced at Penny as if to say, 'I told you this would not work' and left the room.

Penny sat opposite Rod and was candid with him. She acknowledged that the two brothers had a difficult relationship that had deteriorated over the years for no justifiable reason. Tom was not the ogre Rod thought he was. He was trying to help. Rod listened but failed to respond in the way Penny had hoped. It was clear she and Tom would have to tread warily if regular confrontations were to be avoided. As Rod finished his tea, Penny took him to the bedroom she had prepared for him. He was going to unpack and shower before coming down.

Penny joined Tom in the study. From his facial expression it was clear he was raging.

"What the hell do I have to do to please him? Is it not

enough that we are putting him up?" Penny looked scornfully at Tom.

"Tom, his wife has been murdered. He has spent the past few days in a cell. He is grieving. You know how much he relied on Mary. We need to be patient with him. Let him get upset. Let him get angry, just ignore whatever he says to you. I know it will be difficult, but it is the right thing to do." Tom knew she was right.

"I know. I will try, I will try hard to contain my frustration."

"He is your brother. We must do our best to support him." Tom grimaced. He kissed Penny on the cheek.

"I think I will go for a short walk, get some fresh air." He put his jacket on and left the house.

Rod showered and returned to the drawing room. Penny was waiting for him.

"Do you feel better after the shower?"

"Yes, thanks." He sat on the sofa and Penny sat in an easy chair. She looked at him and smiled as he became emotional once again.

"Do you think I killed Mary?"

"Of course not. We know you loved Mary, why would you want to harm her?"

"The police think I did. I know they do! I can tell by the way they talk to me. Why would anyone else kill her? She had no enemies and there were no signs of robbery, not that we have anything to steal. They asked me about the letter they found, written by you, Penny. I told them it was nonsense, but then, who else would write it? How did they get into Mary's chest of drawers in the bedroom? They also told me about the engraved locket they discovered, and asked if I was aware of an affair Mary was having with Tom! Again, I said it was nonsense, but why was there a locket in her personal things, and how did it get there?"

Penny wanted to re-assure Rod they had nothing to do with the items the police found.

"I agree. The letter and the locket are a mystery. Whoever did this wanted to implicate Tom and me in Mary's murder, but we just cannot think who would do such a thing or why?" Rod went quiet for a moment. He was reminded of the reality of his situation, something he had thought about over and over while stewing in the police cell.

"My life is over, Penny. I have lost Mary. I will lose my house. I have no way of paying the increased mortgage payments after extending the mortgage to invest in the car business. I have borrowed so much money from so many people with no prospect of repaying them. Everyone thinks I deliberately conned money from them and had no intention of repaying them. It is not true, but that is how it looks. I have no friends to speak of, not even a brother who really believes I am innocent!" Penny listened sympathetically.

"Oh, of course we do not think you murdered Mary. I said that earlier. You will work your way through all this, you really will. It will take time, but you need to remain positive. One day at a time. Set yourself daily goals…" Rod became agitated and interrupted her…

"…You do not understand. I have nothing, absolutely nothing. What have I got to look forward to? The best thing would be for the police to charge me with Mary's murder, and I could go to prison where I would not have to think about anything." Penny sat next to him.

"I know you are hurting, and I know everything looks so bleak right now, but it will get better. You will get through this Rod, and we will help you, of course we will."

"I cannot see Tom helping. He loathes me, always has. I am a waster as far as he is concerned."

"You have had your differences over the years, but Toms'

not the person you think he is. You must let him help you. If you continue to row with him, it will just make things worse. You need him right now."

Penny offered to make more tea, which came as a welcome respite. As she busied herself in the kitchen, Rod stared into space, reflecting on what Penny had said. Losing Mary, his rock, had left him vulnerable. Added to the loss of his wife, he also had huge debts perhaps forcing him to default on his mortgage. His prospects were bleak.

Tom returned from his walk and went into the study. He had cleared his head and decided how he was going to deal with his brother. He composed himself, then joined Penny and Rod in the drawing room.

"Good walk, darling?" Before he had a chance to respond, Rod blurted out.

"I am sorry, Tom. I know you are doing your best for me. I have been ungrateful. Can we start again with a clean sheet?" This came as a surprise to both Penny and Tom. They had never heard Rod utter such reconciling words before. There was an awkward silence before Tom responded.

"No. I am sorry. I know things are difficult for you right now and I have not been very sympathetic. On my walk I was trying to think of a way of helping you out of this situation, to give you a fresh start. I know returning to your house after the police have released it is uncomfortable for you; there are too many memories. I would feel the same. Assuming the police no longer see you as a suspect, and that is certainly what Peter thinks, then we need to plan a future strategy for you. I have not discussed with Penny what I am about to propose, but I am sure she will agree… We will take the responsibility for paying off your mortgage in full, and we will settle all your outstanding personal debts. We will deal with the sale of your house and will pay for a rental property for you for twelve months to give you time to get on your feet, find a job, and effectively start your life afresh. I know it will be difficult at first, starting again, but we will provide as much encouragement and help as we can."

Listening to Tom's reconciling words brought tears to their eyes. This was a grand gesture, and just what Penny would have wanted Tom to do. Rod found it emotionally difficult to respond. He got up off the sofa and embraced his brother. Tom awkwardly returned the hug as Penny looked on, nodding affirmatively. She gave them a few seconds, then joined in the embrace. It seemed the perfect solution.

"Tom, and you too, Penny. Thank you both. This is so very generous. I already feel a weight has been lifted off my shoulders. This will help me, as Tom says, to make a fresh start. I know it will be difficult coming to terms with the loss of Mary, but I know I need to! Thank you… thank you." He sat down and forced a smile. Tom continued.

"My suggestion is that over the next couple of days you draw up a list of your debts and how pressing they are, as best as you can recall, so that we can determine the extent of the liability. Once the police allow you access back to the house, you can gather any details that verify how much you owe and to whom. I can then settle the debts as quickly as possible."

Rod nodded in the affirmative. Penny smiled broadly.

"Let us have a glass of champagne." She was eager to celebrate the new accord between the brothers. Rod was happy to celebrate, although Tom would have preferred his gesture was not seen in celebratory terms; in truth, it was more a way of relieving him of the burden of his brother in the longer term than anything else. The last thing he wanted was for Rod to live with them for any length of time and be a constant thorn in their side. His theory was that by allowing him a fresh start, unencumbered with debt, he would get on with his life and, hopefully, leave them in peace. That possibility would come at a hefty price, but it was a gamble Tom thought he had no choice but to take. Time would tell if he was right.

Penny brought a bottle of champagne and three glasses in from the kitchen. They toasted the arrangement, albeit awkwardly. Tom announced he had to go to the office. After his gracious gesture, Penny was not about to complain.

As he got into his car, he reflected on what he had just agreed to. Despite pleasing Penny and elating Rod, he was frustrated that he had just agreed to give his brother, a brother he was less than fond of, what he believed would be a few hundred thousand pounds. On balance, he concluded he had little option. He did not want his brother in his life. He wanted him to settle as far away as possible, and aside from exchanging Christmas cards, he never wanted to see or think of him again.

It was also on his mind that a few days earlier, he had concluded the only way of amicably parting company with Susie was to gift her the apartment. This also came with a hefty price tag and there was no guarantee the strategy would work she could still tell Penny about the affair. Emotions run high with Susie. He knew how unpredictable she could be. She loved Tom and would do anything, simply anything to keep a hold over him. If he were to go ahead with his plan, distancing himself from her would be vital, but he lusted after her, and the temptation to spend a few hours with her at the apartment was addictive. He was in dangerous territory, and he knew it, but he called her anyway. He needed sustenance.

"Hi Susie. Are you in the office or at the apartment?" He was desperately hoping it would be the latter, and so it was.

"Okay. Would you like me to pop round for a coffee?" Coffee was never on the agenda. It was a less than subtle term they used instead of 'I would like to come around for sex, are you in?' Of course, she would metaphorically put the kettle on, but she would spend the time she had before he arrived changing into something alluring.

Tom arrived at the apartment and parked. He looked up and saw Susie waving from the bedroom window. He knew being there was a mistake, as it had been on so many occasions in the past. The more he saw her, the more she wanted him. She opened the door and hugged him tightly and he responded accordingly. This embrace was very different from the one he exchanged with his brother an hour or so earlier. For several hours, they had sex, the best sex they had had in quite some time, and Susie was the first to comment.

"What has come over you?" And then, that familiar vulnerability, "You do want me Tom, you do love me?"

Tom had had his fill, and the very last thing he wanted was to get embroiled in yet another discussion about his feelings for her. She was his mistress, and nothing more. Why can she not accept that. If only it was that simple.

"Sure."

"Is that all you can say? I thought you enjoyed me. Say we are good together." Did he tell her he loved her and wanted to spend the rest of his life with her, which would certainly quell her anxiety for the time being albeit it would be untrue making it even more difficult to part company with her when the time came; or avoid answering direct questions he knew would lead to a row. It was a predictable scenario. He tried to change the subject.

"Have you been to the office today?" It was clumsy. An innocent question, although in truth had no interest in her answer. Susie would not be fobbed off so easily.

"Tom. Answer my question. Are we good together or not? Tell me you want me, please! You used to say you loved me all the time, but now you just want sex. Is that what our relationship has come to?" This was the predictable part. Now, whatever he said he knew it would end in a row.

"Why do you constantly put pressure on me, Susie? I voluntarily came around to see you; does that not tell you what you need to know? Every time we are together you do this. It just pushes me away. You must see that." As he finished the sentence, he looked at Susie, her facial expression morphed from vulnerability to anger.

"You bastard! So, you only use me for sex! That is what you are saying. You have no love for me, it is just sex. A prostitute and her client. Over and over, you said you loved me and wanted to spend the rest of your life with me…" Tom had heard this line of attack many times before, and was bored and frustrated with her words, but in his heart, he knew she was right. In her mind she was no longer his mistress, his plaything, she had transcended the divide between casual sex and a permanent mate.

"Just listen to you, Susie! No, really! Whenever we spend time together, we end in a row, and it is always the same subject. I have said over and over, I have a lot on my plate right now, but you are deaf to what I say. If you just enjoyed our time together without all this pressure, everything would be fine."

"Fine for you. So, what you are saying is that I am your mistress, at your disposal, and I should be grateful for your attention. Is that it?"

"Of course, it is not like that…"

"…Then what is it like? Answer me this question, Tom. Do you intend to divorce your wife and marry me, yes or no?" Tom rolled his eyes and stood up.

"Why, oh why do you have to look at things in such a dramatic way? You see, this is the pressure I am constantly referring to!"

"It is pressure, because you know in your heart Tom, you have no intention of divorcing your perfect Penny. No intention of leaving her for me. You have strung me along for two years because you enjoy having an affair, it is good for your ego. Whenever you are at a loose end or crave sex, you turn to me, and I have had enough of being used in this way." In an instant, Tom saw an opportunity to put her resolve to the test.

"Okay. We will end the relationship if that is what you want. It would save you any further anguish and you can get on with your life."

"No, that is what you want, Tom. You have had your fun and now you want to discard me. Well, I will not go that easily!" The last few words sent a shiver down his spine. He had been a fool to provoke the row, and he now regretted it, and wondered how to salvage the situation.

"Susie, can we stop this bickering? We have been through this so many times. I am not using you as a convenience…" Susie was quick to respond.

"…That is precisely what you do. You use me! Tell me, and I ask the question again; Do you intend to divorce your wife and marry me, yes or no?"

Tom was not about to provide a single word answer. He knew that just saying yes may well get her off his back in the immediate term, but it would also store up problems for the next row they had. To say no, would reveal his true hand, and the consequences could be far more dramatic than if he were able to carefully orchestrate the parting. The fact was, he did not want the relationship to end at all. It suited him, and as far as he was concerned, she lived rent free in the apartment with a nice Porsche outside. A fair trade? For some it would be, but not for Susie. She wanted Tom, and marriage was her only goal.

"I know you have heard this before, but the time is not right to be contemplating a divorce. There is too much at stake. If our relationship is to work long term, you need to be patient. If you cannot agree to that, then in fairness to you, we should end the relationship." He had played his trump. Instead of answering her question, he had turned the tables on her for her to decide. Patience or end the relationship!

"You always do this to me, Tom. You string me along and I have no choice but to bend to your will. I will be patient, but in fairness to me, you must answer a slightly different question.

Tom wondered what was coming next and how he would be able to extricate himself.

"Can you assure me that within, say, the next twelve months, you will be divorced?" The twelve-month reprieve would give Tom enough time to manipulate her further without having to worry about the immediate and mid-term fallout if everything came to a head.

"Darling, of course. That is just what I need. Time to ensure a smooth transition."

"I am not sure a smooth transition is necessarily the most romantic expression for the circumstances, Tom…" But she stopped and smiled. She was back on side. He had, once again, won her over. He thought he would chance his arm further.

"So, can we agree that the subject of my divorce and our marriage will not be a topic of conversation in the months ahead? It just undermines what we have together. I love you, Susie; you must know that." This was music to her ears. She nodded in the affirmative. He had won the battle. Of course, whether he would eventually win the war was another matter, but he could at least park the Susie situation for the time being. He smiled.

"Are you hungry? We could grab a quick meal at the Italian if that suits you?"

"That would be lovely, darling. I will get dressed."

Susie went to the bedroom and Tom slumped down onto the sofa. Within the hour, they were having a meal, and to mark their reconciliation Tom bought a bottle of champagne. All was well.

After supper, they walked back to the apartment hand in hand. Susie asked Tom if he could stay the night, knowing full well what the answer would be.

"I would love to, but I really must get back. Rod arrived at the house today and I need to be there. I hope you understand." His loving, caring attitude went down well with her. He made a mental note to remember this was the way to manage her in the future to avoid confrontation. How the relationship unfolded in the longer term was of no concern to him, at least for now.

As Tom returned to the house, Penny was there to greet him. Ordinarily, she would have questioned him for being away for a prolonged period, but not today, his magnanimous offer to help his brother gave him immunity. It had been a good day for Tom. He had managed to manipulate the Susie and Rod situations extremely well and could relax without everything imploding.

"Are you hungry, darling?" Penny had waited for Tom to return to cook supper."

"Actually, no. I have no appetite at all. Do you mind if I miss supper? You go ahead." He had just eaten an Italian meal laced with garlic with Susie and would need to keep his distance from Penny to avoid questions, but after the successes of the day he believed he could invent a story about eating a sandwich earlier to satisfy any curiosity.

Penny went to the kitchen to fix herself something. Tom called out from the sofa.

"How is Rod?"

"He has just gone to bed. He was a changed man after you left. I have never seen him so positive and upbeat. He was overjoyed that his financial worries, aside from losing Mary of course, would disappear once his creditors and mortgage were paid off. He was looking forward to making a fresh start. I say it again, Tom, it was a very generous gesture offering Rod the money and I am proud of you!"

She came into the room and kissed him on the cheek.

"Any idea where he will move to?" Tom was eager to discover if Rod had given thought to the subject.

"We only briefly spoke about it. He thought it would be good if he lived locally, somewhere within walking distance, so we could all spend more time together." Tom's lip dropped. That was the worst possible news. He looked blankly at Penny as she looked quizzically at him.

"What is the matter, darling?" Tom tried to control his emotions.

"I do not want him living on our doorstep." Penny was surprised by his reaction.

"Why not? Now you have reconciled your differences, it would be good to see more of him."

"Darling, you have no idea, do you? I do not want to spend more time with him. I would like to spend as little time as possible, in fact, no time at all. My offer to help was designed to give him a fresh start somewhere else. A place, a town, or a village a distance from us where he could start all over." Penny was shocked.

"I am lost for words! Why are you being so cruel? Rod believes you offered to help him because you wanted to mend fences, and a part of that reconciliation was to spend more time together, quality time.

"Darling," Tom could not contain himself. "I am horrified at the thought of spending time with my brother. We are past all that. There is no way I want him living within walking distance, nor do I want him to think that he has a new relationship with me. Of course, we could see him occasionally. He could come here every few months and once he has settled in a new place, we could pay a visit, but that is as far as I want to go." Penny was visibly upset.

"Oh dear, then we have a problem. Rod is so excited, almost childlike that you will be spending so much more time together. He said he wanted to take us out to dinner to celebrate and would plan a round of golf with you."

"Bloody hell…! This is not what I had in mind. Not only will my foolish gesture cost us a substantial amount of money, but we are also expected to spend time him! I am sorry I cannot do it. I will explain to him in the morning the terms on which I am prepared to bail him out. One of the conditions will be that the accommodation that we rent for him will be a minimum of twenty miles away!"

Penny knew this was brewing into a disaster. "Darling, you cannot say that. Paying off Rod's debts is a kind gesture and cannot be subject to terms like that. How do you think he would feel?"

"I do not fucking care! He must relocate somewhere else. I absolutely do not want to spend time with him. He can forget the meal to celebrate and the round of golf…"

"…This is so unlike you!" Penny snapped. "After all the years we have been married, I cannot recall you being so mean, so selfish." She repeated, "This is so unlike you."

"I am sorry darling, but you know Rod and I are incompatible in so many ways. I cannot bear to be around him. I am sympathetic about Mary's death, I really am, but that does not change the way I feel about the relationship; brother or not."

Tom and Penny were completely unaware that Rod was

on the stairs, listening to their conversation. He was mortified and angry but controlled his emotions.

"Well, well. Now I know how you really feel about me, Tom!"

Tom got up from the sofa, shocked that Rod had overheard the conversation. Penny immediately went to Rod and tried to pacify him.

"Tom has a lot on his plate at the moment, Rod, ignore everything you heard…" Rod interrupted, his emotions no longer under control, he was welling up.

"I should have guessed your offer to bail me out, as you put it, was your way of getting rid of me. And here I was, only an hour ago, believing things had changed between us, that we could be close for the first time in our lives. What have I done to deserve this, Tom?"

Under the circumstances, Rod was quite measured in his questioning. He did not lose his temper, which was so often his response in such situations. Instead, he was desperately hurt that his only brother would treat him in this way in his hour of need.

Metaphorically speaking, Tom had his back against the wall. After applauding himself for the way he managed the Susie situation, and the offer to Rod earlier in the day, he was now confronted with chickens; one chicken, to be precise, that was coming home to roost.

Despite being a great manipulator when under pressure, he struggled at that very moment to think of something he could say that would in any way get him out of the very delicate situation in which he now found himself. He knew that to retract his statement about his relationship with Rod would carry no weight. He also knew that to offer an apology would be viewed as a pathetic gesture, only given as a way of saving his embarrassment. He had to confront the truth head on. "I am truly sorry you overheard our conversation, Rod, but I cannot and will not retract anything I said."

Penny knew this was an incendiary statement and would cause an almighty row. She was frozen to the spot, at a loss for words. Anything she said at this point would be unhelpful. Rod stared at Tom, then looked over at Penny, who attempted a half-smile and gently shook her head to convey that she did not agree with Tom's words.

"I appreciate you not insulting me by making excuses or backtracking on what you said, but then that is not your style, is it Tom? I have been a fool, but that is nothing new to you; I have always been a fool in your eyes. Stupid, ignorant, Rod, Tom's older and needy brother who cannot hold down a job. Unable to provide for his family! That is worth a laugh. What family? Mary's dead, but that means nothing to you. You are a heartless fucking bastard, and I will never make the mistake of ever calling you a brother again. As far as I am concerned, it is you that is dead!" He took a deep breath.

"If it is okay with you, Penny, I will stay tonight but leave in the morning and report back to the police station. I will stay there until they decide what to do with me. After that, you will never see me again." With that, he turned on the stairs and purposefully walked up to his bedroom, slamming the door behind him.

Penny was distraught. "Oh, my God! My God! What have you done?! How could you say that to him? Are you completely without feeling?"

"I am sorry, but I had to tell him the truth. He had heard everything I said…"

"…But why did you have to say…"

He went to comfort Penny, but she withdrew from him. "Darling…"

"Please do not call me darling! Do not say another word

to me, Tom! Nothing you can say now will make any of this right! You have acted like a monster! I thought I knew you, but you have a dark side, a split personality. You are a callous, insensitive, unfeeling man and I fear nothing will ever be right between us again." She burst into tears and ran into the kitchen, slamming the door just as Rod had done moments earlier.

Tom stood motionless wondering what the hell had just happened. Ordinarily, even when he acted impulsively, he was able to articulate his feelings well and was canny enough to shield his dark thoughts. In all the years he had been married to Penny, she had never seen him like this before. Her vision of him was an intelligent, kind, caring, loving, thoughtful man who did his best to take a balanced view of the world. Within the space of a minute or two, though, all that had unravelled, and she was now questioning her trust and belief in him. Nothing he could say or do in the immediate term would change any of that. If he wanted his marriage to Penny to last, and he fervently did, he would have to mend fences one by one, one day at a time. There was no quick fix. He could not expect her to respond positively to any kind of affection he offered, nor could he buy his way out of this dilemma with expensive gifts. He knew, in addition to all the other challenges he had in his life, especially with Susie, that rebuilding trust with Penny was a key priority, but how?

He poured himself a large whisky and swallowed hard. Then, he poured another and repeated the exercise. He knew Penny had gone to the kitchen to escape him but would want to go to bed. Rather than provoke the situation further, he decided to sleep in a spare room. It would be the first time in all their married life that they had slept apart when they were in the house together. After a while, Penny opened the kitchen door, checked to see that Tom had left the room, and went to bed.

It was 7.30 am and both Tom and Penny had had a restless night sleeping apart. Penny wished she could erase the drama of the day before from her mind and rewind. Tom had also spent the night awake, but he had been trying to work out his next moves. Unlike Penny, he was not saddened by his exchange with Rod. He did not regret anything he said, but he knew that to win back Penny's affection, he had to carefully plan how he could rebuild her trust and affection. That would not be easy.

He had weighed up his options as far as Rod was concerned. There was no going back on what he said, because it was the truth and Rod knew it. There was little if nothing to be gained by dribbling out an apology at this stage. Rod was not about to forgive him, and even if he did, he would be back at square one, having to spend time with his brother and make amends. That was not what he wanted, nor prepared to do. He would however stand by his decision to pay off Rod's mortgage and debts. That way, when they parted company, hopefully for good, Rod would be able to reboot his life unencumbered with debt, and Tom could salvage his own conscience, if indeed it needed salvaging.

Tom showered. He had a plan. He would wait in the drawing room until Rod came down and would deliver a short speech confirming that he would go ahead and settle his debts. If he declined the offer, he would have saved a considerable amount of money. If he accepted, even with gritted teeth, at least Penny would have seen him make the gesture, and he would be on the first step to recovering his integrity. That was the idea anyway.

It was almost 10.15 am when Rod came down, dressed and with suitcase in hand. Penny was already in the kitchen making Rod's breakfast. Earlier, she had ignored Tom in the drawing room making no effort to exchange pleasantries.

The moment had arrived when the two brothers were in the same room again. Tom started.

"Rod, if you would let me, I still want to pay off your mortgage and all your debts to give you a fresh start." It was a short statement and very matter of fact. No apology, no emotion, just the hard facts. Rod paused, visibly shaking. The emotion of the day before had not passed. He was clearly angry, but he tried to control his feelings. He knew that leaving their home empty handed, with the prospect of returning to his family home where Mary had been murdered, and then trying to deal with debts he could not repay, was too much to bear. A long prison sentence was also in prospect.

Penny had heard Tom make his offer and walked into the room. She said nothing but waited for Rod's response, it came quickly.

"As far as I am concerned, nothing has changed. I never want to see you again, Tom. I am sorry, Penny, you are not blame for any of this." His voice was wavering as he held back the tears.

"I did what you asked when you made your grand gesture, Tom. I have written down my debts, and yes, I will accept your money as your apology for the way you have treated me over the years." Penny looked anguished. She did not believe that Tom had treated Rod badly over the years as he claimed, but saying so would serve no useful purpose. Tom was desperate to lay into his brother and tell him precisely what he thought of him, but he knew that would be a pointless exercise. Instead, he glared at Rod and held out his hand.

"How much do you owe?" Rod reached into his pocket and pulled out a scrap of paper on which he had listed his debts. He thrust it into Tom's hand.

Tom could not resist reading it out loud. In his mind, doing so would achieve two objectives. Firstly, it would expose how pathetic his brother was in getting himself into such a precarious financial situation. Secondly, it would reiterate, both to Penny and to Rod, how generous Tom was about to be.

"Outstanding mortgage, £462,000. Loans from friends, £56,000. Three credit card debts, £17,400, £11,700, £16,500. Two bank loans, £191,500, £41,000. Building Society loan, £10,600. Payday loan, £4,500. Total, £638,200."

Tom looked across to Penny for a reaction. There was none. The total amount was staggering. He had been anticipating a figure well under half the amount at tops. Tom was seething. It was a serious amount of cash to throw to the wind, but what could he do? Negotiation was not an option!

"I will write you a cheque." He walked into his study tightly clutching the scrap of paper. Penny half-smiled at Rod.

"I have made you some breakfast before you leave. Come with me." Rod smiled back at her and followed her into the kitchen.

As Tom entered his study, he screwed up the paper, threw it onto the floor and stamped on it. He was fuming. He wanted to shout out, 'You bloody fool!' but at himself, not Rod. £638,200 was an enormous amount of money, even for him. It was the most idiotic gesture he had made, or would ever make, and it was unnecessary. Rod had won. He was claiming the prize for the way Tom had treated him over the years. In Tom's mind, it was a totally misguided view of the relationship. He had tried desperately, well, not too desperately, to help his brother over the decades by offering him sound advice and guidance with the objective of him rebooting his life, gaining some self-respect, and getting a job that he could hold down for more than a few months, but his reward was a slap in the face and substantially more than a half million-pound bill.

As he wrote the cheque Tom's hand shook with anger.

He marched into the kitchen, where Rod was eating a hearty breakfast. Penny watched over him like a mother encouraging a child to eat before leaving for school. Tom flicked the cheque onto Rod's toast on a side plate, turned and started to leave. As he did, he uttered, "Enjoy your breakfast. I would like you to leave as soon as humanly possible!"

As Tom exited the kitchen, Rod stopped eating, looked at Penny, smiled, and tore up the cheque. Penny's lower jaw dropped. That impetuous act took a second, no more. He was throwing away the opportunity to reboot his life. Penny knew Rod was incapable of looking after himself. He was certainly incapable of dealing with the financial issues he faced. This was a gesture of bravado. It would serve no useful purpose.

"Penny. Thank you for being so kind, so thoughtful. As a sister in-law, I really love you, I always have, but I cannot accept his money. I could not live my life knowing that my benefactor, my brother, who hates me so much, paid for my existence. I will deal with my issues in my own way. I do not need him. I never have." He continued with his breakfast. Penny attempted to calm things down.

"Rod, I know you are angry with Tom, but please I beg you take the money. Pay off your debts. Without worrying about money, you will be able to think more clearly about the future and have a decent life. Please, let me ask Tom to write another cheque. I beg you!"

"You really are so kind." He started to sob. Penny hugged him.

"You are so kind. If only my brother was like you. You have been so good to Mary and me over the years."

"Come on, no point being upset. It is often said that time is a great healer, you know. You will come to terms with Mary's death and move on with your life, but you can only do that if you are free of worry, especially money worries. Please, let me speak to Tom."

Rod was adamant he would not accept Tom's money. He had always acted irrationally in life. His decision making over the years was rarely based on sound, thoughtful judgement. Instead, it was based on emotion. That mindset was the root of his problems. He always acted before thinking.

Years ago, Rod had confided in Penny that he struggled with relationships. He could not understand why he lacked the respect Tom engendered. He had been unable to hold down a job for any length of time, and as a consequence had bouts of anxiety and low self-esteem which led to frustration and anger that spilled over all too frequently. On this occasion, his ill-placed pride would deny him more than a half million pounds and the opportunity to get his life back on track, but to Rod, that was a price worth paying. The simple act of tearing up the cheque made him vulnerable, but he just did not care.

He finished his breakfast, hugged Penny, picked up his suitcase, and left the house. Penny was insistent that she drove him wherever he wanted to go but he refused. He said he had enough money for a bus fare into town and would head for the police station. As he walked down the drive, he turned briefly to look back for the last time. Penny attempted a wave, but Rod did not see her at the window. She watched him arrive at the electric gate and let himself out.

Penny was tearful. The last thing she wanted was to see or speak to Tom. He was in the study having just phoned the bank to inform them to expect a cheque for a substantial amount to be presented for cashing, which they should clear. Little did he know that his instruction was unnecessary. Penny decided to put the torn cheque in a drawer rather than binning it. She would tell Tom later, when she thought she was able to face him.

Tom had calmed down. He had seen Rod leave and

sighed with relief. He knew it was not the right to attempt a conversation with Penny, so he chose to go to the office instead. Just as he had chosen to sleep in a different room from Penny the previous evening, a first in the time they had been married, so it was the first time that he had left the house when she was there without saying goodbye or kissing her on the cheek. He packed his briefcase, left without a word, and headed straight for his car. Penny heard the door close and looked out of the window to see him drive away. She was heartbroken. She knew the significance of what had just happened.

For the first time in their marriage, their relationship was being tested. Of course, Penny knew nothing of Tom's infidelity with Susie, or indeed any of the other affairs he had had over the years. For her, she was married to the perfect man, and was secure in feeling loved and protected, and wanted for nothing. Now, she felt alone and isolated, fearful of whether she could ever forgive Tom, and accept that he was fallible.

Would they be able to reconcile the events of the past twenty-four hours? What happened between Rod and Tom would not be uncommon in many families, an accepted way of life, but not for Penny. Tom had destroyed the illusion she had of him as a human being. Life with Tom would never be the same again.

CHAPTER 5 – PENNY'S DILEMMA

For an hour Tom drove aimlessly before arriving at the office. His mind had been consumed by mending fences with Penny. He wanted to convince her that he was not an ogre. Time would tell if he could achieve that objective. Busy with thoughts of Penny, he barely noticed Susie as he entered the office. She was bright and breezy.

"Hello, darling. I was not expecting you in today; I thought you were dealing with your brother's problems?"

Tom was not in the mood to exchange pleasantries, his mind was elsewhere, but he knew he had to appear affectionate, or she would wonder why the new, loving partner that he had promised to be the last time they spent intimate time together had changed. "I was not sure I would make it in, but I had to escape."

"Oh, poor baby, what has happened, is she giving you a hard time?" Susie went to cuddle him. Reluctantly, he accepted her affection; he had no choice.

"No. Nothing wrong with Penny."

Susie was about to say something negative about her as she always did, but thought the better of it, reminding herself of the pact they had agreed.

"What is troubling you, my love?"

Tom could feel frustration welling up. The last thing he wanted to do was pour his heart out to his mistress, the mistress he wanted rid of, but he had to control his emotions, otherwise it would lead to another row.

"Can we not talk about this now; I have a lot to do. I will update you on everything later, is that okay?" The words came out in a caring, loving way and as a result she had no idea what he was really thinking.

"Of course, darling. I will let you get on. We could go for a drink after work and chat about it?" Tom failed to answer but managed a brief smile to keep her happy.

Back at the house, Penny was miserable. She had gone over the events of the past twenty- four hours, repeatedly, in a vain attempt to understand how they had ended up where they were. Was it her fault that she had misunderstood Tom's sentiments? Had she just assumed that he would want to reconcile with Rod after all those years of antipathy? Or had she witnessed an unpleasant side to him, one she had not seen before? If so, it was a side she did not like and was slightly fearful of. She did what she always did in such circumstances: she phoned Ginny for a chat. Ginny came across to the house. Penny made coffee and told Ginny the whole story.

Momentarily, they stood looking at each other. Ginny was so shocked by Penny's story she was lost for words. Penny realised she had been talking uninterrupted for over ten minutes and said,

"I am sorry, Ginny. I did not mean to burden you with my troubles. What is happening with you and George?" Ginny, being Ginny, was eager to tell her everything since they last spoke.

"After George said he was leaving, he came back on three occasions to pick up some clothes and a few other items he wanted. He told me he had taken a hotel room while he figured out what to do next. I asked him if he was moving in with his girlfriend, and he said he had no plans to. He repeated over and over that they had not slept together, but admitted he was in love with her. After the shock of discovering his deceit, I was better able to cope with his admission of being in love with another woman, but I admit I could have stabbed him in the heart at that very moment, then poured a gin and tonic to celebrate his death!" Penny could not help but laugh.

This was Ginny's sense of fun seeping through.

"Anyway, he left, then two days later, he phoned and asked if he could come round. He sounded like a naughty schoolboy. Of course, I agreed. He arrived in the car, and I watched him tentatively walk to the front door and ring the bell. I waited a couple of minutes before I answered it, I wanted him to sweat. No sooner had he arrived he told me the affair was over, and he wanted to come back home. He begged my forgiveness and said he would be eternally grateful if I would agree and would do all he could to patch up the relationship. Anything I wanted to buy, anything I wanted to do, anywhere I wanted to go on holiday, he would arrange it. I listened and burst out laughing. I could not help myself!"

"Oh Ginny, you are terrible. Poor George!"

"None of it! Poor George? No, poor me! I decided not to respond immediately. I wanted answers to a list of questions I had. Why was the relationship over? Who ended it and why? Did he still love her? He told me that she, Angelique, that is; what a silly name! She is not French, you know, An English girl, clearly with pretentious parents… anyway, she decided she was going back to her previous boyfriend who had proposed to her. Penny knew Ginny so well. She knew George would have been dragged through her inquisition, remaining submissive throughout.

"He repeated he had never slept with her. He now said he had an affection for her – different from being in love, and that he knew he had been stupid thinking he could be happy with a younger woman; and how much he missed me and all we had accumulated over the years. I was unsure if he meant household possessions, household dust, or memories?" Again, Penny laughed.

"So, what did you say?"

"I said it was highly unlikely that I would take him back, but I would have a think about it. I asked him to go back to his hotel room to ponder, really ponder, how stupid he had been and start adding up how much his fling with that child had cost him in restaurant bills, the cost of the hotel room so far, and how much more it may cost him until I arrive at a decision. More importantly, the hurt and anguish he had put me through since he decided to have the affair!"

"You will take him back; of course you will."

"Not sure. I have got used to my own company these past few weeks and I really think I could be happy without him."

"Well, you have changed your tune! When he first left, you were devastated."

"It was you, Penny, who said time is a great healer and you are right. Three weeks is long enough for me to bounce back and get on with my life! Who knows, I might find a twenty-five-year-old hunk on an internet dating site that would be extremely happy to have this over-weight, slightly saggy old lady that can cook?" They laughed together.

"I am not sure I could survive without Tom."

"What?! Nonsense. You are so resourceful, Penny. You would miss him of course, but you would soon find another gorgeous man." Penny smiled, but beneath the surface she was worried if she and Tom would ever get back to the nurturing relationship they had before the saga with Rod.

"I hope I will never have to go looking for another man, but you never know, I suppose."

"Oh, cheer up. You will sort things out with Tom, and I am sure things will be resolved with Rod. Tom will come round."

"It's not just Tom I am worried about – they are at absolute loggerheads. Both of them are too proud to back down and try and reconcile the relationship. Rod craves Tom's attention, but that desire to have a good brotherly relationship is not reciprocated. Tom has a closed mind as far as Rod is concerned." Ginny looked at her sympathetically.

"Oh well, it will all come out in the wash I am sure… My mother used to say that all the time. 'It will all come out in the wash.' As a child, I used to go to the washing machine when it was working and look to see if 'it' was coming out. A funny memory!" Penny laughed. Ginny stood up.

"Anyway, I had better get back, I am baking."

"Thanks for coming across and listening, Ginny. Do let me know what you decide to do about George?" Ginny smiled. "I will take him back, of course I will, after I have let him suffer for a few days. And keep me posted on the Brothers' Feud?"

"I shall." With that, Ginny left for home.

CHAPTER 6 – FIRE

After Ginny returned home, Penny started to worry again about her and Tom, and how best to deal with their relationship from here. A divorce or leaving Tom through separation was not in prospect as far as she was concerned. She loved him and would counter all manner of personal challenges in their marriage before that ever became an option, but all the same, she knew she had seen a different side of him that both surprised and worried her. She wished she could go back in time.

The afternoon was wearing on and she had not heard a word from Tom. She was hoping he would call with an apology or at least attempt to put things right, but the phone remained silent. She thought of calling him, but decided it was not for her to make the first move. She made some tea and settled down with a book but found it difficult to concentrate.

Tom had completed several phone calls in the office and caught up with some correspondence. Unusually, Susie had remained at her desk rather than bobbing in and out of his office making concentration difficult for him, which is what she did. She loved being with him in the office, and aside from dealing very efficiently with her roles and responsibilities, she also enjoyed flirting and the everyday banter of office life. Tom was grateful for the respite on this occasion, as it allowed him to be more productive with his time. He often wondered if his other employees were aware of his relationship with Susie. If they were, they were discreet.

It was close to 5.00 pm when she finally wandered in and sat provocatively on the edge of his desk.

"Are you ready for a glass of wine at the bistro, Boss?"

Tom knew he had unfinished business with Penny at home, and he should have called her earlier. Like Penny, he wanted to make things right, but was uncertain of how to go about it. Susie looked gorgeous. She had taken the opportunity prior to entering Tom's office to top up her scarlet red lipstick. She knew Tom liked the look. He smiled at her. She walked around the desk and kissed him, and he was not about to deny the contact. The rest of the staff had left the building, and they were alone. Within a few minutes, they had undressed each other and were having sex. Eventually, they dressed and made their way to the bistro.

When they arrived, it was quite busy. They knew quite a lot of the people there. Susie was always under strict instructions to act in a manner that told everyone she was an employee, his PA, not his mistress. Susie knew the score and rarely stepped across the divide. They had a light supper and a bottle of wine. They were both in good spirits. Tom had forgotten about the challenges he had waiting for him at home. He would let that take its course. After the meal and drinking half a bottle of wine each, neither were legally able to drive.

Susie was always pleased when Tom agreed to drink because she knew he would not risk driving under the influence. That invariably meant they would get a taxi back to her apartment, and if she were lucky, he would stay the night. It was only very occasionally that he did stay, though, because he knew it would be difficult to explain his absence at home to Penny. He usually made the excuse that he was dining with another publisher, an agent, or a writer, and had therefore had a drink and taken a room at a local hotel to be safe. Penny would rather he did that than risk driving back. Little did she know.

Susie was delighted when Tom arranged for a taxi. They left the bistro and within ten minutes, they were at her apartment and having sex, again. It was too late to phone Penny, and too late to go home only to have heated words about Rod. It would also mean a taxi ride all the way home. Staying with Susie overnight seemed the only option.

The following morning, they got a taxi to the office. Tom always kept a change of clothes there, where he could also shower. It was very convenient. Susie was in fine form. She had spent quality time with her man, and that always put her in a good mood. Tom could do no wrong, so when he announced he needed to go home, she was fine with it, and avoided any caustic remarks about Penny or his marriage.

Tom set off for home. Upon arriving, Penny was out; her car was not in the driveway. In some ways, he was relieved. He did not want to be seen to be returning with his tail between his legs. No, it was better that he was already at home when she returned. In his mind, this would put him in a position of control.

Twenty minutes later, Penny arrived. Rather than call out as she usually did, she thought better of it on this occasion. Tom was in the study. Penny walked through to the kitchen and switched on the kettle. Tom decided it was time to make his entrance. He had already concluded he would not make an apology about his exchange with Rod; he had meant every word he said, but he would be apologetic for the upset he had caused her. "Hello. Before you say a word, I want to offer an apology for the upset I have caused you. I never meant for all this to happen." She cut him off.

"Tom. You have hurt me. This is so unlike you, to be so callous and uncaring. The way you treated Rod was despicable!"

"Sorry darling, despicable? Giving him well-over half a million pounds cannot be described as despicable!"

"The way you treated him was despicable and for your information, if you did not already know, Rod tore up the cheque. He refused to take your money!"

"What? Tore up the cheque. Well… I have to say that is the best news I have had this week!" Penny was outraged. She stormed out of the kitchen as Tom rushed after her, asking her to stop. He failed to understand why she was upset.

"Darling, what is the matter?"

"If you do not know what the matter is, then I really do not know you at all!" He was stunned. He knew his comment had appeared somewhat glib, but she had just told him that they had been spared over half a million pounds. Surely that was good news. It was evident they were on a different wavelength.

The landline rang. Penny answered it. Tom stood nearby. He took the opportunity to turn his phone on and immediately received three ping's, text messages from Susie. He glanced at the screen but ignored the messages.

"Hello, Penny Taylor?" It was Peter, Tom's solicitor.

"Hi Penny, is it possible to speak to Rod?"

"I am afraid not. Tom and Rod had a falling out and Rod left us early yesterday morning. He said he was going back to the police station to see if they planned to hold him." Tom looked quizzically at Penny.

"Ah, that is not good news. You will recall I told you both there was a strict requirement for Rod to stay with you at your home until the police were satisfied, he was no longer a suspect, and if he were to leave, the police should be informed in advance. Did you call and tell them?" Penny looked worried and turned to Tom passing him the phone.

"Hello, Tom here. What is the problem, Peter?"

"Morning Tom. I was just explaining to Penny that the basis of Rod's bale was that he was to stay at your home and the police were to be advised in advance if he had to leave for any reason. I gather you did not tell them that he left yesterday morning?"

"Well, no. It did not occur to me to call them." He turned

to Penny.

"Did you call the police, darling, to let them know about Rod's decision to leave?" Penny glared at Tom. He knew she had not.

"No, neither of us did. The bloody idiot had a tantrum. It was impossible to get through to him. Why, what is the problem?"

"I am afraid, the police have CCTV evidence of Rod smashing a window, breaking into a Mini Market, and walking off with half a dozen bottles of whisky. They are out looking for him." Tom was incandescent, and he could not help but show it.

"Fucking idiot! What is the fucking matter with him. Is he totally stupid? I am sorry, Peter, both for my language and the antics of my idiot brother!"

Penny was eager to know what happened.

"Sorry, let me just update Penny… Rod has broken into a Mini Market and stolen six bottles of whisky. The police have CCTV evidence." Penny was beside herself. She marched around the hallway in a state of flux.

"So, Peter. What happens next?"

"The police will find him, and he will be detained again. But this time, they will not bale him until their enquiries are completed and they are satisfied he is not their key suspect. He will be charged for breaking and entry and theft. I have to say this episode does not help his case!"

"All I can do is thank you Peter for your intervention. Please keep us informed?"

"I will. Once they have him back at the police station, I will arrange to see him and will report back." The call ended.

Penny screamed at Tom. It was usually her nature to be cool and calm, always maintaining the ability to take heat out of situations, but on this occasion, she just lost it.

"This is all your fault! I hope you are proud of yourself! What is the matter with you, Tom? Have you had a personality transplant?" Tom was angered by her attack.

"What the hell are you talking about?! It is you that has lost the plot! I offered to help that idiot brother of mine with a very substantial amount of money, but he threw it back in my face…" During the heated exchange, Tom's phone had rung twice. The third time, he chose to answer it. It was Susie. He was still wound up and not in the mood to be interrupted by her, who wanted to know if he would have sex with her again in the office when he returned. He let loose on her.

"What the hell do you want? Why are you bothering me?!" As he was yelling, she was trying to talk over him…

"The office and warehouse are on fire. Listen to me, Tom. The warehouse is on fire and the fire brigade are here. You must come to the office, right now!"

Tom's emotions hit the roof. He had unfinished business with Penny, but this was far too important to ignore. He shouted at the top of his voice, "FUCK, FUCK, FUCK, FUCK!

Penny was still extremely angry with him and would not ask what the phone call was about. He, too, had no inclination or time to waste explaining.

"I have to go."

"What, right now; where?" He snapped at her.

"The fucking office and warehouse are on fire!"

Penny dropped onto a chair in the hallway and burst into tears. She put her hands over her face and dropped her head to her knees. Tom ignored her distraught state, grabbed a set of car keys from the rack, and rushed out of the house, attempting to put on a pair of shoes at the same time.

He made a point of picking up the keys to his scarlet red Porsche 911 Turbo, which he used infrequently. When driving the Range Rover, he had a calm attitude to driving and always adhered rigidly to traffic laws. In the Porsche, though, it was as though he assumed a different personality. He was incapable of adhering to the law and rarely, if ever, stayed within the speed limit. He had two previous convictions for speeding in the Porsche and for that reason, Penny refused to ever be a passenger when he was driving that car.

He jumped into the car in double quick time. His heart was pounding. He started the car, revved the engine loudly, and roared down the driveway, cobble stones spreading everywhere across the manicured lawn as he did. As he approached the electric security gate at speed, he braked hard to allow time for the gate to open fully so he could pass through.

Once on the main road, he put his foot down and within a few seconds he was approaching sixty mph. He fumbled around in his trouser pocket for his phone to call Susie and temporarily lost control. In doing so, the car bounced off the verge, almost careering off the road. The engine raced, as did his heart rate. Eventually, with one hand, he managed to call her and prayed she would answer, but his luck was out. He tried again. He was entering a built-up area with speed limit signs indicating forty mph. He was clocking seventy. In his manic state, anything could happen. Fortunately, on the third attempt to call her, she answered.

"Where are you, Tom?" She was frantic, speaking through tears and gulps of air.

"I am less than fifteen minutes away. What is going on?" He could hear a great deal of activity in the background with people talking and some shouting orders. It did not sound good.

"I am not allowed near the building, but I am sure at least half of the inventory in the warehouse has gone up in flames already. Nigel, the warehouse manager, has been taken to hospital and two others have joined him with smoke inhalation. Tom, it is awful."

By now, Tom's driving had become increasingly dangerous for other road users. He was so focused on his conversation with Susie that he narrowly avoided colliding with a car coming in the opposite direction. He was shaken; but high on adrenaline and lacking any sense of danger. He was desperate to get to the office at almost any cost.

He approached a local village centre at almost sixty miles an hour, passing a parade of shops and parked cars with pedestrians milling around. The legal speed limit there was only twenty. People were shocked that someone would be driving at such speed. He had also attracted the attention of a police car which had taken up chase. He roared through the village and out onto a busy road, where he continued talking to Susie on his phone. His speed increased to eighty mph.

Just five minutes from the office he saw a flashing blue light in his rear-view mirror. The police siren bellowed out and he knew he had to stop. As the car ground to a halt, he punched the steering wheel in frustration. Instantly, he knew how stupid he had been. He had lost any rational sense. A policeman got out of his car and approached as Tom lowered the window. He tried to adopt an apologetic and relaxed demeanour, but he knew there was no chance of getting off lightly.

"I am so sorry, officer. I know I was speeding. I am trying to get to a fire…" Before he had time to complete his sentence, the police officer took out his notepad and pen.

"So, a fireman, are you? And this red Porsche 911 Turbo is your fire engine?" The irony was not lost on Tom.

"Look, I know this is unusual but is it possible that we could discuss this later? I need to get to my business, which is on fire. The fire brigade is there now, and it is only a few minutes away… you know, the small Hazelwood Industrial

Park?" Tom was visibly shaken.

"Is there any way you could escort me there so I can see what is going on and I will provide my details when we arrive?" The urgency of his tone was not lost on the policeman, who agreed to his request. He followed the police car to his office, painfully adhering to the speed limit the entire way. As they entered the small industrial estate, a plume of smoke greeted them. Two fire engines and several police cars were in attendance.

Tom parked up as Susie approached the car in tears.

"It is awful, Tom. They are doing their best, but it is out of control, an inferno in there!"

He hugged her and tried to calm her down. Tom spoke to the policeman who had provided his escort and asked if he could speak with the officer in charge before sorting out his driving offences. Again, he agreed. For twenty minutes, he attempted to ascertain what had happened, the extent of the damage, and the well-being of his staff some of whom had been injured.

The fire brigade's initial assessment was that it was an electrical failure that had sparked the fire, although they were not ruling out arson. They wanted to reserve judgement until a forensic examination could be undertaken once the fire had been extinguished.

Tom had calmed down completely and was now thinking and acting more rationally. He insisted that Susie went back to the apartment and promised he would join her later. She agreed and left immediately.

For another two hours, the fire brigade worked hard to bring the fire under control and were eventually able to extinguish it. The incident had attracted a lot of attention from local businesses, many of whom came across to offer help. Tom gave a statement about his earlier driving offence and the mitigating circumstances. The officer had no option but to book him for dangerous driving and cautioned him.

Tom knew it was highly likely that he would lose his driving license, but that seemed the least of his worries.

The events of the past few hours had taken a toll. When it was safe to do so, he was given a brief opportunity to survey, from a distance, the damage the fire had caused. It was extensive. None of his inventory would have survived. Most of the machinery and equipment in the warehouse had obviously been destroyed. The internal fabric of the building had gone and there was speculation whether the building itself would need demolishing. Either way, there was no quick fix. His business and his future livelihood were on hold and for a considerable time.

Tom was an astute businessman taking out maximum insurance to cover fire losses and business disruption, but claims were always complicated and took time to settle. He had the ability to rise from the ashes, but his business challenges were not the only ones he faced. He had his brother, Penny, and Susie to deal with, and there was no way of predicting how everything would unfold.

The building was cordoned off. The fire brigade and police left, leaving the estates' security guards to watch over what was left of the building. Tom had arranged for anything that could be salvaged to be taken to a storage depot. It would not amount to much. He took one last look at the smouldering remains, got into his Porsche, and headed in the direction of Susie's apartment. Before arriving, he stopped the car and called Penny. There was no answer. He tried again but the phone kept ringing. Next, he called her mobile but again there was no response. He decided not to leave a message. His plan was to spend an hour or two comforting Susie before heading for home.

When he arrived at the apartment, he let himself in. She had gone to bed but woke immediately. Little was said, they were both exhausted. Within a few minutes, Tom had stripped off and got into bed with her and they both fell into a deep sleep.

CHAPTER 7 – ANGELIQUE

Several hours had passed. The doorbell rang and they both woke with a start. Susie slowly got up, put on her dressing gown, and went to the door. Tom heard a voice.

"Hello, Angelique. I hope it is okay for me to call on you…" Susie cut the visitor short and whispered her response.

"What are you doing here? How did you find me?"

"I am sorry if it is inconvenient…" Again, she cut him short.

"You must go away, please..." Before she had time to finish her sentence Tom appeared at the door, dressed only in his underwear. He was utterly shocked to discover George; his neighbour and Ginny's husband standing on the other side of the threshold.

"Tom? Why are you here, how do you know Angelique?"

"Angelique? George, have you gone mad? And may I ask the same question; what the hell are you doing here?" Susie tried to shove Tom back into the hallway and close the door on George. It was the first thing she could think of doing in the hope that it would resolve the situation, but of course, it would not. Tom stepped back and brushed Susie to one side.

"George, it is obvious we are both somewhat surprised to be meeting like this, but why are you here?"

"I was hoping to have a word with Angelique…" Tom was exasperated.

"For fuck's sake, George, Angelique, whoever she is, is not here! You have the wrong address.

"But Tom. That is Angelique…" He pointed right at Susie.

Tom was utterly baffled by this bizarre exchange and looked over at Susie for an explanation.

"Can you tell me what the hell is going on, Susie?"

"Susie?" George's voice went up an octave.

"But you told me your name was Angelique?"

Susie had lost the power of rational thought. She blurted out, "Tom, will you please get rid of this man? He has been stalking me for weeks! I had no idea he had my address! I should have gone to the police!"

It was George's turn to be totally confused. He whispered, "Tom, may I have a word in private?"

This was the last thing Susie wanted. She did not want Tom to know that she had led George on a merry dance. She had the idea some months earlier when she thought her relationship with Tom was on the rocks, to flirt with and encourage one of Tom's friends. Her rationale was that she could use the encounter as a way of making Tom jealous, and consequentially win back his affection. It was an absurd idea, and she later knew as much, no more so than right at that moment. George had indeed fallen for her, so her ruse had worked, but then she and Tom had become close again. George had told her that he was leaving his wife Ginny to be with her, and she was horrified.

The events rapidly unfolded, and she found it difficult to keep George at bay. She ended the relationship with him on the pretext that she was going back to her boyfriend who had proposed to her. With that, George realised he was left stranded and begged Ginny to take him back. After pleading his case and promising her anything and everything to reconcile the marriage, Ginny said she would only think about allowing him back home. He waited for her call with her decision, but the call never came.

Increasingly, he feared she would decline his request and he would be left on his own, and the whole episode with Angelique would be for nothing. So, on the assumption that Ginny was going to reject him, he was there to make a last-ditch attempt to plead his case hoping she would give up her boyfriend and they would live happily ever after.

Tom agreed to George's request to talk and invited him in. Susie went into a rage and locked herself in the bathroom. Tom decided it would be appropriate for him to put on some trousers and two minutes later they were sitting on the sofa. Tom was keen to try, for what it was worth, to explain why he was at Susie's apartment, and why they had obviously just got out of bed. What better cover than the emotion they were suffering with the business burning down.

"George, let me start off and tell you why I am here. Susie, or Angelique, as you prefer to call her, works for me. She is my personal assistant. Earlier today, my business caught fire and burnt down. We were both distraught and once the fire brigade had done their bit and put the fire out, I offered to drive Susie back here to her apartment. We dropped onto the bed and fell into a deep sleep, that is until you rang the doorbell. So…, now it is your turn!"

Susie was still locked in the bathroom and could only hear snatches of conversation. She feared that Tom would discover why George had turned up on her doorstep. Desperately, she shouted at the top of her voice,

"Tom! Come in here NOW! I am going to cut my wrists! NOW! COME IN NOW!"

Tom could not ignore her demands. He went to the bathroom, she unlocked the door, and dragged him in.

She sat him down on the toilet seat and looked at him, the fear written across her face. "Tom. You must listen to me. Whatever he says is untrue. He has been stalking me for weeks and I felt afraid of what he may do to me. He seems to think I want a relationship with him. I bumped into him with my trolley a few weeks ago in the supermarket. I apologised and smiled at him. He immediately latched on to me. He asked if I would like a coffee with him. I thought it was innocent enough, so I did. As we left the café, he gave me his business card and asked me on a date. It was creepy. I knew then it had been a mistake having coffee with him. I declined of course, the date, that is, and left. He followed me. It was awful…"

Tom listened intently. He was baffled by such an implausible story, but then the entire day had been one crazy episode after another. But George, a stalker? That notion was one that had to be set aside but he did want to hear what George had to say.

"Okay. I will not let him anywhere near you, but I am still going to find out why he is here."

"Tom, no, please ask him to leave. I beg you." Tom insisted she join them in the sitting room. She had no option. If there was a chance of Tom believing her, she would need to argue her case defending her story. Susie glared at George, hoping, praying he would not say anything that would compromise her relationship with Tom.

"So, George. You were going to tell me why you are here?"

"Tom. I am as baffled as you. Did you know I have been having an affair? Well, it was with Angelique… Susie…"

Susie needed to deny his claim. "That is not true! Tom, he is lying!"

"If I may continue. It was her that pursued me. After I had told Ginny I was divorcing her, Angelique, sorry, Susie said she did not want to see me anymore because she was planning to marry her ex-boyfriend.

It is embarrassing, I should have accepted that, but I was, emphasis on was, fond of her. It was only right to try and find her to explain my feelings. That is why I am here."

Tom turned to Susie. "So, you totally deny what George has said?" Before she was able to respond, though, Tom's phone rang. It was Penny. He had to take the call. He left George and Susie and went outside the apartment. Susie rushed to the bathroom and locked herself in.

"Penny. I am so sorry." Penny did not want to hear an apology.

"Tom, where the hell are you?"

"The business has gone up in flames. I am at Susie's apartment. She was so heroic when the fire started and helped the fire brigade and police before I arrived at the scene. She was distraught so I thought I would drive her home and make her some tea. She is a lot happier now and I was planning to leave and come home. Shall I meet you back there in forty-five minutes?"

"Tom. All this, everything that has happened over these past few days… it is awful. I feel so stressed, I just do not know what to do about Rod, you, the business…" Tom tried to reassure her.

"Everything will work out, trust me. We will get back on our feet and I promise to sort everything out. You know I am good at problem solving." Penny was not prepared to acknowledge anything so positive. There were too many challenges facing them and she was not convinced he could make that much of a difference anyway.

"Okay. I will make my way back home." Penny ended the call. Tom returned to the sitting room.

"George, I am sorry, but I need to go. Penny has just discovered the business has burnt down and is distraught." He went to the bathroom.

"Susie, I am going home. I will call you. George will leave with me." Susie decided to say nothing. He added… "I am going to assume you are okay. I will call you."

The two men left the apartment. On the way to their cars, George asked Tom if he would say nothing to Penny about his appearance at the apartment, knowing it would get back to Ginny. If nothing else, he knew, definitively, that he had no chance of establishing a relationship with Angelique. It was as if she had never existed, which was true, of course, at least in name.

Tom also suggested it would be wise if George did not mention their encounter to anyone, not that he had anything to hide of course, but he did not want Penny to think there was anything to be concerned about between him and his PA. They got in their cars and drove off.

Throughout Tom's journey home, his phone kept pinging. There was no need for him to guess who the messages were from. He certainly was not about to read or answer them. He made a point of driving as sedately as he could avoiding being stopped by the police again. He crawled home, barely changing out of second gear. His mind wandered as he drove, trying to reconcile the events of the past week starting with Mary's murder. Only that morning, he had discovered from Peter that Rod would be taken back into custody once the police had found him. The consolation for Tom was that Rod had torn up the cheque. The six hundred thousand pounds he had earmarked for Rod would come in very handy to help rebuild the business. In a euphoric gesture to himself, he slapped the steering wheel and laughed. He needed something to cheer him up, even if it would be short-lived.

The main concern he had was rebuilding the relationship with Penny, which he knew would not be an overnight task. He knew what she was like. She was a predictably good person, moral and upstanding, truthful, and totally trustworthy, and she loved him. She would do anything for him, and he felt the same for her, aside, of course, from his dalliance with Susie and the other sexual encounters he had engaged in since they first married.

He knew his weakness. It was not his business acumen or his persuasion skills, it was his insatiable appetite for new and exciting relationships. Susie had occupied that role over the past two years but, like most dalliances, they become complicated by emotions. Tom needed young women to find him attractive. He wanted a steady provision of sexual encounters with no strings attached, and of course, that commodity was in short supply.

There were challenges ahead but they had not changed since yesterday. He knew he would have to end his relationship with Susie if he had any chance of mending bridges with Penny. If Penny were to find out, his marriage would be over. There would be no way back. No matter how much she loved him, there was only so much she would accept, and infidelity was not a flaw she would accept in any man, Tom included.

As he approached the driveway, he pledged to himself that we would do everything possible to get Penny back on side, resurrect his business, somehow sort out his brother and, most difficult of all, part company with Susie. As he entered the house, Penny ran toward him, and they embraced. "Tom, can we put aside everything we have said to each other these past few days? I hate conflict of any kind and especially with you!" This was music to Tom's ears.

"Of course. That is exactly what I want, too. We have a lot going on at present including losing the business, at least temporarily, but I will make sure we get up and running again as soon as possible. We have insurance, although how much we will be able to claim and how long it will take to get a settlement is anyone's guess. Fortunately, we still have the money I pledged to Rod, that will help enormously…" Penny's face dropped.

"What is the matter, you have lost colour in your cheeks?"

"After you stormed out the other day and Rod had left after tearing up the cheque, I felt so sorry for him. I phoned the bank and made an appointment. I already had his bank details, because some months ago I had transferred a small amount to their account after Mary bought something online for me. I am sorry, Tom. I transferred the money you pledged to Rod's account, so the money has gone!" Tom stood stock-still. Anything he said in response had to be compatible with his aim of winning back Penny's affection. But was this revelation too much to take in? Tom perfectly masked his anger at hearing the news.

"Oh, right. So, to be clear, Rod has the money?" Penny nodded.

"Oh dear. We could have used that… but never mind… we will make do!" Penny was hugely relieved that Tom had taken it so well. Tom, meanwhile, had bitten his lip so hard in silent anguish that he had drawn blood.

"Are you okay Tom? You have blood on your chin."

"Yes, I will pop to the bathroom to sort it out."

As soon as the door was closed, he silently shouted a series of obscenities aimed at his brother, he would not have wanted Penny to hear. He could not believe the money resided in Rod's bank account to resolve his problems, faced with their own challenge of resurrecting the business from the fire. Hitherto, the business had been financially sound, although any reserves they had would be wiped out in the coming months to pay for a new warehousing facility and office.

The inventory of books and other vital equipment had perished, but the fundamentals and integrity of managing and monitoring the business were intact. Everything was stored on external servers and The Cloud. In theory, the business could still function; Tom still had all his contacts, his distributors, and his authors. What he did not have, though, were physical books to distribute, so delays in servicing demand were inevitable. He was confident he could use his charm and diplomatic skills to keep his stakeholders on side, but it would be a slog to get the business back to where it was pre-fire.

The timing of the fire could not have come at a worse time. Tom had toyed with the idea of selling up and retiring in a couple of years either to retire abroad with Penny, or start afresh with a new business venture, using the cash proceeds from the sale of Taylor Publishing. He had plenty of business ideas or partnerships he could pursue, but did he want to start all over again?

As far as resurrecting the business, quite literally from the ashes, he needed the insurance pay out more than ever. He had always wanted to keep his business and personal finances separate from each other. Now, that would be possible.

Having accepted, with gritted teeth, that the money was sitting in his brother's account for him to pay off his debts or blow it all on drink and gambling, he returned to Penny.

"Shall we have a drink, darling? G & T, or would you like me to open a bottle of champagne to celebrate our future beyond today's and yesterday's events?"

Penny knew there were challenges ahead but agreed to the champagne. She was pleased they had repaired their relationship. She had dreaded days or weeks of difficulty between them. She never wanted to argue with anyone, especially Tom, but after recent dramas she knew how high emotions were running, and that in those moments of madness, all manner of things can be said and done.

Tom went to the kitchen to open the champagne. He returned to the drawing room and handed Penny a glass. She mustered a smile for him and kissed him on the cheek.

"Tom. You will overcome the challenges of the fire and before you know it, you will be back on top. I have every faith in you!" Tom smiled and raised his glass.

"Oh, Mary's father called yesterday to say her body had been released and the funeral is next Wednesday. I said we would attend. I am not sure Rod is invited, although I suppose they cannot stop him if he wants to go, that is assuming the police have found him by then?" Tom hesitated.

"Oh dear, poor Mary. I must admit with everything that is going on I could do without attending a funeral." Tom wanted to avoid seeing Mary's parents and the distinct possibility of seeing Rod ever again.

"We must go, Tom. We really, must." Tom looked at Penny.

"I know this is a delicate subject and I am not blaming you or looking for any kind of confrontation, but you do recall me saying to Rod that the money I was giving him was only to be used to pay off his mortgage and his many debts?"

Penny paused.

"In front of me, although you may have said something else to Rod privately, you said, 'Prepare a list of all your debts and let me have it and I will pay them off,' or words to that effect."

"So, if you are right, implicit in that statement is the fact that the money is only for paying off his debts and not for any other purpose?"

"Tom, what is on your mind?"

"I am concerned, especially in his state of mind, that he will just blow it all on drink, drugs, and gambling and his debts will remain unpaid. I need a way of ensuring the money is not squandered, especially now, at a time when we could do with it. I was thinking of speaking to Peter about it."

Penny knew Tom was not blaming her but wished he had not raised the matter.

"I believe I did the right thing in transferring the money to Rod. You had given him the cheque, so it was clearly your intention he had it, but I am sorry I failed to discuss the transfer with you. We were not exactly on speaking terms at that point, and in fairness, I called you several times but could not get hold of you. I was so upset and angry at the time… Hindsight is a wonderful thing, if I had known the business was going up in flames, I think I would have thought twice about giving him the money."

Tom nodded. At least his questioning had not caused a rift between them. It was typical of Penny to be pragmatic. It was a trait he loved about her. She was honest and dependable and had no bad side to her. In fact, she had all the qualities that Tom lacked, and in abundance.

After drinking the whole bottle of champagne between them, Penny decided she would have a nap in the bedroom. Tom went to his study. He knew he had to speak to Susie. He had received numerous text messages from her, frantically trying to find out what happened between him and George. She was desperate to reaffirm her story of George being a stalker. The last thing she wanted was to lose Tom.

Tom, however, was thinking differently. He was wondering whether he could use the drama at the apartment with George as a way of ending the relationship with her. It could be the perfect solution, after all she had been unfaithful to him. On the other hand, he desperately needed her in the business to help salvage what was left. She was a good planner and executor of tasks, and they were valuable skills at a time like this. He could give her a list of things to do knowing she would tackle them efficiently, effectively, and in a timely manner. There was never a need for him to check her work. He also knew that whatever the circumstances, she would not go quietly. He did not need reminding that she loved him. She was besotted with him. She was in awe of him. No, if he ended the relationship even on the pretext that she had been unfaithful (and he knew she had not, at least not with George; that was too much to believe) she would not accept the rationale of him leaving the relationship.

She would fight hard to defend her right to him. If she

were to go down, then Tom would go down with her. She was his wife-to-be, not a casual girlfriend or mistress. She was emotionally invested in the relationship and would pay whatever price was necessary to keep her man, which included losing her job, her apartment, and her shiny red Porsche Cayman.

Having weighed up the options, Tom knew it was impossible to end the relationship with Susie in the immediate term, or indeed at any point in the future if he wanted to maintain his marriage to Penny and hang on to what assets he had left. On balance, he needed her just as much as she needed him. He decided to call her. As she answered the phone, he could detect she was fearful of what he might say. She was tearful upon hearing his voice.

"Tom, Tom, please can you come over so that…" Before she had a chance to plead her case, he cut her off.

"Susie, look, just calm down. I know you are worried what George and I spoke about. I do not believe for one minute that you were seeing him. He is a neighbour, and I know him well enough to know that he is… how do I put it, a little immature when it comes to matters of the heart. Aside from his wife, Ginny, he has never been with another woman. So, if you showed him any interest or flirted with him for even just one minute, I could imagine him falling for you, hook, line, and sinker. Anyway, fear not, it is of no consequence to me." There was a brief silence before Susie responded.

"Tom... I love you. I love you. I love you! I was so worried you would want to end our relationship believing George and not me…" Tom was intrigued.

"Why did you call yourself Angelique?"

Susie was about to make a big mistake in answering that question.

"I know it sounds silly now, but I was worried we were

quarrelling, and you would end our relationship, and I was frantic. I thought if I could flirt with a friend of yours, and George seemed the best option as I had met him at your house on one occasion, it would make you jealous. So, one morning, I decided to wait at the end of his drive and flag him down as he drove into the road. It worked. I told him my car had broken down and asked if he would drive me to the Porsche dealership in Guildford…" On the way I offered to buy him coffee. He gave me his business card and invited me out to dinner. We had a meal together the following week and at that point, I knew I had made a big mistake.

"He genuinely thought I was keen on him. He told me he had not been able to think of anything else since he first met me, and that he loved me! I was horrified. He said he would leave his wife and we could be together, and unlike you, I believed him! I tried to push him away but the more I did, the more he wanted me. He had arranged to take a hotel room in town and had moved some of his things out. I was shocked. Anyway, I told him any thoughts he had of the two of us being an item were pure fantasy on his behalf, and that my boyfriend, that is you, Tom, had asked me to marry him… I thought I had resolved the situation until he turned up on my doorstep."

Tom listened to her account and was amused by the inventiveness of the plan. On the other hand, it reaffirmed to him the lengths she would go to maintain their relationship. He was not a jealous man. He had no reason to be. Sex was the motivator. Sex with a young, attractive, intelligent woman whenever he wanted it without complications. It was the latter, without complications, that was impossible to achieve, at least with Susie. She loved him and would never deceive him. As Susie waited for Tom's response he smiled.

"Susie, I am flattered you would go to such lengths to

maintain our relationship. I am not angry with you, but I do want you to know that doing, saying, and demanding the things you do of me does not improve our relationship. It does not make me want you any more than I do. I am not a jealous man. Please, please, let us have an understanding that if you ever want to end the relationship with me for whatever reason, you just tell me. I will accept it. I would never try and change your mind. You are a free agent. In such circumstances, you would not lose your job, I would not expect to take your car back, and I would not even contemplate charging you rent on the apartment or asking you to move out. That is life, people move on. Equally, though, if it was in my best interest to end our relationship, then you must allow me to make that decision without threats and dramatic interventions such as the one you described with George. I would like to think whatever may happen between us in the future, we would be mature about it, but always remain close friends. Are you in agreement?"

"But Tom, you still love me, just say you love me. You said in the next twelve months you would divorce Penny and we would be together. Nothing has changed, has it?" Tom's jaw dropped.

"This is precisely what I am talking about. You must see by bringing this up yet again, you are not helping yourself. All you are doing is pushing me away."

"Why do you say that? I simply do not understand the way you think, Tom. If you love me as you say you do, you should be flattered that I want to marry you!" Of course, what Susie failed to grasp was that she was his mistress, and to him, that was it. He had no intention of divorcing Penny and wandering off into the sunset with her. So, she was right not to understand why Tom saw her commitment to him as negative.

As far as she was concerned, he should be happy, ecstatic even, that he had a much younger, attractive, intelligent woman who was so interested in him. Many a man, including George, would sacrifice a great deal to take his place!

Tom knew where she was coming from, so he was back to square one, and he could do nothing about it. He was cornered. Whichever way he turned or tried to manipulate situations, Susie was both an asset and a worryingly long-term liability. She was a firework waiting to explode that could do far more than burn down his business. No, she could completely undermine, or worse still, wreck his marriage and, make his life a misery.

"Look, let us not go over old ground. We have both cleared the air. Can we change the subject and talk about the business?" Susie knew she had taken her concerns as far as she could. Now he had forgiven her for the George saga, the last thing she wanted was for him to turn cold on her.

"Of course, I am sorry Tom. What can I do? How can I help?" Tom put his business hat on.

"Firstly, I want you to check on the team. See how they are. See if we can do anything for them. You will need to go to the hospital, too. Reassure everyone they still have a job, and they will be paid as normal. Ask those that can work and did not suffer any injuries to report to you daily in case we can use their assistance. I have already made plans for everything that can be salvaged from the fire to be shifted to a temporary warehouse. As you know, what is left of the building has been cordoned off and security are there twenty-four hours a day, but I am concerned there may well be stuff that we need to retrieve that could be stolen or affected by the elements. Could you go to the site and have a look around, assuming security will allow you to, and make a list of things that need sorting?" Tom could hear her writing notes as he spoke.

"Can you also contact by phone or email all our authors, distributors, suppliers, and anyone else that needs to know about our current circumstances and reassure them that we will keep them informed of progress. Please word your communications in a way that it is 'business as usual' despite the challenges. Could you also cancel any appointments I have you think can be postponed for a while? I am happy for you to decide who I see and where I go over the next few months, so we make the most of business opportunities, but at the same time, it gives us enough time to find new premises and get the infrastructure of the business up and running. Okay?"

Apart from her special time with Tom in their personal relationship, Susie loved nothing more than getting her teeth into the challenges of the business. Right now, there was a lot to do, and she relished the opportunity. She was excellent at her job and Tom knew it.

"Yes, boss. All noted. I will get on with it. I have everything stored on my laptop so I can work from home until we have a new office. I love you, boss. Thank you for being so understanding. I will do everything I can to get us through this!"

"Thank you, Susie. Stay in touch." With that, he ended the call. He felt he could relax a little. With Susie dealing with the immediate consequences of the fire, it allowed him to think more strategically about the future. He did not want to replicate and rebuild what he had. The fire was an opportunity to think laterally and produce better ways of running and developing the business. If he chose to retire in the next few years and capitalise on his assets, what he did now with the business would determine the level of reward he could expect. There were several things he could immediately bring into effect or build into the new business structure, which would have a positive impact. He smiled to himself. Suddenly, the future did not look so bleak. Quite the contrary; he could see that the fire could well prove to be a godsend.

CHAPTER 8 – THE ARREST

For the next two days, Tom worked tirelessly on his plans, uninterrupted, until one afternoon, when he and Penny were in the drawing room having coffee, the phone rang. It was his friend and solicitor, Peter.

It was not good news. The police had found Rod semi-unconscious under a canal bridge. He had consumed the whisky he stole from a mini market. Tom was furious. Rod was arrested and was being charged for the offence and faced further charges for breaking his bail conditions. Peter warned Tom and Penny they should expect a call from the inspector after what Rod had claimed during a brief interview.

The last part of Peter's statement was brushed over by Tom, he was quick to say there was no way he would accommodate Rod in the house again.

"You misunderstand me, Tom. There is no possibility of the police allowing Rod to leave their custody in the foreseeable future…" Tom interrupted him.

"…Well, thank God for that! He can stay in the cell and rot for all I care!" Peter could see Tom had not grasped what he was trying to tell him.

"Tom. We are talking about two different things. Other than being charged with breaking and entering and theft, he is not a suspect for Mary's murder. I cannot say more, but you should expect a call from the inspector at any time. I must go." Peter ended the call abruptly. Penny was anxious to know what was said.

"What was all that about, Tom?" Tom paused for a moment and tried to get beneath the meaning of what Peter had said to him.

"Rod is being charged with breaking and entry and for theft, but Peter appeared to be warning us that we should expect a call from Inspector Gale at any time, but he was reluctant to elaborate further. Rod is a hopeless case, surely you must see that now, darling? We should have nothing more to do with him. In fact, I will phone Peter later to see what our chances are of getting the money back from Rod, or, at worst, make it illegal for him to spend the money we gave him on anything other than his debts. I cannot tell you what I would do to him if he used it for any other reason!"

Penny looked out of the window and saw a police car approaching. Tom must have disarmed the electric gate and forgotten to rearm it when he returned.

"A police car is coming up the drive, Tom." Tom went to the window as the car drew up and Inspector Gale and another policeman got out. He went to the door.

"Inspector Gale, what can we do for you?"

"Thomas Taylor, I am arresting you on suspicion of murdering Mrs. Mary Taylor at her home on Wednesday May 19th at approximately 9.30 am." The inspector proceeded to read Tom his rights.

Tom was flabbergasted. "Arresting Tom, why are you arresting Tom, inspector? Of course, he is not Mary's murderer. This is preposterous!" Tom found his voice.

"Inspector, this is bizarre. I am just in the process of dealing with a major fire at my business…" The inspector was insistent.

"…Yes, I am aware of the fire, and we shall be looking into that. Our forensic team are there as we speak. I would be grateful if you would take with you any medication or anything else you may need for the next few days." The reality was sinking in.

"I need to call my solicitor, Peter…" But before Tom had the chance of giving Peter's last name, the inspector interrupted.

"Is he the same solicitor representing your brother?" Tom paused.

"Yes, why?"

"I am afraid he cannot represent you and your brother at the same time. You will have to secure the services of another legal representative."

"In that case, may I make a phone call?" The inspector agreed to his request. Tom went into his study and phoned Peter immediately.

"Peter, I am being arrested for Mary's murder! This is ridiculous! The inspector said you are unable to represent me, is that true?"

"I am sorry, Tom, he is right. You asked me to represent Rod and he accepted my appointment as his legal representative so I cannot act for you both. Would you like me to recommend someone for you?"

"This is all too much! Yes, please, if you would. Can they meet me at the station within the hour?"

"I will arrange for the best person I know. I am sorry, Tom. Really, I am."

Despite Penny and Tom's assertions, it was clear the inspector would be arresting Tom whether they liked it or not. While he was on the phone to Peter, Penny was keen to continue with her questioning.

"Inspector, can you at least say why you think Tom murdered Mary?"

"I am not at liberty to say." His response was short, sharp, and to the point. Five minutes later, Tom was escorted to the police car, and they drove off, leaving Penny in tears on the driveway.

Having arrived at the police station, he was led to an interview room, where he was told to wait until his legal representative arrived. Within the hour, Charlotte Minchin-

Hart, Peter's recommended solicitor had arrived and introduced herself. She was in her late thirties She immediately took control of the situation and requested she spend time with her client before the inspector interviewed him. Having told her all he knew and briefed her about his relationship with his brother, Inspector Gale and DC Jon Benn entered the room and switched on the recorder.

"Time of interview is 3.43 pm on Wednesday 28th June. In attendance are Inspector Nigel Gale and DC Jon Benn and the accused, Mr. Tom Taylor and his legal representative, Charlotte Minchin-Hart."

The reality of Tom's predicament became apparent in that instant. He knew he had nothing to hide. In fact, he had no idea why he had been arrested at all, but the fact that he was being interviewed under caution for murder made him nervous.

The inspector got underway.

"Would you please state your name for the record?"

"My name is Tom Taylor."

"Thank you, Mr. Taylor. Can you tell me what kind of relationship you had with the recently deceased Mrs. Mary Taylor, your brother's wife?"

"Relationship? Well, as you said inspector, she was my brother's wife and that made her my sister-in-law."

"Yes, I understand, but what kind of personal relationship did you have?"

"My brother and I have never, well, we have never really got on, so we spent little time together over the years. Mary was pleasant enough. We, that is my wife and I, made every effort to keep the relationship going but there was no real chemistry between the couples."

"So, you did not spend much time together as couples?"

"No. As I said, I did not get along with my brother in a social context, and that meant we had little to do with Mary?"

"When you did meet up with your brother and his wife, what did you talk about?"

"Not much. Idle conversation. On the occasions they came to us for lunch, or on rare occasions, to one of our dinner parties, we would always end up arguing."

"So, you argued with Mrs. Taylor?"

"No inspector I argued with my brother."

"What about?" Tom sighed.

"Where do I start? We argued about everything. Rod has always been jealous of our lifestyle. Not that we are that well off."

"Oh really? You have an extremely nice house Mr. Taylor, I would say you were extremely well off in my book."

"Everything is relative, inspector. My brother is not like me. I have worked hard all my life to have a lovely home and a successful business while he has sat at home feeling sorry for himself. He has been totally incapable of holding down a decent job for any length of time. He is lazy in my view, expecting everything to land in his lap, but that is not how the world works."

Tom was allowing his frustrations with his brother to cloud his emotions. The inspector was happy for him to pour his heart out.

"There seems to be a lot of deep-felt anger in you, Mr. Taylor, as far as your brother is concerned?"

"Not anger, inspector. Frustration. I have spent years trying to help him, advising him on a way out of his situation but he ignored me."

"He is older than you, is he not? Is it a surprise to you that an older brother might take exception to being lectured by his younger sibling?"

"Possibly… inspector, forgive me, but where is all this leading? You have arrested me for Mary's murder, which I have to say is absurd, and yet, you have not said why you think I murdered her or what evidence you have gathered to show that I did?"

"All in good time, sir."

The questioning continued for an hour when the inspector, having garnered enough information about the background to the two brother's relationship, dropped the bombshell.

"Mr. Taylor. Were you in a relationship with Mrs. Mary Taylor?"

"No! The notion is quite ridiculous! What makes you think I was?"

"Your brother, Rod, says you were."

"Rod told you I was having an affair with Mary?! That is nonsense, why would he say that?"

"You tell me Mr. Taylor?"

"Inspector, what else has my so-called brother told you?"

"He told me that you were having an affair with his wife, and he caught you one day having sexual relations." Tom laughed until he noticed that the inspector was clearly deadly serious.

"Are you denying your brother's account?"

"Absolutely, unequivocally! Has he gone mad? I assume he was drunk when you found him. I can only imagine he was having a mental aberration… No, inspector, I was most certainly not having a relationship with Mary, nor have I ever had sex with her or been caught by my brother doing so!"

"Tell me about the locket you gave Mrs. Mary Taylor."

"I explained when you came to my home, inspector, I did not give Mary a locket, inscribed or otherwise. I am sorry, inspector, you really are barking up the wrong tree."

"It is alleged Mr. Taylor, that not only were you having an affair with Mrs. Mary Taylor when your brother found you in bed with her, but that you also offered him a bribe not to tell your wife about the affair. Your brother was prepared to take your money for staying silent, but Mrs. Mary Taylor refused to be traded for money and said she would tell your wife anyway, irrespective of how much you offered them. It is also alleged that whilst your brother was out of the room attending to someone knocking at the door, you got into an argument with Mrs. Mary Taylor, which resulted in you strangling her with a scarf. Is that true, Mr. Taylor?"

Tom looked incredulously at his solicitor, and she promptly asked the inspector for some private time with her client. The two police officers agreed to leave the room and the recording was stopped.

"Charlotte, if I may call you that?"

"Of course, Tom."

"This is all nonsense. It is a complete fabrication. I cannot believe my brother would say such things. The alleged story is a lie from start to finish."

"Tom, the inspector has not made it up. Your brother has implicated you in her murder. You have not been charged, though, it is clear they only have your brother's word for what allegedly happened and no hard proof."

"And they will not find any proof because I did not do it!"

"I understand, but what I was about to say…"

"Sorry, for interrupting you, Charlotte. As you can imagine, this has come as a great shock to me."

"I am sure. I was going to say, the inspector's line of questioning is designed to get you to talk freely in the hope that you will incriminate yourself. I believe you have answered his questions so far in an honest and direct way, but I still think it wise from here if you adopt the response of 'No Comment' in answering further questions."

"Surely, if I do that, it indicates that I am unwilling to cooperate, and I am trying to hide my guilt?"

"No. That is not the case. It is for the police to gather enough tangible evidence to build a case to charge you. If you did not commit the crime and there is no evidence to prove you did, they will eventually have to let you go."

"How long can they detain me?"

"Twenty-four hours. Then, if they believe they have enough to justify holding you for longer, they can apply to the courts for an extension of thirty-six or a maximum of ninety-six hours."

"Okay. I will follow your advice."

The police officers returned and resumed the recorded interview. Charlotte spoke directly to the inspector. "Inspector, my client maintains his innocence of the crimes you have alleged. Up until now, he has been cooperative in his answers to your questions but no longer wishes to comment further."

"Mr. Taylor, before we stopped the interview earlier, I asked you if you strangled Mrs. Mary Taylor with a scarf. What is your response to that question, for the record?"

"No comment."

"So, again I ask you, did you have an affair with Mrs. Mary Taylor at any point in the past?"

"No comment." The inspector smiled.

"Thank you, Mr. Taylor. It is our intention that you remain in custody for further questioning for the next twenty-four hours. If, during that time, we believe there is justifiable reason to detain you for longer, we will apply to the courts for an extension. Interview terminated at 4.52 pm."

Tom asked Charlotte if she would call Penny to update her and reassure her that all was well. She agreed to do so. He was then taken to a cell and Charlotte left the building to call Penny.

"Mrs. Taylor. Hello, this is Charlotte Minchin-Hart, the solicitor representing Tom. Tom has asked me to call and reassure you that he is okay." Penny was sick with worry.

"Oh, thank you so much, I have been so worried. So, what is happening?"

"The police have interviewed Tom and have decided to detain him for further questioning."

"How long will he have to stay there?"

"They can hold him for a maximum of twenty-four hours, after which, if they want to question him further, they can apply to the courts for an extension."

"Golly. Can you tell me why they think he killed Mary?"

"I am afraid not, but you can be rest assured that I will do all I can to have him released. Tom will have an opportunity to call you shortly."

"Thank you, Charlotte."

"It is my pleasure. Goodbye."

Within the hour, Tom was able to call Penny. He relished the opportunity to update her.

"In a totally bizarre way, the process is quite novel. It is as though I have been hired as an actor in one of those crime series you love to watch. You know, the interview room with the accused and their lawyer on one side, and the two police interrogators on the other. The tape machine…"

"Tom," she cut him off abruptly. "Tell me what happened?" It was clear she was worried about him. He was a strong character, mentally, but in the very crime series he was referring to, she had also seen tough people crack under pressure and wondered if Tom was buckling.

"Well, if I gave you three, or indeed thirty guesses, my darling, on how this scene is unfolding, I guarantee you would fail with every attempt." He took a deep breath and told her everything that had happened. When he finished, there was silence on the other end of the line before Penny said,

"Tom... that is crazy!" In her heart, she knew it was all a

lie, but in the back of her mind, there was a nagging doubt, especially after the way Tom had acted toward his brother in recent times.

"Of course, it is a complete fabrication, utterly crazy, but I saved the punchline. After Mary refused to accept hush money and threatened to tell you about the affair, I strangled her whilst Rod was out of the room. Horrified by what I had done, Rod went to call the police, but I persuaded him to accept over a half a million pounds if he kept quiet!"

"But why would Rod say such things?"

"It is obvious. After our spat a few days ago, when he tore up the cheque that I gave him, he must have reflected on what happened and wished he had taken the money. His pride would not allow him to come back to me, cap in hand, asking me to write another cheque, so he masterminded a plan to get his revenge anyway. Of course, I am only speculating. But what complicates things is that you deposited the money in his account, and I sense that he is totally unaware he has that money deposited in his account, but if the police investigate, and they will, they will find the deposit."

"Oh, Tom, you were right, I should never have transferred the money. I am so sorry. But look. We know the truth, and it will come out. The police are not fools. They will meticulously go through the detail, and it will be obvious that Rod has lied. Despite what he said, they have no proof, no evidence that you murdered Mary! I still cannot believe, even after your spat with him, that he would make up such a story to implicate you! Charlotte called me and said they were planning to hold you for twenty-four hours, have they told you when they will interview you again?" Tom changed the subject.

"Look. Do not worry. I have had time to think about the business, this drama at the police station unfolded just as I was about to sort out the fallout from the fire at the warehouse.

Fortunately, I have already briefed Susie to undertake a lengthy list of tasks which I am sure she is getting on with, but would you be kind enough to call her and let her know that I will be out of contact over the next day or so? Call the office number. We have transferred all calls to her mobile."

"Should I tell her where you are? Incidentally, your mobile, which you left in the study, has pinged several times and you also have voicemail messages. I think some of the text messages are from Susie, but I cannot open your phone to look at them without your security code."

This revelation made him anxious; the last thing he wanted was for Penny to trawl through his messages, especially the many steamy exchanges he had had with Susie.

"Yes, there is no harm telling Susie where I am." He paused to think. "Darling… there is no security code on my mobile, I use fingerprint recognition, so the messages will have to wait." His off-the-cuff response proved to be a stroke of genius. He knew Penny was less than comfortable with technology and would not know if he was telling the truth of not.

"Okay, darling. I will call Susie. Please call me again later if you get the chance. I love you, Tom."

Tom ended the call with a degree of apprehension. Was it wise to ask Penny to call Susie? Susie loathed her, simply because she had Susie's man. Susie was manipulative, especially with people she did not like, or when she was frustrated with Tom. She had a way of saying one thing but meaning another, and there was always a risk the person on the receiving end would work out what she really meant and be offended. He was concerned that she would use the conversation with Penny to tease her or reveal something about her relationship with him. That said, he knew it was pointless speculating now on what may or may not happen.

Penny made a cup of tea and called Susie. She had always

liked her. She was extremely hard working and dedicated to the business, a true asset. The perfect replacement for her when she stepped back from working in the firm. She took her tea into Tom's study, where she found a notepad and called Susie.

"Hello, Taylor Publishing, how may I help you?"

"Oh, hello darling Susie. Penny here, how are you coping?"

"Oh, it is you, Penny. I thought it was Tom calling?"

"No, it is me, dear. Look, I do not want you to worry, but Tom was arrested and taken to the police station for questioning about his brothers' wife's murder. You may remember Mary was murdered a few weeks ago, I am sure Tom would have told you?" There was a brief silence.

"Tom… arrested? Were you not arrested?"

"Me, dear? No. Why would they arrest me?"

"Why have they have arrested Tom… it must be a mistake?"

"Of course it is. I am sure he will be released any time soon. Listen, I do not want you to worry. I understand Tom has left you a list of things to do?"

"I hope they release him soon… I could not bear to be without him for long."

"You are sweet. You underestimate your ability. You can cope without Tom for a while. He has often told me he could not do without you." Susie paused.

"So… why are you calling me?" Susie did not want to speak any further to the woman that occupied the same bed as her lover. Penny was slightly taken aback by her abruptness, although she had been on the receiving end many times before, but she put it down to her direct approach, which was part of what made her good at her job.

"Oh… just to let you know about Tom's situation and to see if there is anything I could do to assist you? I know how stressful it must be for you after the fire."

"No, I am coping fine. The best thing you could do is get Tom out of jail."

Penny laughed. Again, she was taken aback by Susie's direct communication.

"I wish I could wave a magic wand and have him home safe and well, but I do not think the police will listen to me."

"Well, they should do. You of all people know he is innocent."

Penny's laughter turned to slight annoyance. Susie's tone was uncalled for. It seemed odd that she would think that Penny could change Tom's current predicament.

"Susie, dear. Of course, I know Tom is innocent of Mary's murder.

The notion that Tom would kill anyone, let alone Mary, is absurd, but if I am honest, I am slightly upset by your tone of voice." Susie had let her emotions get to her. Her venom for Penny was spilling over and she needed to back off.

"I am sorry… I am just worried for Tom. I just want him back." Of course, what she really meant was that she wanted him back in her life. What Penny heard was that she was desperate for him to be back at the business as she was struggling to cope.

"I understand, dear. I know you want him back, but I have every confidence that you will cope. He should be released within the next twenty-four hours, so it will not be long before you will see him again. If you need any assistance, do call me."

"Okay."

With that, Susie put the receiver down. Strange girl. Highly strung, thought Penny. It did not enter her head that the abruptness reflected anything more sinister. The last thing she would imagine was that Tom would be having an affair with his PA. He was an expert at masking the truth and covering up his infidelity. Penny felt ill at ease, so she did what she always did in times of stress and called Ginny over for coffee and a chat.

"So, what is the latest with George?" Penny was desperate to disclose information about Tom's arrest but knew Ginny was just as eager to update her on George's affair.

"He came to the house yesterday evening after I agreed I would talk again about him returning home. I left it a couple of days for him to sweat before contacting him. You remember, I said I needed time to think over whether I wanted him back or not?"

"And…?"

"Well, I have never seen him so desperate. George is not exactly the most romantic man. Rarely over the years of our marriage has he ever expressed his feelings for me. Well, you know what some men are like! Not Tom, of course, he is a treasure. Well, anyway, he looked at me with dewy eyes as though we had met for the first time and fallen in love. He hung on my every word. It was funny to see him the way he was, but I gave the impression I was taking the whole thing very seriously. We talked for an hour," Ginny was keen to string out the drama, "and I read him the riot act. I told him that if I allowed him back, I wanted to see a different man, a different relationship, and he agreed. I said if I got an inkling that he had an interest in that Angelique or any other woman, our marriage was over, and I would cut off his appendage with a pair of scissors. He agreed."

Despite Penny worrying about Tom, she found Ginny's remark very funny and laughed.

"So, when is he coming back?"

"He is moving back tomorrow!"

"Well, that is great news! I am so pleased for you. George's fling is just what was needed to rejuvenate your relationship with him? And now you have taken control."

"I have, but a part of me just cannot accept that he was unfaithful. He still pleads his innocence that he never slept with her, but I just do not believe him. I mean, why would any man announce he wanted a divorce and move into a hotel to be with another woman if he had never slept with her? It makes no sense to me."

"Either way, I would put it out of your mind. Make the most of your new and hopefully reinvigorated marriage?" They both laughed.

"And you, any news about your brother-in-law?" Penny came back down to earth with a bump.

"Tom's been arrested for murdering Mary!"

Ginny gasped audibly. "What?! You are joking! Tom? Arrested for murdering Mary? Tom would not harm a fly, why would he do it?"

"Exactly. You would not believe what I am about to tell you."

Ginny was so desperate to hear that she refused Penny's offer of coffee. She listened mouth half open, without so much as an interjection throughout. When Penny was finished, she asked, "Goodness me! You could not make that up… well, of course, Rod did make it up, but you know what I mean?"

"I do. I spoke to Tom earlier and tried to reassure him that the truth will come out; it always does. Well, mostly."

"Are you suggesting there is a chance the story is true?!"

"Absolutely not, but I am fearful that innocent people are sometimes mistakenly found guilty and go to prison. I just hope and pray this all works out."

Ginny tried to reassure Penny. "When are you expecting him to be released from custody?"

"They have the right to hold him for twenty-four hours.

They have interviewed him once with his solicitor present, but he expects they will want to interview him again, otherwise why detain him?"

"And what about Rod?"

"I have absolutely no idea, and after this, I do not care what happens to that man. Over the years, we have both tried to help him and this is the way he treats us. I told you that Tom offered Rod over half a million pounds to pay off his debts so he could make a fresh start. Well, after saying he would accept the money, he tore up the cheque when Tom gave it to him. Later, when I told Tom what he had done, he was delighted because, truth be told, he did not want to give it to him. It was clearly an impulsive gesture that he regretted. We had a row. Tom stormed off and stupidly, later that day, I went to the bank and transferred the money to Rod's account, believing it was the right thing to do. Tom had offered it, and Rod certainly needed the money to pay off his debts.

How I regret that now. And despite Rod having all that money, he still tries to implicate Tom in Mary's murder! It is beyond me."

"Golly. Like you, I am completely lost for words. But did Rod know that you had transferred the money before spinning his story to the police?"

"Well, that I do not know. On reflection, probably not, because he had been arrested for breaking and entering, and stealing bottles of whisky from a Mini Market. So, perhaps he is unaware of his good fortune."

Penny and Ginny nattered for another hour or more before Ginny returned home. It was later in the day when Ginny called on the phone.

"Hello Pen. Nothing much, but I forgot to tell you when George was pouring out his affection for me yesterday evening, he told me that 'Angelique,' his mistress with pretentious parents… really, who would name someone 'Angelique…' was in fact not called Angelique. She had lied about her name to protect her real identity. She had used George… silly man… as a way of making her boyfriend jealous. Anyway, George confessed; he said he wanted to get everything out into the open. He had made enquiries and found out where 'Angelique' lived. He went to her apartment and found her in her dressing gown in the middle of the day and her boyfriend, an older man, in his underpants. That scared him off. I just thought I would tell you."

Penny thought for second.

"Do you think it was her boyfriend? She might be a prostitute. What is it with men? Why are they so afraid of long-term relationships?"

"Maybe, like Georges' tart, she needs to find a younger man, someone her own age, and leave our men alone!"

CHAPTER 9 – FREEDOM

Tom had more than enough time to think about the challenges that were stacking up in his life as he sat quietly in his cell. He was innocent of Mary's murder, so he knew his chances of release over the next few hours or at worst, the next day or so, were good. The police needed evidence to detain him for much longer and applying to the courts for an extension was not a given; it would only be granted if they had enough to substantiate their belief that Tom was guilty. Of course, they would not find anything to incriminate him.

What did concern him was Susie's volatility, and the chances of George disclosing information to Ginny or Penny. For Tom, these were the same thing. If Ginny knew, Penny would know, and vice versa. He worried about the fragility of the business. The fire had destroyed the fabric of the business, but not the records and data, which were backed up on an external server, but still, being able to put all the pieces together like a jigsaw would take time. He needed to be released, not locked up in a cell.

He had supper and been informed that he would be interviewed again and that his solicitor was on her way. Charlotte arrived ten minutes later and spoke to Tom privately.

"Tom, this second interview is also under caution. I sense that the inspector has something new to talk to us about. Remember, if you are asked questions, you feel uncomfortable answering, or that you feel may compromise your position, you simply say: 'No Comment.' If I feel the questioning steps outside the usual permitted boundaries, I will say so; otherwise, I will remain silent."

Tom felt anxious. He sensed the next interview might prove more challenging. They were shown into the interview room.

Inspector Gale and DC Jon Benn entered the room and switched on the recorder.

"Time of the second interview is 7.57 pm on Thursday 28th June. In attendance are Inspector Nigel Gale and DC Jon Benn and the accused, Mr. Tom Taylor and his legal representative, Charlotte Minchin-Hart.

"Mr. Taylor. In our first interview, you told us a good deal about the relationship you had with your brother and the deceased Mrs. Mary Taylor. You said that you had a strained relationship with your brother, is that true?"

"Yes. Inspector. We have never really got on. We are poles apart in our thinking on most subjects. We were never close even as children. I tried over the years to help him, although I admit it was not to win his affection as a brother; I did it to genuinely help him out of his predicament."

"Describe the predicament, as you put it, that your brother was in?"

"He was always moaning about having no money. He failed to hold down a job. He lacked focus and motivation. He seemed to drift through life, that mental state is alien to me, inspector. We are all wired differently, I suppose."

"Yes, I suppose we are. We do not all have your talent to run a successful business, Mr. Taylor, do we?"

"Precisely what I just said."

"But if you did not get along with your brother, why bother at all?"

"My wife, Penny, wanted us to at least be civil rather than we remove them from our lives completely."

"That is an interesting expression, Mr. Taylor. 'Remove them from our lives completely?"

"A figure of speech, inspector, nothing more. If you are about to ask me again, did I murder my brothers' wife, I can save you the trouble and give you another emphatic, no." The inspector dived straight in.

"So, let me be clear. You had a strained relationship with your brother and the deceased?"

"No, I did not say I had a strained relationship with Mary although, unlike my wife, Mary made no effort to encourage Rod to have a good relationship with me. I sensed whenever we met as couples, Mary had primed Rod to get into an argument with me about politics, the environment, and such things… She stirred things up if you know what I mean?"

"I do. Why would she do that?"

"Because she envied our lifestyle, our assets, and the fact that we were successful as a couple while they spent most of their lives living from hand to mouth…"

"But your brother will not be living hand to mouth any more, will he, Mr. Taylor?"

"What do you mean inspector?" Tom was nervous. He knew the inspector had uncovered the money Penny had transferred into Rod's bank account and he would now have to explain how it got there.

"Well, during our investigation, we discovered that you deposited a significant amount of money into your brother's bank account only two days ago, totalling over six hundred thousand pounds. Now, that is a lot of money, Mr. Taylor. Why would you do such a thing? Why would you give a brother you do not like such a considerable amount of money?" Charlotte intervened.

"I think my client would prefer not to comment, inspector." She looked over at Tom he immediately shook his head. He had nothing to hide so he would answer the question.

"No, thank you, Charlotte, but I am happy to answer the inspectors' question. I have nothing to hide. After my brother had gone on his drinking binge, you will recall you had to bring him in, the first time, I mean…"

"Yes, Mr. Taylor. Do continue."

"Well, after that, my wife and I took pity on him. As you know, he had got into a lot of debt and there was no way he could pay his way out of the problems he had, so we offered to clear them for him… to give him a fresh start. I also offered to find and pay for rented accommodation for him for twelve months."

"Goodness. That is a very generous thing to do, almost noble."

"Thank you, inspector, we thought so too."

"But would you not agree, Mr. Taylor, that to most people, me and DC Benn included, that giving away so much to a brother you had no time for stretches credibility? I put it to you that you transferred money into your brother's bank account as a bribe to keep him quiet after you killed his wife. Is that not what happened?"

"No, inspector. That is not why I transferred the money into his account. I have explained why I did it."

"So, you admit to transferring the money?"

"Goodness me, inspector, I did not realise you were hard of hearing." He cut himself off and took a breath. He knew insulting the inspector was the wrong call. "My apologies. I did not mean to be rude, but I thought I had already explained…"

The inspector interrupted him. "Strictly speaking, Mr. Taylor, you have lied to me, have you not?"

"Lied? No!"

"We have evidence that the money transferred into your brother's account was actually executed by your wife, Mrs. Penny Taylor."

"Semantics, inspector."

"Is that so? Or are you covering up for your wife, Mr. Taylor? Would it not be unreasonable to assume that you both plotted the murder of Mrs. Mary Taylor?"

"Yes, it would, inspector. It would be most unreasonable."

"So, as far as you are concerned, we can discount your wife, so that only leaves you. Did you kill Mrs. Mary Taylor?"

Tom was getting frustrated and looked across to his solicitor.

"We are going around in circles here, inspector. No, I did not kill Mary Taylor."

The inspector had tried his best to get Tom to confess or slip up in his story, but to no avail. He knew he was clutching at straws, but he still wondered if there was any significance in Penny Taylor transferring the money instead of Tom, so he decided to question her later.

Penny was watching TV when the inspector buzzed at the gate to gain entry.

"Hello. May I help you?"

"Mrs. Taylor. Inspector Gale and DC Amanda Ross. I wonder may we have a word with you about a few matters? Can you let us in?"

"Of course, do come up. Penny pressed a button, and the gate opened. As she opened the door and welcomed them in, she offered to make tea.

"No, that is kind of you, but we will just press on if we may. We shall try and be brief."

"Do take a seat, inspector." They both sat on the sofa as Penny perched awkwardly on an easy chair. She was nervous.

"Mrs. Taylor. We are aware from the interview with your husband that he did not get on with his brother, is that true?"

"Inspector, I am happy to answer your questions, and I would be the first to admit I am not an expert in law, but should I not have a legal representative, as Tom does?"

"Why, do you think it would be necessary? You are not under caution. You are not under arrest, Mrs. Taylor. I merely want to ask you a few questions to clarify various statements that have been made by your husband. Is that okay?"

"Yes, of course. I did not mean…"

"I understand it can all seem a bit official."

"Yes. I am not sure what Tom would want me to say?" Penny was getting increasingly agitated. Instantly she knew saying what she had just said sounded as though she would only repeat what Tom told her to say, irrespective of the truth. In other words, she would lie for him. Of course, this was an innocent enough statement from a woman who was nervous and loved her husband, a husband that had been arrested for murder, but it was music to the inspector's ears.

"What might you say that would incriminate your husband, Mrs. Taylor?"

"I am not good at all this. I was not suggesting he has done anything wrong, or I would lie for him if he had…"

"Alright, Mrs. Taylor. Let me ask you this question. Did you or did you not pay over six hundred thousand pounds into your brother-in-law's bank account yesterday?"

"Yes. I did."

"And why did you do that?"

"Tom had promised to settle Rod's debts. After Mary's murder, when Rod was staying here, the two of them had a row about something and nothing, and when Tom gave Rod a cheque to cover his debts, Rod tore it up. It was all confused at the time. Anyway, if I am honest, I was unhappy with the way Tom spoke to Rod, which caused him to pack a bag and leave the following morning. After leaving us, of course, he broke into the Mini Market, and you arrested him. Tom and I had a row about it all, something we never do normally, and Tom went off to his office. In a moment of madness, I decided to go to the bank and deposit the money into Rod's account so that he could use it to pay off his debts. I was a little uneasy not telling Tom what I had done, but I worked on the premise that he had written the cheque in good faith, I was doing what was intended. When I told Tom, he raised an eyebrow, but then, he was fine about it. That is really all I can tell you, inspector."

He smiled, "That was extremely helpful, Mrs. Taylor. Thank you. So, just to clarify, the reason for giving your brother-in-law such a huge amount of money was to pay off his debts?"

"Yes."

"The debts of a brother your husband loathes?"

"Yes. This is partly what we argued about. Rod saw the money as a way of Tom repaying him for the way he had been treated over the years. At least, that is what he said. It seemed odd to me because we had always tried to help them, in a modest way. Tom would always give advice to Rod, but he never accepted it in good faith. It was awkward most of the time, when we were together as couples."

"So, your husband treated his brother badly, did he?"

"No. I think you are confusing my words, inspector…"

"My apologies, let me rephrase that question. If Rod thought he had been treated badly by your husband, what do you think he meant by that? Had Tom done something to his brother that his brother found hard to forgive?" The inspector was again in the territory of clutching at straws, but he thought by probing in this way, Penny might reveal why they were parting with such a huge sum of money. Had Tom in fact murdered Mary and this was Rod's compensation?

Penny was confused to say the least. She had already asked if she should have legal representation but had been assured it was not necessary. Still, she felt she may have said something she would regret.

"Inspector, I am a little worried that I may be saying things that you are misinterpreting. My husband is an innocent man. He would not harm a fly. He is a loving, faithful man, and someone I would entrust with my life. He is not a murderer. I really do not think I can help you any further."

"Well, thank you again Mrs. Taylor. We will be on our way. Incidentally, you are not planning to go anywhere over the next few days, are you? In case we need to speak to you again?"

"No, inspector. I am not going anywhere."

"Thank you. When we leave, do you need to open the electric gate for us?"

"No, just approach the gate slowly and it will open for you automatically."

"Good evening, Mrs. Taylor." The inspector and DC Benn left.

Penny poured herself a large gin and tonic and sat on the sofa. She was extremely worried. Had she said anything that Tom would be unhappy with? What had Tom told the inspector in his interview? Had he fabricated a story for any reason, and if he had, had she undermined him? She started to read a book but there was no way she could concentrate. She wanted Tom to ring so she could discuss the content of the interview. Eventually, Tom rang.

"Hi darling. I had a second interview with the inspector. It all went well."

"Tom, did you know the inspector was planning to come here to the house to question me?"

There was a pause before Tom responded.

"No, but I assume from what you just said that he paid you a visit?"

"Yes." With that, she burst into tears.

"Penny, what is the matter?"

"I am really confused. The inspector asked me questions and I told him the truth, that is all I could do."

"About what? What did you say?"

Penny explained in fine detail what the inspector had asked her and the responses she gave. Tom was happy about most of what she had said, although from what he could determine, Penny may have given the inspector reason to think that the money they deposited in Rod's account was put there to bribe Rod in some way. Of course, Rod had already fabricated the story that Tom had tried to bribe him to keep him quiet after he had allegedly murdered Mary. He wondered what the inspector would make of it.

After twenty minutes, he had to end the call but promised to ring back in the morning. Hopefully, he would know by then if they planned to release him or seek an extension for his detention.

The following morning, the inspector knew he had only a few hours left to either charge Rod or release him from custody. He faced the same dilemma with Tom, although he had more time to play with, as well as the option to seek a court extension if he thought it justified.

After Tom's emphatic denial of his brother's allegations, the inspector was keen to find the underlying cause of the matter. Had Rod lied, and if he had, why had he done so?

After Rod had been arrested for breaking and entering and theft from the Mini Market, he needed time to sober up. He had never been a heavy drinker in the past, but he had discovered that alcohol, especially in enormous quantities, allowed him to escape temporarily from the challenges he faced in life, which were becoming more acute. Of course, like most heavy drinkers, there was a price to pay for over-indulgence: irrational thinking, memory loss, and the prospect of a hangover that could last for days.

Rod was only now beginning to emerge from his last drinking bout. It could be argued that his first interview with the inspector had taken place when he was less than mentally alert, but that said, Peter had sanctioned the interview with his client. The inspector called Peter and arranged a second interview with Rod. After the notifying formalities were complete, the inspector and DC Benn got the session underway.

"Mr. Taylor, when we last interviewed you, you told us that your brother, Tom, had attempted to bribe you to keep you quiet after he had murdered your wife. Is that true?"

"Yes, inspector."

"Yes, he attempted to bribe you or yes, he murdered your wife?" Rod paused for a moment.

"That he attempted to bribe me for murdering Mary."

"So, you stand firm on your assertion that he both murdered her and attempted to bribe you?" Rod looked at his solicitor.

"I thought I had just answered your question, inspector?"

"I just wanted to hear that on both counts, according to you the allegations are true."

"Yes."

Ordinarily, Rod was a conformist. He tried desperately hard in life not to step out of line and certainly not where the law was concerned. With recent events, though, that principle had been put aside. He seemed prepared to say and do anything without rational thought or an understanding of the consequences of his actions. He believed his life was over and the difficulties he faced over the years, especially in the couple of weeks since Mary was murdered, were in some way his brother's fault. He had entered that space in his mind where he was able to convince himself that the stories he made up, were true. He lacked the ability to differentiate between fact and fiction.

"Mr. Taylor, based on the statements you made in your first interview, the facts of which you have just confirmed, we arrested your brother on suspicion of murdering your wife and took the opportunity to interview him. He flatly denies ever bribing you or indeed murdering your wife. So, who is telling the truth? You, or your brother?"

Rod seemed stunned that Tom had been arrested and questioned. Of course, in his mental state, he had not thought that his statement would have such an effect.

"So, you arrested Tom?"

"Yes, Mr. Taylor, why would we not arrest the man you allege murdered your wife? I thought you would be pleased to know he is in custody?"

"Yes, I am, of course." Rod was hesitant in uttering the words.

"In light of his arrest and denial, do you wish to change your statement?"

"In what way?"

"Do you wish to retract your allegation that your brother bribed you and murdered your wife… or not?"

Rod was becoming increasingly agitated. He was not confused by the inspector's question, that was straightforward enough, he was confused because he was unable to remember what he had said and why. Why had he tried to frame Tom? He struggled to remember the incident at Tom's house, when he had overheard Tom uttering disparaging comments about him to Penny, or when he was with Penny in the kitchen and had torn up the cheque. He had an overwhelming feeling of remorse that he was making untrue statements that would alienate him further from his only family, his brother. He wondered if he should come clean at this pivotal moment or press on with his assertion that Tom was guilty. He chose the latter; what did he have to lose? His life was a mess, he had lost Mary, he was penniless, and he would be on the streets in no time at all. Why should Tom continue to prosper and not pay a price for the way he had treated him over the years? It was his fault that he was a failure, and he should suffer for it.

Rod looked the inspector squarely in the eye.

"I have no intention, inspector, of retracting my allegations, because they are true."

"We also spoke to Mrs. Penny Taylor in our enquiries, and I have to say she corroborated your brother's statement to us concerning recent events between you and your brother. This includes the fact, and we have verified this, that she deposited over six hundred thousand pounds into your personal account, to help you clear your debts..."

Rod interrupted the inspector, "Penny transferred the money into my account?! You mean I now have the money?" He smiled with relief.

"You have a very generous brother, do you not Mr. Taylor?"

"He was only paying me what he owed me..."

"So, had he borrowed the money from you and was now repaying his debt to you?"

Rod did not listen closely to the inspector's question as he was still soaking up the good news that he had the money in his bank account.

"It was payment for the way he has treated me over the years."

"Is that the case? Nothing to do with bribing you to keep quiet after he murdered your wife?"

Rod could see the inspector's questioning was unravelling his story. Now he had the money, was it even necessary to persist with his lies about Tom?

"No, inspector."

"So, I put it to you, Mr. Taylor, that you lied to us about your brother trying to bribe you. Is that true?"

Rod did not believe he could continue with his story and get away with it.

"Yes, fine, I lied but..."

The inspector interrupted him. "And did you also lie about your brother murdering your wife?"

Rod looked at his solicitor, then back at the inspector. He sighed.

"Yes."

The inspector had got a result. He was no further forward in knowing who murdered Mary Taylor, but he had unravelled several lies that could have wasted a good deal more of his time.

Rod and his solicitor were left in the interview room to discuss what had transpired and what would happen next.

Rod had already been charged with the Mini Market robbery and would certainly face an additional charge of perverting the course of justice. Peter knew Tom well and had been convinced of his innocence. Within the hour, Tom had been released from custody and was on his way home.

He looked a little dishevelled as he arrived back, and after greeting Penny, he took a shower and changed. Penny was thrilled to see him home.

"You unfortunate thing. Are you okay? It must have been a terrible ordeal?"

"I could think of better ways to spend my time! Look, darling, can we catch up at later? I really need to get on top of things, business wise?"

"Of course. Oh, when you called to say you were on your way home, I arranged a treat for us."

"Oh yes, what is that?"

"Well, Ginny and George are back together, thank goodness, so I have invited them over this evening for supper."

For Tom this was anything but a treat. In fact, it was the last thing he wanted to do. Having a social gathering with all that was going on in his life would be bad enough, especially after just being released, but supper with George after the incident at Susie's flat…? No. That was not a clever idea.

"Oh... no. I just want to spend the evening with you."

"Please, please darling. I have asked them already and Ginny was thrilled by the idea and has accepted."

Tom wondered if George had been as enthusiastic, but then, as he was serving his penance for straying, he could hardly refuse.

"Honestly, it is kind of you darling, but I would rather not have them round."

Penny was insistent it was just what they needed, a small social get-together with good friends. Both couples had reasons to celebrate – George and Ginny's reconciliation and Tom being released from custody.

"Tom, I am sorry, but on this occasion, I insist. It will do you good, and if I am honest, I need to unwind too after recent events!"

Tom had lost. Supper with George and Ginny would not be an unwinding for Tom. In fact, he would be spending the evening with someone that had seen him with his mistress in nothing but his underpants.

He retreated into his study and picked up the phone. There were sixteen messages and several voicemails. Most of the messages were from Susie, and others from some of his contacts who had heard about the fire and were offering their support. Susie's messages, if Penny had had access to them whilst he was being detained, would have been enough to reveal the true relationship Tom had with his personal assistant.

'I love you, Boss. I cannot wait to see you. Stay strong and think of me naked,' and other similar messages that Tom saw as incendiary.

He phoned her.

"Hi, just got home. How is your work schedule going?"

He was not about to get smoochy with her. His priority was the business, but of course, Susie had other ideas.

"Oh Tom, I am so pleased you are out! I have missed you so much! That awful brother of yours…"

"Yes, all is fine. So, what news?"

Susie sensed she would have to wait until Tom visited her at the apartment to celebrate having him back.

"I have covered off most of the things you wanted me to do, including speaking to the staff, but getting to the hospital has been impossible because I have had so much to do."

"I will call the hospital to make enquiries, no need to worry."

"The fire brigade came back, and the insurance assessor has also looked over what is left of the warehouse. The chap from the fire brigade confirmed that the cause of the fire was an electrical fault, and commented that from what he could see, we had not maintained conformity to latest fire regulations. To be honest, I did not really understand what he was telling me, it was all too technical." Tom was taken aback.

"Goodness! Who on the team is responsible for such matters, Susie?"

Susie was Tom's right hand woman, and he had loaded so much responsibility on her shoulders that they had both lost sight of who was doing what.

"To be honest, Tom, I have no idea. I suppose I assumed you were responsible?"

He was mildly irritated.

"But Susie, you have responsibility for everyone's job description in the business… a part of your own job description, if I remember correctly, is health and safety, insurance, and that sort of thing, is it not?"

Susie went on the defensive.

“Tom, that is really unkind…”

“Is it? Is it your responsibility or not? If I am wrong, you have my apology.”

Susie was angry.

“But everything ends up on my plate. You cannot expect me…”

Tom was bearing down on her unfairly, but he was not about to let up.

“Yes, I can. That is why I employ you. You are my personal assistant, and I expect you to perform the duties that fall within your remit.”

Susie had heard enough. She slammed down the phone. As she wiped the tears from her eyes, she was determined not to call him back. He had been totally unreasonable and vile toward her. Despite his affair with her, he had no compunction in tearing into her if he felt she had failed in her duties. Tom could not believe that she would hang up on him and was tempted to call her back to continue his assault but thought better of the idea. Within a few minutes, he received several emotional text messages from her, which he immediately deleted. He decided that in future, he would always delete Susie’s text messages and voicemails as a precaution. Fortunately, in his conversation the previous day with Penny, when she had informed him that he had several text messages, she had been unable to access his phone, which had come as a great relief. However, it made no sense to keep messages which could, one day, be his downfall.

Tom opened the letters that had arrived in his absence, one of which was a court summons for his dangerous driving offence. That was all he needed. The prospect of losing his license came with its own challenges. Frustrated, he punched the wall in his study and immediately regretted the action. His knuckles were sore.

After Susie's revelation that the fire brigade had announced that the warehouses electrical system was non-compliant, and that the insurance assessor had visited the premises and would certainly have come to the same conclusion, he thought it best to confront the situation and call the insurer to see where he stood. Susie had already told the insurer that a claim would be on its way. Despite being released from custody, nothing else that day had gone Tom's way.

He was able to establish with the insurance assessor that they had identified that the electrical system was non-compliant and for that reason, only a part, if any of the claim would be met.

He was told that on two previous annual checks, the insurer had raised the issue in writing, recommending immediate remedial work be undertaken. This advice had not been acted upon. Tom stood to lose hundreds of thousands of pounds if he were unable to claim against his insurance policy. This was devastating news and added salt to a gaping wound named Rod, and the cash that he now had at his disposal courtesy of Tom's generosity. He was tempted to punch the wall again but decided against it.

Only two days earlier, he had been motivated by the prospect of re-building the business after the fire, but this had been predicated on the insurer paying out against a substantial claim. Now, it seemed highly unlikely they would, although any attempt by the insurer to back away from a full settlement would be something he would fight vigorously. In truth, though, he knew he would stand little chance of winning a case, even if he paid for the best legal representation, which would not come cheap. The only way of realistically investing in a partial business re-build would be drawing down from his and Penny's personal finances and that would be something that Penny would resist.

Penny was not a risk taker and would argue that Tom should retire or find investors to make the business whole again. Whichever way he turned the future looked far bleaker than it did only a few hours before.

Tom sat staring out of the window onto the driveway, where his Porsche 911 and Range Rover were parked alongside Penny's Mercedes SL and wondered how long they could maintain their lifestyle. With the prospect of losing his driving license, he would have no need for two cars. He thought selling the Porsche would be the immediate best option. That alone would raise almost £80,000, as it was almost new. It was small fry compared to the amount he would need to raise to fulfil his ambitions in the business. He felt weary. The past few days had taken it out of him, and he wondered if he had the motivation and energy to start over again.

Penny popped into the study to remind him that George and Ginny were due to arrive within the hour, as if he needed reminding. He chose not to tell her about the likelihood of a dispute with their business insurer, or that he had received his summons. Instead, he changed, put a smile on his face, and waited for their guests to arrive.

Penny was excited at the prospect of seeing Ginny and George. Tom decided he would indulge her for the evening, knowing he would have to break unwelcome news to her soon enough. He had no idea how the encounter with George would go, but decided he would act normally, as though the incident at Susie's apartment had not happened.

Ginny and George arrived carrying flowers and a bottle of champagne. Penny bounced to the door, excited, with Tom apprehensively following behind. After exchanging pleasantries, they made their way to the drawing room for canapés and champagne, which Penny had put on ice.

Tom looked at George to get a sense of his mood and his feelings toward Tom. Better that he knew now, at the beginning of the evening than find out later.

Ginny and Penny were engrossed in idle conversation, so Tom took the opportunity to take George into his study. He would not confront him over Angelique/Susie, but he would instead enquire about him moving back home.

"When did you move back in then, George?"

"Yesterday. Look, I know this is difficult, Tom, us being here, I mean. But I want to…"

"Not at all, it is good to see you. I was taken aback when Ginny announced you were leaving her."

"Yes, it was foisted upon me. I had no intention of leaving her really but…"

Tom knew what George wanted to say, but he stopped him in his tracks.

"Look, George. We agreed at the apartment that this would go no further, and I appreciate your discretion so far. You obviously know I am having an affair with Susie, despite my pathetic claim when you arrived at the front door. I want to be frank and honest with you. I have no intention of leaving Penny. Susie is, well, to put it politely, she is a plaything! You know how engaging, well, how gorgeous she is. Like you, I could not resist her…" He slapped George on the back. "A shame I beat you to her!"

George was comfortable back at home with Ginny. He had got over his infatuation for Angelique and responded positively to Tom's quip.

"Look, we are grown up. It was mad of me to think I stood a chance with… I will call her Susie from now… with Susie. I am not cut out for affairs; I quickly discovered that. No, I am happy to be back with Ginny. But I do worry about you, Tom. I will not ask how long you have been seeing her, but you are risking a lot with Penny and the business by carrying on like this?"

Tom was relaxing. He knew George was onside and would not leak his indiscretion.

"We have been seeing each other for two years and I admit it is great fun, if that is an appropriate way of describing it, but I accept what you are saying, it is risky. I have been able to manage that risk up until now, but I sense it is getting more difficult by the day."

"Well, let me drop that subject for now, Tom. I am sure you will keep me updated when we next play golf?"

George was eager to hear about Tom's arrest.

"Ginny, the font of all knowledge of course told me about the difficulties with your brother and you being arrested. What on earth happened there?"

Tom relaxed and told him the whole story. He was quite well versed in it now. As he finished, he quipped… "and that's how I ended up being arrested! It would make a good movie!"

Tom was pleased he had managed to get back on side with George and felt comfortable he could trust him to say nothing about Susie. They went back to the drawing room as Penny called them for supper.

The dining room, like Tom's study, faced out onto the driveway, albeit a distance apart. Ginny and George were facing the window. As they were about to start their main course, Ginny spotted a car entering the driveway. Tom had forgotten to put the electric gate system on again.

"Oh look, you have a visitor."

Tom and Penny turned round to see Susie in the red Porsche, speeding toward the house. Penny was surprised to see her, even more so that she was driving so fast, scattering stones over the lawn as she went. Tom was also taken aback, and George's face fell.

"It is Susie. Tom, did you know she was coming to the house? Why is she driving so fast?"

Tom had to think on his feet.

"No idea, but it must be important. Look, you all continue with the meal, and I will sort things out and be back soon."

With that, he left the dining room and shut the door behind him so he would not be heard. He went to the front door just as Susie was about to ring the doorbell.

Susie was in a state of high tension.

"Tom, why have you not answered my text messages or returned my calls? I had to come over; I was worried you did not want me anymore… I was only doing my best… how was I to know that I needed to get someone to check the electrics?"

She threw herself into Tom's arms.

"Tell me you still love me, Tom! Please tell me…"

This was all too close to home, quite literally. It was fortunate that the dining room door was made of substantial oak with a good latch, so it was firmly closed, and they would only be heard if they decided to shout. He hoped, desperately hoped, that Susie would not do that.

"Look, come into my study."

He took her in and closed the door. He knew his mission was to dispatch her with a smile on her face as quickly as possible if he were to extricate himself from this latest drama.

"I am sorry. I have been totally tied up with the insurer all afternoon…"

"But Tom I have not spent any time with you since you were released. I waited at the apartment hoping you would visit, and assumed you were still angry with me."

"Of course, I am not." He embraced her, kissing her passionately as if he really meant it. It worked.

"Darling, I will see you first thing in the morning. In fact, put breakfast on for 7.30 am and we will spend the day in bed together. To hell with work! We deserve some quality time together. Is that okay?"

Of course, it was the perfect thing to say. She hugged him tightly.

"Oh, I love you so much Mr. Bunny!" She had never said that to him before, but he was not about to complain. Anything, but anything to send her on her way.

"Come on, I will show you to the door. I will see you tomorrow morning on the dot of 7.30 am, and make sure you open a bottle of champagne before I arrive!"

Like a lamb to the slaughter, she did as she was told. She made no mention of Penny and was certainly unaware that her other suitor, George, was in the next room. Of course, his own stress was double that of Tom's.

Tom opened the door and hugged her once more. He waved her goodbye and as she drove off, he closed the door with a thud, composed himself, and returned to the dinner table.

"Sorry, she was desperate to discuss some papers… have I missed anything?"

When it was time for the final course, Tom went into the kitchen with Penny to give her a hand. She took the opportunity to interrogate him.

"Darling, why is Susie coming to the house unannounced? Surely, she could have called in advance. I do not like her assuming she can turn up whenever she likes. You have a private life just as she does."

Tom nodded but said nothing. He dutifully carried the meal into the dining room and exchanged a nod with George to indicate that all was well.

The rest of the evening was taken up with Penny and Ginny, both in high spirits, chit chatting about nothing much that interested either George or Tom. They left the women and went to play billiards. Tom was exhausted. It had been quite a day, one way or another. After the guests left, Tom was keen to get to bed, saying he would clear up in the morning, knowing full well that Penny would insist that she did the chores. He was relying on her saying she would, as he had that important appointment early in the morning with Susie and he knew he had to keep it. He embraced Penny in a way that he had not done for some time. She was delighted with the affection he gave her in that moment. The embraces he shared with Susie were different; the hugs and kisses were sexually motivated. The moment he embraced Susie he knew what it would lead to. She was always very accommodating with his demands. For Tom, there was a sense of power and control. He knew she loved him more than anything else and would do anything to win his affection. He could turn the tap on and off at will. It felt good to be needed and, for an older man, desired.

Penny decided to relax and read her book for a while before retiring to bed. As Tom climbed the stairs, he looked down at her, she caught his eye, and they both smiled lovingly. Tom continued his journey to the bedroom. As he entered, he sat for a moment on Penny's dressing room chair and reflected.

He had enjoyed decades of success in the business, in his marriage, with friends, and he had much to be proud of. He was not a rich man by modern day standards, but he could have retired some years earlier and still lived very comfortably without the possibility of running out of cash. Since Mary's murder, though, so much had changed in his life, and it had only been a couple of weeks.

He had been arrested for Mary's murder, his business had perished in the fire, and he had given a brother he had little in common with, and now detested, a substantial amount of money to pay off his debts, at a time when his own financial challenges were only just beginning, and he could least afford it. He was also about to lose his ability to drive. It was a given that he would receive a sizeable fine and a driving ban, for one, or even three years. Added to all that, his marriage, which he desperately wanted to keep intact, was in jeopardy, as Susie's demands for him to divorce Penny and marry her were intensifying. There were so many balls in the air, but time would tell how good a juggler he was.

His most immediate plan of deception had to be crafted before he went to sleep. He could not expect to wake in the morning and idly announce to Penny, just a day after his release from custody, that he was going out for the rest of the day. There would be too many questions and few plausible answers. No, he had to decide before dropping off what he would tell her in the morning that would allow him to leave for the day without generating suspicion?

Over the two years he had been having the affair with Susie, he had fabricated dozens of stories to tell Penny so that he could spend time at her apartment. She had accepted them all without challenge. He had mastered the art of deception, and it now came easily to him.

It would be the same on this occasion. He decided when they woke at around 6.00 am, he would tell Penny that he had forgotten to mention that he was meeting the insurance assessor at the warehouse at 7.30 am and it was unlikely that he would return until late afternoon. Of course, he was sorry he had to go out and would rather spend the day at home with her, but he had no choice. It was perfect! Satisfied, he slept soundly.

CHAPTER 10 – HANGING BY A THREAD

They had never fitted curtains in the bedroom that completely darkened the room, preferring to wake quite naturally at daybreak. When either of them got up to make tea, they would go to the window and look across their beautiful garden. It was a moment of immense joy and a good start to the day.

It was 5.50 am. Penny got up and performed the usual ritual. It was a warm morning, and the sun had been up for some time. She quietly opened a window for a breath of fresh air. Then, she slipped on her dressing gown and went down to make some tea. When Tom woke, the first thing on his mind was telling Penny of his early morning meeting with the insurance assessor. Within ten minutes she had returned carrying a tray with the tea, and two glasses of champagne she had salvaged from the dinner party. She offered Tom a glass, which he accepted with a smile.

"Darling, let us toast our new future. I know it has been tough on you these past few days, but we will recover. I want you to be happy and stress free, Tom. I have every confidence you will do the right things to get the business going again. She was eager to reassure him about their future.

"Thank you…" Tom's muted response was understandable; he had some theatrics to perform if he were to escape for the day without a fight.

"And darling, once the insurer pays out and the business is running smoothly again, I want you to promise me that you will consider selling the company and retiring?"

Tom's luck was in, at least he thought so. This was the perfect opportunity to tell Penny he would be out for the rest of the day.

"You have just reminded me I agreed to meet the insurance assessor at the office at 7.30 this morning. It is likely to be a long session, but I will get back as quickly as I can."

"Oh, Tom. I wanted you at home all day today, I had planned a lunch for us. It is not every day your husband is released from custody!" She smiled.

"Sorry darling, I will make it up to you, I promise."

"I suppose the food will keep… well, I have an idea. If you are to endure a boring morning with the insurance assessor, then it is only fair that I share the boredom with you. I will come along."

Tom was horrified by Penny's suggestion, of course he would be. His mastery of deception honed over the past two years having an affair with Susie, demanded that he now pulled a rabbit from the hat. Not just any rabbit, but a pure white rabbit wearing a diamond encrusted necklace, not unlike the one he had recently bought for Penny in Guildford.

"That is really kind of you, but I will not hear of it. You go and play a round of golf with Ginny; I am sure she would be thrilled if you asked her."

"No, not this time, Tom. I want to spend the day with you, boring insurance assessor or not. What time is the meeting planned?"

"Look…" Tom was struggling to think of the next line that would hopefully get him off the hook. "It makes no sense. Let me sort out the assessor, I will insist the meeting is as short as possible, and I will be back in time for the lunch you have planned."

He thought this would do the trick and the necklace-wearing white rabbit would not be required. But Penny had other ideas.

"Tom, you are not listening to me. I want to be with you today. You can still chivvy the assessor, and we can be back for the lunch."

Tom's attempts to detour Penny's insistence that she

accompany him had failed to the last. There was no corner left for him to hide in; no rabbits to pull from the hat. His mastery of deception had failed on this occasion, and he now had think on his feet to manage the situation and remain credible. Of course, Penny was not the only challenge he had, though. How could he extricate himself from the champagne breakfast Susie would be preparing? In a flash, he saw the irony of the two woman each presenting champagne at breakfast. One could argue he was a lucky man to have two women so smitten with him, but like so many things in life, one man's meat, or champagne, in this instance, is another's poison. He could not contemplate phoning Susie to announce he was no longer coming for breakfast, or the carnal day he had planned in bed with her. There would be no way she would accept any kind of excuse, no matter how original or plausible.

Tom had no option but to accept Penny's generous offer. They drank their tea and sipped the champagne, then Penny went down to the kitchen to make breakfast. They had forty-five minutes to shower and dress before they set off for the thirty-minute journey to the burnt down warehouse to meet the imaginary assessor at 7.30 am.

At almost 7.00 am, Penny was ready to leave. Tom was in his study and had planned his strategy. He would suggest to her that they should take two cars, allowing him to go from the meeting with the assessor onto Susie's apartment, to discuss her progress on contacting all his stakeholders, while Penny would return home to prepare lunch.

Again, credit where credit was due, it was a brilliant idea. Admittedly, he would be late arriving at Susie's apartment for the champagne breakfast, but she was used to him being late for everything. At least he would arrive. Of course, he would have to fabricate a story that allowed him to leave around lunchtime so that he could get back home for Penny's lunch.

Alternatively, he could phone Penny after she had returned home and say that he had been delayed at Susie's, as there were business issues that he had to deal with and, unfortunately, he would have to miss lunch. On balance, the latter was by far the better option.

He knew disappointing Penny was just that: disappointing her. With Susie, however, disappointment would manifest itself into anger and threats of exposing his relationship with her. Of course, that was the last thing he wanted, especially as he was struggling to keep his head above water anyway.

As Tom came out of his study, Penny was in the hallway. He picked up two sets of keys, Penny's Mercedes SL, and the Range Rover. The Porsche was too risky. He knew he was incapable of staying within the speed limit and the very last thing he wanted was to be stopped again by the police.

"We will take two cars. That way, I can briefly catch up with Susie on some business stuff after the meeting with the assessor, and you can return to prepare lunch…"

"Oh, no Tom! I do not want to drive!"

"Oh, come on darling it makes sense…"

"No. Tom. We can both go to Susie's after the meeting with the assessor. I am sure she would be okay if I just sat and read a magazine or something while you do your business."

If he had not been having an affair with Susie, Penny's idea would have made sense. Why take two cars? Of course, what was likely to transpire at Susie's apartment had nothing to do with business, at least not in the traditional sense of the word, and certainly not as spectator sport that Penny would want to watch. Again, Tom's plans backfired. How on earth could he get around this one? Despite all the odds being against him, he tried once more.

"Darling, that is a bit unfair on Susie, I mean, the apartment might be untidy and the last thing she would want is for you to see it. No, we should take two cars."

Penny had made it clear that she wanted to spend the day with him no matter what happens, and she was now getting frustrated that he was trying to fob her off. She would not relent; shc was insistent that she would accompany him. It was now 7.12 am and within eighteen minutes, Susie would be at the apartment preparing a champagne breakfast, dressed to kill. His phone pinged. He knew it would be her.

"Who is texting you so early in the morning, Tom?"

"Probably the assessor; let us get going or we will be late."

Tom was resigned to taking the one car to a non-existent meeting at the burnt-down warehouse. He had no other option.

"If it is the assessor, darling, he might be texting to stay he is running late. Shall I read it for you?"

It was the last thing Tom wanted her to do. He got the phone out of his pocket as it pinged for a second time and looked at the messages as Penny got into the Range Rover.

'Morning, darling bunny. Breakfast is cooking and champagne is cold, but I am hot for you… please be on time!'

The second message read, 'I have the door unlatched, you can come straight in. I have nothing on!'

Naturally, Penny was eager to know what the assessor had said in his messages.

"Is he running late, darling?"

"It seems so." It was all he could say. His mind was racing, trying to fathom a way out of the situation he now found himself in.

"How late, darling?"

"Oh, not too late."

They drove away from the house to the main road and Tom headed toward the warehouse. It was a twenty-five-minute journey, the same journey he had taken in the Porsche a couple of days before when he had discovered the warehouse was on fire. At that time, he had been in a heightened state of stress; anxious to get there as quickly as he could. This time though, he was under a different kind of stress, trying frantically in his mind to work out how to control the situation. He was sailing close to the wind, something he enjoyed doing on his yacht when he felt in control, but in this instance, he had no control, no plan, no way out in his head. The next few hours could take him to the brink.

Penny attempted to make conversation on the journey, but he remained silent.

"Darling, are you cross with me for wanting to be with you?"

He was not cross with her, as she put it; he was berating himself for getting into such a mess of his own making. His lies and deception over the past couple of years in seeing Susie and, if he were honest, far longer than that with a string of other short-lived affairs, were coming home to roost. He was a condemned man waiting for his sentence to be handed down. How fickle life can be, he thought.

He had everything a man could wish for. A loving wife, a successful business, and everything that comes with it, but it was not enough. No, he craved the affection of young women, knowing he could afford to indulge them as he had done with Susie with the rent-free apartment and the Porsche. He loved living on the edge, believing that he was an expert manipulator and would never get caught. He was a proficient juggler who could pull white rabbits from a hat at a stroke, but no longer…

They arrived at the warehouse. It was in a forlorn state. What had been a smart warehouse and office building, was now a heap of rubble. Only part of it was still standing, but it had been cordoned off and was waiting demolition. The security guard knew Tom and waived him onto the site. He parked the car. It was now 7.34 am. Penny was keen to get the meeting over as quickly as possible.

"I wonder how long he will be?"

Of course, Tom knew he was never going to turn up.

"We will have to wait a while…" Just then, his phone pinged. Penny reacted.

"Ah, that must be him."

Penny looked at him, waiting for him to look at the text message. He knew instinctively who the sender was. He also knew in broad terms the content of the message. He had no option but to look down at it.

'You are already late, big boy. I am ready and waiting xxx.'

Tom avoided Penny's gaze. If there was a more momentous time to think on his feet, he certainly could not recall it.

Then, the phone rang. Text messages were one thing but dealing with a call from Susie as Penny sat next to him was an impossible ask without giving the game away. Very carefully, he managed to end the call but put the receiver to his ear as though he were having a conversation with the insurance assessor.

"Hello, Tom Taylor? Yes, Mr. Smith…"

Not an inspired choice of name but it would do.

"Oh, I see. Right. Well, I am sorry to hear that… have you called your breakdown company? Okay. Look, it is better that we reschedule the meeting for another day rather than us waiting here for you… Okay. No, it is fine. So, you will call me to rearrange. Yes, no, not a problem. Bye."

Penny had been listening intently to the non-conversation.

"Oh dear, poor man. That was a wasted journey, then?"

Tom quickly turned his phone off without Penny being able to see it. He was as white as a sheet.

"Are you okay, darling, you look pale?"

He should have said, no. I feel dreadful, and they could have been on their way home. Instead, though, he said, "No,

I am fine, darling."

At that precise moment, he believed he had just got away with a stroke of genius and had, at least for the time being, resolved the drama. What he had failed to remember was their earlier agreement. Penny spoke.

"That is good. At least we do not have to hang around here for hours. It is so sad seeing the building in this state. Shall we head to Susie's apartment, then?"

Now, he thought it was a good moment to feel physically sick.

"You were right, I do feel unwell. I have a bad headache coming on. Would you mind driving us home? I will catch up with Susie later!"

Penny changed seats with Tom and drove them back. On the return journey, Tom stayed quiet, feigning a headache. In his head, though, he was rejoicing. He had managed, through luck rather than judgement, to pull of his greatest deception.

Happiness was not his current state, but he was hugely relieved that he had managed once again to avoid being found out. He knew, though, that only part of the jigsaw puzzle had been resolved; to complete it meant dealing with the fallout from his non-arrival at Susie's apartment. His phone was switched off, so there was no chance of her text messages or voicemails getting through. They would have to wait until he was on his own.

They drew up outside the house. Penny parked the car after Tom had limped out and made his way into the drawing room. He had to phone Susie. Once again, he would need to find the right words that would smooth over the situation with her. As Penny entered the drawing room, she offered to make tea and said she would get him some pain killers, but Tom declined the offer, suggesting it would be best if he went to bed for a couple of hours. Penny agreed.

A few minutes later, he was lying on the bed. He switched on his phone and downloaded five text messages and two voicemails. The text messages were predictable. Susie was outraged, incensed that he had let her down once again. The champagne was on ice, the breakfast cooked and going cold, and she was there, stark naked, waiting for him.

He played the voicemails. She was beside herself. She screamed obscenities and wept uncontrollably. This was the last time he would do this to her. She planned to drive to his home and tell his precious Penny that he had been unfaithful. She also planned to delete everything on the business server, destroying the very fabric of the business and making it almost impossible for him to get it going again.

He had known in the car, after they arrived at the warehouse and were 'waiting for the assessor,' that the biggest challenge he had was Susie. He knew how emotional and unpredictable she was. There was never any forethought with her as far as her relationship with Tom was concerned. She never weighed up the outcome or consequences of her actions. No. She was in love with him, and when he failed her, as he often did, she said anything that came into her head. What was even more alarming for Tom, was that she was capable of, and willing to act upon her instincts, and there was absolutely nothing he could do about it.

Ironically, he was now genuinely getting a headache. Was it psychosomatic? He thought long and hard before he called her. He had to face the situation for fear of her driving over sooner rather than later. For all he knew, she was already on her way. He called with some trepidation. Fortunately, she was not in her car, but in the apartment. Tom knew he could not risk being overhead by Penny, so he shut the bedroom door. Penny would not think it odd after all he was sleeping off a headache. Susie answered the phone and there was a momentary silence between them. Surprisingly, Susie was calm and measured.

"Why are you calling me?"

Tom took a deep breath.

"I know you are angry with me, and I completely understand, but on my way to you, the police arrested me again. Some trumped up story my brother had told them. I had no opportunity to call you…"

"Where are you now, Tom?"

"At the police station. I am only allowed one call, and I immediately called you."

Susie's tears came immediately.

"Oh, Tom! I have been so angry, beside myself! I thought you had just let me down again."

"I had no plans to let you down. I was looking forward to spending the day in bed together." Susie was ecstatic to learn that Tom's no-show was not him being cavalier about their relationship, but that there was a genuine reason why he could not be with her.

"I am so sorry I have acted in this way, Tom. Will you forgive me?" Of course, he would forgive her.

"Nothing to say sorry for, really."

"When do you expect the police will let you go?"

What he did not want to say was 'any time soon,' because she would expect him to go straight to the apartment.

"No idea, but certainly by morning. Shall I come across tomorrow, although I cannot give you a time?"

"Darling, come across whenever you can. I love you, Tom. You know I love you…"

"Of course, love you too."

With that, he ended the call and sighed with relief. Oddly enough, his headache had disappeared, but for how long, he had no idea. What he had always avoided, unless under extreme pressure, was to tell Susie that he loved her, but on this occasion, it was a fair trade for getting him off the hook, once again.

He rested his head on the pillow, smiled to himself, and fell into a deep sleep.

CHAPTER 11 – UNRAVELLING

Tom woke with a start. He was fully dressed. He looked at his bedside clock; it was 11.27 pm. He had been asleep for almost fourteen hours. Penny was also asleep, next to him. He quietly got up and went down to the kitchen to make some coffee, then headed for his study. His phone had been in his pocket all that time, switched on. There were no signs of text messages or voicemails, so he concluded his tale to Susie had obviously worked.

He had been so stressed with the day's events the uninterrupted sleep had been the tonic he needed to recharge his batteries. It had worked; he felt more like his old self.

The uncertainties and worries of what may happen next in the Susie saga had subsided for the time being and he was back in control. He knew how lucky he had been and could not contemplate a repeat of the day's events. One way or another, he had to find a way of dealing with Susie.

His mind focused on the conversation he had had with the insurance assessor when he discovered the electrical system was non- compliant and wondered how much he could expect to receive by way of a claim? He had registered the incident with the insurer; hence the assessors visit but receiving a settlement inevitably took time. Too much time, and there was the real chance he would get nothing.

His phone pinged. It made him jump. It was Susie, wishing him a good night. This was a good example of how she had put aside any concern that Penny might see the message or question who was texting him. In the initial stages of the affair, Tom had made it clear that if she wanted to have a relationship with him, she would have to agree to a set of rules. He was married, happily married in fact, and it was important that he was able to distinguish between the two relationships. She was not to go to his home.

She was not to leave text messages or voicemails unless they were business related. She should in no way do or say anything that would undermine his relationship with Penny. Susie agreed. She was his mistress and mistresses behave.

But very quickly, those rules crumbled away as emotion took over. It was difficult for her to accept that Tom was not solely hers. That he belonged to another woman.

That he could continue with his everyday life, sleeping with that other woman while she had to put up with snatched moments with him or the occasional overnight stay at the apartment. She became increasingly jealous of Tom and Penny going away at weekends and leaving her in the apartment alone. She was also frustrated seeing them take long holidays to exotic locations or sail away on their yacht while she had to stay behind and keep his business going.

She had given up her long-term boyfriend, who she had been planning to marry, to be his mistress. He had demanded that she did so. He did not want to share her with anyone else. She was a beautiful woman and could have her pick of young men, but she wanted Tom. On a couple of occasions, she had signed up to an online dating agency and attracted a substantial number of eager men wanting to take her out, but had abandoned the idea, fearing Tom would find out and the relationship would be over. In the early days of the relationship, he knew he had his cake and could eat it at any time. As time wore on, the familiarity and predictability of the relationship became a little tedious, but he knew it would. He had been there before. Despite enjoying the comforts of a beautiful mistress, it was not enough long-term. There had to be more; and more meant finding new young women to seduce.

The trap he had fallen into was allowing the relationship

to continue for as long as it had, but the complication was that they worked together, and while they were able to define roles and get on with their jobs in the business, the two began to merge, business and pleasure. Susie had become increasingly flirtatious with him in the office and saw nothing wrong with it, he was her man. The staff in the business certainly knew what was going on, but that did not deter her from taking risks despite Tom's insistence that in the office, they had to put the relationship to one side.

Penny had undertaken Susie's job before her and knew the staff well. That, too, was not lost on Tom. Overall, it was a mess. With the other affairs he had had, the women in question had never worked for him for any length of time. It was easier to administer and manage.

Tom went back to bed, carefully avoiding waking Penny. It was just after midnight, and he was wide awake. He spent the rest of the night thinking about his plight.

It was just coming up to 6.00 am. He had obviously fallen asleep, although it did not feel as though he had. He was tired, but he needed to get on with the day. He made tea for Penny and woke her. They chatted for a while before she made breakfast. Once again, he had to make an excuse to be out for the day and dreaded raising the subject. He could not contemplate a repeat of the day before.

Whatever Penny said, he certainly would not be leaving the house for Susie's apartment with her in toe. Penny was in her usual caring mode.

"How are you feeling today, darling?"

"Oh fine. The sleep did me good…"

"You were out like a light when I came up. I thought of waking you to get out of your day clothes but decided against it. You obviously needed the sleep to clear your headache. Do you think it was a migraine?"

"I am not sure, but it knocked me out… I shall be out this morning into mid-afternoon. I am going to see Peter to find out what is happening with Rod. I am also going to the bank to have a chat with them about the fire and secure an interim loan to tide us over, and then I want to catch up with Susie."

If he was expecting any resistance from Penny, he was mistaken.

"Okay, darling. I have arranged to play golf with Ginny today. I am really looking forward to it." Tom was relieved there would be no push back on his plans.

"Great stuff, you enjoy yourself and give her my love."

Tom got showered and dressed, then headed off to Susie's just after 9.15 am. He called her to let her know he was on his way.

Of course, she was thrilled with the news. He wanted to give her sufficient notice to ensure that she prepared for his arrival. The thought of spending several hours with her in a relaxed, but highly sexual encounter pleased him.

It was almost 10.00am. Soon after he arrived at Susie's apartment, Penny received a telephone call on the landline. She was due to play golf at 10.30 am with Ginny.

"Hello, Penny Taylor?"

"Oh, I am glad you are there, Penny. Rod here." Penny was shocked to hear his voice.

"What do you want, Rod, why are you calling?"

"I just wanted to let you know that the police have released me from custody…"

She stopped him mid-flow. "But why are you telling me, Rod? You have caused us, especially Tom, enough problems and you are the last person we want to hear from!"

"I know you must think badly of me…"

"Think badly of you? That is an understatement. Tom was arrested for murdering Mary because you told the police he had killed her! What kind of brother does that?" Rod persisted.

"But you must understand I have been grieving for Mary? I had no idea what I was doing or saying! I am sorry! Please forgive me, Penny."

Penny knew there was no chance that Tom would ever forgive him for what he had done. He had offered to pay Rod's debts on the basis that he would go away and start a new life, preferably as far away from Tom as possible. To think that he would entertain the idea of an apology was absurd.

"No, I cannot, and I can assure you that Tom will never forgive you. I am sorry but this is of your own making!"

Rod persisted.

"Are you attending Mary's funeral?"

"Why are you asking?"

"We will see each other there."

"Have Mary's parents invited you?"

Rod got mildly angry.

"It is nothing to do with them whether I attend or not; she was my wife! I am going, and no one will stop me!"

"That is your problem, Rod. I must go."

With that, she put down the receiver. She was visibly shaking. She had to tell Tom.

Tom and Susie were intertwined when his phone rang at the side of the bed. Susie did not want him to stop what he was doing to answer the call, and Tom was not about to displease her. After a few rings, it stopped. Penny never liked leaving voicemail messages; she decided she would call a few moments later. She called again. Tom had more than an inkling it would be her, but they had reached a delicate moment in their encounter.

"FUCK, FUCK, FUCK… do not answer it, Tom, not now…"

Tom knew he could not stop what he was doing, and again,

the phone went silent after a few rings. Penny was running late for her golf date with Ginny and gave up the call for the time being. For the duration of the golf session, she could not get Rod's call out of her head. She discussed the call with Ginny, and Ginny agreed that she had done the right thing in dismissing him.

She was surprised he had the nerve to call.

Ginny's encounter with Rod the previous year at a dinner party that Tom and Penny had hosted, was still fresh in her mind. She found Rod creepy, weak willed, and lacking in social skills. Moreover, he had spent most of the conversation with her trying to undermine Tom in one way or another. She thought it very odd that he would do such a thing, Tom was a lovely, charming man in her eyes.

Tom and Susie had spent four hours in bed and took time out to talk about the progress she was making on her list of business tasks. He was mindful that in her fit of anger the previous day, she had threatened to tell Penny about their affair and destroy all the business data on the company server. Such an action would be devastating, making it almost impossible for him to reignite the business quickly after the fire. The thought of her doing such a thing worried him. He was extremely aware how volatile she was, and in hindsight, he knew he had abrogated too much power to her. She had control over every aspect of the business in one way or another. She was the touch-point for the bank, accountants, lawyers, insurers, distributors, printers, and the staff. It was her they would go to, not Tom. He had worked himself out of the everyday activities of the business entirely and now concentrated on PR and relationships with his existing authors and international contacts, freeing himself of the mundane, day-to-day running of the company. The mistake he had made, though, was avoiding responsibility rather than delegating it. If he had been clear with Susie on her job description, he would have his finger on the pulse and be able to take over from her if she were out of the business for any reason. Instead, he had chosen to let her get on with it and over time, he had found he knew less and less about the systems, processes, and procedures. In fact, left to it, he would not know where to start.

Not only had he let her get on with it, he had done so while taking her as his mistress. A fatal combination. He had been a fool. His flings were usually short-lived, before moving on to the next prey. With Susie, whether he liked it or not, she was strategically important to him in running the business. Ending the relationship meant potentially ending or debilitating his livelihood, not to mention also potentially leading to his divorce. It was a conundrum to which he had no answer. Like it or not, Susie had become an integral part of the metaphorical furniture, and time would tell when, not if, it would all blow up in his face.

"So, give me an update on where you are with your to-do list?"

Susie had poured two glasses of champagne emptying the bottle and handed one to Tom. He had broken one of his rules, not to drink and drive, but on this occasion, after the drama of the day before, he felt he had no option but to accept Susie's hospitality.

Susie ran through her list of actions and Tom was pleased with her progress. He knew he needed to wrestle away some of her power in the business. He needed to be able to access every facet of the business from his laptop, just as she could, but he needed to do it without causing her any consternation.

"Great stuff. Thanks… and well done!"

Susie looked pleased that her boss was impressed. Then, he said, "I spoke to the insurance assessor after he surveyed the remains of the warehouse, and it is not good news. He picked up on the fact that the electrical system had not been updated and would certainly invalidate a claim."

Susie was shocked and looked worried. They had already had a heated conversation about whether it was her responsibility or not to keep such matters up to date, and she was now fearing that the last few hours they had spent together, cementing their relationship, would be undermined by another row.

"But Tom…"

He was keen to reassure her that he was not about to blame her again.

"Before you say anything, I am not blaming you. Really, I am not! But it did set me thinking. Over the past couple of years, you have done a fabulous job for me. The business could not have achieved what it has without your superb management. But I have been unfair. I have dumped everything on your shoulders, and I think it is time I freed you up a little and shared the burden. The fire has also made me see how vulnerable the business is when only one person has access to the servers and all the business data. I would like to be able to access everything on my laptop so that wherever I am in the world, I can see how we are doing, and connect to all our stakeholders. In other words, to have the same access you have. That way, if you are unavailable for any reason, the business could continue without interruption."

At first, Susie was pleased that he was not now blaming her for the electrical system failure, and not heeding the insurance company's advice to update the system. However, she was less than pleased that having patted her on the back for a job well done, he now wanted to wrest back control of the business, which would inevitably dilute or diminish her responsibilities, and the power she wielded over him and his livelihood. She chose not to hear the bit about the importance of business continuity, what was the problem? She was not planning to quit. She and Tom were an item. In time, they would be married, and she would own half the business anyway, a business that she believed she had built single-handedly.

"Tom. I do not understand why you would need to have everything accessible on your laptop. I am happy to manage the everyday business so that you can be brilliant at what you do. I have no plans to leave you! I am not overworked, really, and I certainly do not want you interfering, I know what you are like."

Tom listened to her response with trepidation. Whichever way he turned his bat he was stumped. He had created a monster that exceeded his own power of control. The principal of master and servant had been reversed. He now worked for Susie. He needed to toe the line or suffer the consequences.

"No, I have no intention of interfering but as the principal of the business, I do need to have a finger on the pulse…"

"Darling, I am your finger on the pulse."

Tom looked at her and smiled. They finished their champagne as Susie dragged him back to bed.

The fact that a successful claim on the insurer was highly unlikely meant that Tom could not invest in the business as he needed to. This had escaped Susie, but it had not escaped Tom. He knew he would be under financial pressure to draw enough cash together to build or lease a new warehouse and office space without relying heavily on personal assets. Still, that thought dissipated as she presented herself to him once more.

An hour later Tom got dressed, said his loving goodbyes, and headed to his car. He knew he would be taking a risk, driving after consuming three quarters of a bottle of champagne and a couple of gin and tonics, but he felt he had no option. If he arrived home in a taxi, it would attract unwanted questions from Penny.

He was driving the Range Rover. Unlike the Porsche, when his adrenaline pumped as he started the car, the four by four did no such thing. He always drove sedately; he took on the mantle of an old man driving a wheelchair rather than a young buck negotiating the twists and turns of a racetrack.

Unfortunately, it made no difference. Fifteen minutes into the journey home, he careered into the back of a stationary car at a roundabout. An elderly man with plenty of time to move into the flow of traffic, had stopped abruptly. Tom had not been expecting him to do so. Of course, it was Tom's fault, but truth be known, it was the other driver's lack of action that had created the drama.

That was not the way the police saw it. With minutes of the collision, a queue of cars had built up and the inevitable happened: a police car appeared at the scene. Tom was asked to take a breath test, and it showed he was well over the allowable limit. He was taken to Guildford police station, where he took the test again to verify the original reading.

This time, the reading was even higher. He was cautioned. He would also be prosecuted for drink driving. Tom's Range Rover had been towed to a local garage, but he was no longer permissible by law to drive. He called for a taxi to take him home.

He had already scheduled to attend court for dangerous driving and expected to lose his license. He now feared that any likely penalty would be ramped up. He was mortified at the thought. He sat back in the taxi and wondered when his run of back luck would end. He dreaded the thought of telling Penny.

He arrived home. Penny was eager to tell him about Rod's phone call earlier in the day and was surprised to see him arrive in a taxi. She went out onto the driveway.

"Hello, darling, where is the car?"

"Towed to a garage…"

"Oh, no. Has it broken down?"

"No. I drove into the back of a stationary car. He hesitated to move into the flow of the traffic and… I hit the bloody thing."

"Oh god, what next? We have had enough to deal with."

"I am afraid it is worse than that. I had lunch with the accountant and, I do not know why, but I had a couple of drinks. It was foolish. The police attended the accident, and I had to take a breath test. I was over the limit, and they plan to prosecute me!"

Penny looked at Tom incredulously, then turned and marched into the house. The taxi driver left, no doubt with a story to tell his next fare. Tom followed her into the drawing room.

"I cannot believe that after being stopped for speeding only a few days ago, you then chose to drink and drive? Are you mad?"

"I am not about to argue with you. I know how stupid I have been…"

"You do know that on top of the speeding offence, you will lose your license?"

"Darling, that is the least of my worries. Two serious offences in such a short space of time could lead to more than that!"

"Oh my god! You are not serious?"

"Look, I will get Peter to represent me, but I think we should hope for the best and prepare for the worst."

"I do not know whether to be sympathetic or shout and scream at you… could it get any worse? Why has our life been turned upside down like this?"

Penny became emotional. Tom attempted to comfort her.

"Tom, please do not try and make things better with a hug… and if I am honest, you smell quite sweaty. I think you should take a shower!"

Of course, after several hours of exercising with Susie, bodily odour was an inevitable consequence. He quickly showered and joined Penny downstairs. It was close to 5.15 pm.

"I am truly, sorry, darling. It was just one of those things. I hope you will forgive me?"

"I do not want to think about it. And it was not just one of those things. You were stupid and should have known better!"

Tom sat on the sofa. He was tired and had already taken a beating, and in many ways, and could do without Penny telling him what he already knew, what a fool he had been.

"And to add to your woes, Tom, I had a phone call this morning from Rod."

"Rod? What? He called here?!"

"Yes. He called to make amends. He was relieved that it was me answering the phone and not you."

"I hope you told him…"

"Yes. I told him we wanted nothing to do with him and he should not contact us again."

"That must have been difficult for you. You are usually so accommodating. How did he respond?"

"Perhaps that is where I am going wrong, I am too accommodating!" She looked Tom in the eyes. Tom offered up a cautionary smile.

"What did he say?"

"He asked if we were going to Mary's funeral tomorrow and I said we were. He plans to attend despite Mary's father saying he did not want him there."

Tom's expression changed.

"Bloody idiot! Why would he go. He must know how

people feel about him."

Penny had a slightly different view.

"As Mary's husband, he has every right to attend, but if he does attend, I hope he behaves himself."

"I hope he changes his mind. You do know that the media will be there at the crematorium in force, just as they were when Rod and I were arrested?"

"Oh god, I hope not! It is the last thing any of us want or need. It was wise of Mary's father not to have a church service first."

Tom was tired, in fact exhausted after his marathon with Susie, and with a hangover looming wanted nothing more than to go to bed and sleep it off, but he thought better of the idea.

Despite her disappointment in Tom, Penny made some coffee and offered to cook an early meal, but he declined. He was not in the mood to eat. The doorbell rang. They looked at each other; Penny headed for the front door. It was Rod. He was drunk. He had taken a taxi to the bottom of the drive and staggered up on foot.

"So, you are both in then?" He was slurring his speech. Tom rushed to the door and was immediately angry.

"What the hell are you doing here?! We want nothing to do with you!"

"Hold your horses, little brother!"

Penny was terrified and went back into the sitting room hoping, praying, he would just go away.

"Will you let me in so we can talk for a while…" Tom stood squarely in the doorway.

"…Abso-bloody-lutely, not! Any chance of us reconciling our differences disappeared after you framed me for killing Mary. As far as I am concerned, I never want to see you ever again, now please go, or I will call the police!"

Unexpectedly, Rod took a sudden swing at Tom and hit him

squarely on the jaw. Tom staggered backwards but managed to recover himself. Stunned, he pushed Rod backwards, went inside, shut the door, and fell to his knees.

Penny rushed into the hallway and saw blood pouring from Tom's mouth.

"Shall I call the police, Tom?"

"No. I have seen enough of them these past few days. Leave him, he will soon tire and hopefully leave."

Rod stood outside the front door, shouting obscenities at Tom for some considerable time. He was keen to let him know that he planned to enjoy spending the money he had given him. Failing to get them to open the door, he grabbed handfuls of stones from the driveway and threw them at the drawing room window. Tom was seething. Penny had gone upstairs to the bedroom and covered her ears.

"Let me in Tom… I only want to talk to you; say sorry… say sorry for everything…"

Tom watched him from the window wondering what he would do next.

"Are you going to let me in? If not, I will smash the windows of your fucking Porsche!"

Tom was incandescent. He opened the front door and leapt on Rod, punching him several times.

Neither man was experienced in the art of street fighting, and to any casual observer they would have witnessed a comedic scene, a sketch from a Monty Python episode. Tom was in a rage, and nothing could stop him. Rod fell to the ground as Tom stood over him, shaking uncontrollably. This was the first time in his entire life he had hit anyone, and he had no regrets. He was just pleased Penny had not witnessed the attack. Rod was in no fit state to respond. He remained on the ground, moaning. Tom left him there, closed the door, went back into the drawing room, and slumped onto the sofa.

Because of the adrenaline rush, he was exhausted, and his hands were sore.

When Penny eventually came down, she found Tom staring into space, his knuckles bleeding. She had heard them fighting from the bedroom but covered her ears fearful of what may happen. Tentatively, she looked out of the window and saw Rod staggering down the driveway. Every few steps, he fell, got up, then fell again. Eventually, he left the property boundary and faded from view.

Tom was shocked by what had happened. Penny sat next to him.

"Are you okay, Tom? I was so worried when I heard you both fighting."

"Where is he? Has he gone?"

Penny confirmed that she had seen him leave the property. Tom was relieved to say the least.

"He has lost it. You know that?"

"What are we going to do, Tom? He will never leave us alone."

"What can I say? Right now, I do not want to think about him. My hands are sore; I think I will go and bathe them."

Tom went upstairs to the bathroom as Penny made more coffee. She would have offered him a stiff drink but thought that was a bad idea, given recent events.

After this latest incident with Rod, Tom was reluctant to go to Mary's funeral the following morning in case Rod turned up and there was trouble. Penny understood his anxiety but insisted they went. It would look bad if they stayed away. Anyway, she thought it highly unlikely Rod would be in a fit state to attend, at least she hoped that would be the case.

As they talked the inevitable happened, Tom's phone pinged, it was Susie. Tom was dog tired, and the thought of concealing Susie's text with a lie was too much for his brain to cope with.

"Susie. I had better call her. She wants some advice."

Tom went into his study. He read the message: 'Hope you got back okay, naughty, naughty boy!'

He knew he had to call her. Failing to do so came with its own challenges. He decided he would make no mention of the drink driving or Rod's appearance on his doorstep. He wanted to get the call over as quickly as possible and have an early night.

"You called?"

"I did. How are you, lover?" That all too frequent feeling descended upon him. Tom was not in the mood for trivial banter, but he knew what she was like after they had spent time in the sack.

He tried to indulge her to avoid an inquisition or to unsettle her from her happy state of mind.

"I am good. It was nice spending time with you."

"Nice? I hope it was better than nice?"

Tom winced. What on earth did he have to say to get her off his back?

"It was terrific, as always. You are so beautiful…"

"I just phoned to say I love you lots, Tom. Hope you love me back?"

"Yes, yes, yes, of course I do. Look, I will call you tomorrow after Mary's funeral at the crematorium."

"Oh. So, the funeral is tomorrow? Why did you not tell me?"

"It does not affect you."

"Oh, but it does. Whatever affects you, affects me."

"Look, Susie, I must go. I have a lot to do… I will call you tomorrow afternoon. Bye."

He hung up and went to bed. Tomorrow would be a long day.

CHAPTER 12 – THE FUNERAL

The following morning, they got ready to leave for the crematorium. They were both apprehensive, fearing the media would be there in droves as Mary's murder still dominated the local media headlines, and of course, whether Rod would turn up. Penny insisted she drove. The last thing she wanted was Tom being stopped for a third time in quick succession.

There was long queue leading to the crematorium when they arrived. It was 11.30 am and the service was due to start at midday. Gradually, they inched their way onto the meandering driveway leading up to the main building. They had no idea how many people Mary's father had invited to the service, but they assumed there would only be a few.

As far as they were aware, Mary had few friends, and the circumstances of her death might put some people off. They were surprised to see so many people congregating.

They managed to find a parking space. Their concern about a media presence was clearly justified. From the moment they got out of the car they were besieged. Tom's face was familiar from when the journalists and cameramen had been there to see him taken into the police station after he was arrested for Mary's murder. They swarmed all over him and Penny, demanding a quote.

Penny was taken aback by the intrusion and had to jostle her way to the crematorium entrance. Tom said nothing. The place was heaving with people eager to witness the comings and goings of the funeral party, knowing Mary's killer had not been caught. Tom was asked if he had killed Mary. Had his brother killed her? Did he know who was responsible? Did he suspect anyone? What kind of relationship did he have with Mary and his brother?

The questions came thick and fast, but Tom ignored

their attempts to get him to speak. As he approached the crematorium entrance, he heard a familiar voice call his name. It was Susie. She was standing at the front of the crowd.

He was irritated that she had come after he had told her it was none of her business…

The solemnity of the chapel was in stark contrast to the media circus taking place outside. As Tom and Penny had suspected, there were about twenty people in the room for the service, although more were due to arrive, assuming of course they were able to navigate their way through the crowd of reporters.

They looked at each other apprehensively and took a seat in the middle of the room. So far, no Rod. Tom acknowledged Mary's mother and father, who came over to speak to them. Her father was clearly upset.

"I had no idea there would be so many people here. Why are they harassing us, especially today?"

Tom responded sympathetically…

"I am so sorry for your loss. We will miss her terribly." Mary's father thanked them both for attending.

The remainder of the congregation eventually assembled as midday arrived. The vicar of Mary's local church conducted the service. He stood and welcomed everybody. Mary's coffin, which was covered with flowers, sat in preparedness for her final journey.

"We are gathered here today to bid a final farewell to Mary, beloved daughter of Frank and Anna, who was so brutally taken from us. Everyone loved Mary. She was a pillar of the community…"

Just as the vicar had got into his speech and emotions were running high, the door at the back of the chapel burst open. It was Rod. He was drunk, and it was obvious he had slept rough after leaving Tom and Penny's the previous day. He was in a high state of emotion. He shouted, "Mary was my wife! Why was I not allowed to pay… pay my respects?" He staggered down the aisle, crying and slurring his words. "I loved Mary. Why was I not invited… I didn't kill my wife…"

The vicar was horrified by Rod's intervention and had no idea how best to deal with the situation.

Tom stood up and stepped forward to stop Rod going any further. Another man joined him, eager to assist. Rod took an arbitrary swing at Tom, the second in twenty-four hours, and caught him again, this time in the right eye, the result was a deep gash to Tom's face that bled freely.

Several people rushed to his aid, others held Rod tightly; dragging him past Mary's coffin and into the vestry, where he was locked in. He continued to shout and scream obscenities at Mary's parents and especially Tom. The vicar continued with the service as best he could.

Tom returned to his seat next to Penny, who tried to mop up the blood flooding down his cheek. The commotion Rod was making in the vestry was far too audible to expect Mary's send-off to be in any way dignified. The speeches from Mary's father and a close friend of the family were abandoned and Mary was quickly despatched. It was nothing short of a fiasco.

Everyone present was visibly upset that the funeral had passed in such an unseemly way. If Rod had wanted to alienate everyone, especially Tom and Penny, he had achieved his objective. But if his theatrics had not been enough, they then had to confront the media and onlookers as they left the building.

The drama that had taken place inside soon became known on the outside and everyone attending the service was mobbed as they left. With a cut to his face and blood still pouring down his cheek, Tom was their main target. In the ruckus, he was separated from Penny. Unable to do anything else, Penny went back to the car and locked herself in as Tom waded through cameramen and journalists eager for a comment. Anything would suffice. He was not about to indulge them.

They were in a state of shock and disbelief at what had happened. It was clear Rod was unhinged. They never wanted to see him again.

As they drove home, they spoke of Mary's parents and how they must be feeling. Not only did they have to contend with the murder of their daughter, but they also had to witness her husband make a mockery of her funeral. They could not go back in time and do it all over again, nor could they fast forward and wipe the memory from their minds. Rod had a lot to answer for.

Once they were home, Penny insisted that she dress Tom's wound. It needed stitches, but he refused to go to hospital. They drank some hot tea and Penny announced she was exhausted and would go to the bedroom for a rest. Tom was still buzzing with anger and needed time to calm down. He had reflected a lot over the preceding few weeks about his crumbling life. He was incapable of putting the brakes on. It was one thing after another, and in truth, it had all started to go seriously wrong after he learnt of Mary's death.

His phone rang. It had to be Susie. Who else?

"Tom, are you okay?" Tom was not in the mood to talk.

"Why are you calling me now, and forgive me, but why were you at the crematorium?"

"To provide moral support for you, Tom. I wanted to be there for you. Is it true that you and your brother got into a fight?"

"Susie. I am really done in. Do you mind if we do not talk about this right now? I just want to unwind. It has been a hell of a day, one way or another."

"Sure, if you feel that way. I was just being kind, that is

all."

"I know, and I am grateful, but I cannot concentrate right now. I am too tired. I will call you tomorrow." He ended the call and switched off his phone.

Was it possible that anything else could go wrong in his life, at least in the short to medium term? He had endured enough drama in recent weeks to last a lifetime, but thought he had to call Peter, his friend and solicitor to talk about his recent driving offences, and the likely penalty he would face. The receptionist connected the call.

"Hi Tom, how are you doing? It was Mary's funeral today, was it not?"

"It was. I will spare you a minute-by-minute account, but suffice to say, Rod turned up drunk, swearing and shouting, and when I tried to restrain him, he punched me in the face. I am now home, nursing quite a deep wound to my right eye. The media were out in force and the place was heaving with onlookers. It was dreadful."

"You are joking, were the police called to arrest Rod?"

"I have no idea, the service was shortened, almost abandoned. We got out as quickly as we could. Rod was locked in the vestry, and he can stay there!"

"Tom, I am so sorry. You have been through enough."

"That is why I am calling you. My plight is not over. In quick succession, over a two-day period, I was booked for dangerous driving, then today I was stopped and charged with drink driving." Peter went silent. He was in disbelief. This was so out of character for Tom, who he knew quite well.

"Bloody hell, Tom. Why? How?"

"Look, it would take too long to explain right now but I wanted to know if a) You would represent me when the offences come to court and b) what kind of penalty I am likely to face?"

"You did say 'dangerous driving,' not 'driving without due care and attention?"

"I am afraid I did."

"Well, Tom, they will both come to court at the same time and be dealt with together. I can tell you that drink driving involves a hefty fine and a mandatory twelve-month ban from driving. Dangerous driving can attract up to two years imprisonment and a hefty fine.

If I am honest with you, Tom, even with representation and a list of mitigating circumstances, which you could certainly argue, you will get a short prison sentence. I cannot see you getting the full two years, but you must be prepared for the worst."

It was Tom's turn to go silent. With all the stresses and strains he had recently put himself through, he could take no more. He was a strong character and took most things on the chin but Peter's revelation that he would serve a custodial sentence for his driving offences hit home, and he started to sob uncontrollably.

"I am sorry, Peter. I have let my guard down…"

Peter knew that he had been under intense pressure and took pity on him.

"Think nothing of it, Tom. You are human! You have had a lot on your plate recently; it is perfectly understandable that you would be emotional over such news. The consolation, if indeed you see it as a consolation, is that if you were to serve time it would be in an open prison."

It was no consolation at all. He had so many balls in the air, the last thing he needed was time in prison, any sort of prison. Penny would be mortified. What would happen to the business? What would Susie do if he were locked away? How could he control her? What would his authors, distributors, accountants, staff, friends, and bank manager think? His chances of resurrecting the business would be over and his days in publishing, numbered.

He politely ended the call with Peter and said he would arrange a date for them to meet up.

Once he put the phone down, he continued to weep. He could not control his emotions any longer. He looked in a mirror which had hung in his study since they moved into the house and saw an ageing man with a scarred face and deep wrinkles on his forehead.

His eyes were tired and bloodshot, and he wondered where his youth had gone. More importantly, he wondered what lay in store for him. Mentally, he was a shadow of his former self. His positivity, quick wit, and charm had faded like a candle starved of oxygen. He was a beaten man and for the first time in his adult life, he felt truly out of control, lacked the confidence, and drive to do anything about it. He wanted to go to sleep and not wake until he knew the dramas in his life were over and he could return to normality. Of course, that was not going to happen. He had accumulated influence and prestige and the trappings of a comfortable lifestyle. He had a good marriage, a mistress, friends, good health, and a business that was financially growing and profitable. Now, it was all crumbling like an ancient building and there was nothing he could do to stop the rot.

This was not Tom the entrepreneur or Tom the magician, able to pull white rabbits with diamonds necklaces out of a hat. He was exhausted and needed to recuperate. He quietly tiptoed into the bedroom to avoid waking Penny, lay down beside her, and promptly fell asleep.

CHAPTER 13 – REVELATIONS

Several days had passed, surprisingly without any further drama. Tom had no appetite for business affairs despite an urgent need for him to resolve a mountain of pressing issues. His phone pinged round the clock and countless voicemail messages remained unanswered. Despite his malaise, though, he knew he could not risk upsetting Susie. He did not want her turning up on his doorstep again. He called and begged her to give him space and not to call or text or leave messages, as he needed to recover from recent events. She was understanding, something that surprised him. She agreed to get on with her tasks and would only email him if there was an emergency. Even more surprisingly, she kept her word.

Penny was worried about him; she had never seen him like this before. He was always full of fun and energy and relished daily challenges. Now, though, he looked a beaten man, and she sensed he needed time to recover from what had taken place in recent weeks. Six days had passed, and his mood had changed little. He spent most of his time staring into space or pottering around the garden on his own, something they usually did together.

Penny felt they needed to get away and suggested they pack a bag for a week and take their yacht, moored at Hamble, across to Cowes on the Isle of Wight, a two-hour sail, to spend time in their cottage and visit friends. Tom was unenthusiastic. He needed to get back to work. He knew he had been distant from her the past week and offered an apology. Penny was fine about his decision; she was just pleased he had remained at home and been able to relax. It had served its purpose. While Tom had to resume work, he saw no reason why Penny should not go herself. She loved sailing solo, enjoyed time at the cottage, and she needed a break from recent dramas, too. At first, she was reluctant to go without him, but he was insistent that she should.

In the end, she agreed and spent the rest of the day preparing for the trip.

The following morning, they were up early, Penny wanted to catch an early tide. The weather was quite good and light winds were forecast, perfect for sailing. In clear weather, it was about two hours from Hamble to Cowes, but as every local sailor knew, the Solent could be unpredictable and the water choppy, even on a good day. It was also a busy stretch of water as hydrofoils and ferries crossed the channel every hour to France and back, and huge cargo vessels navigated their way to Southampton and Portsmouth. Tom helped Penny pack. She was excited. He offered to drive her to the mooring to save her leaving the car, but she declined. She liked the flexibility of jumping in the car and heading back home the moment she had de-rigged and packed everything up.

She left home at 6.40 am. The journey time over the fifty miles was about an hour and a quarter, plenty of time for her to set off and be on the island for a late lunch. As she drove away from the house, he reflected on how lucky he was to have such a beautiful, caring, and loving wife. He knew he did not deserve her.

He had breakfast and went into his study to start work. Today was the first day he had felt motivated to open his laptop and contemplate a day's work. Susie had behaved herself throughout; he had not received any phone calls, text messages, or emails. He hoped this experience would bode well and she would be more circumspect in the future. If only he could go back twenty-four months in the relationship, when they first started the affair. In those days, she had been far more compliant and less demanding. He knew he was in control of the relationship, and it was him that determined when they spent time together. Susie made no demands of him; it was perfect. Familiarity breeds contempt, he thought to himself.

Before calling her for an update, he needed to think about his approach, what he would say and, most importantly, how he would say it. He did not want her to get excited and demand he visit the apartment for an afternoon in the sack, as attractive as that proposition might seem. No, it was important that he focus on the business and ascertain the progress she had made on her list of tasks. He called her.

"Hi, Susie."

Contrary to best laid plans, she was excited to hear from him.

"Oh, Tom! I have been so worried about you and missed you so much!"

"I know it has been remiss of me not to have called earlier, but I needed to recharge my batteries. The Mary and Rod saga really took it out of me."

"Poor dear. Are your batteries fully recharged now?"

"Yes. I feel good, and ready to get back in the saddle."

The wrong choice or words, he thought, and it proved to be.

"I hope so. I want you desperately, right now. Can you come to the apartment?"

His attempt to get the relationship on a business footing had clearly failed.

"Sounds tempting, but I have a ton of stuff to get through. I just phoned to get an update on what you have been up to?"

Susie was disappointed.

"Oh, Tom, please come over. Come over and I will give you a full debrief and then…"

"Sorry, I cannot. I need to press on. Can you email me a quick update and let me know if there are any pressing issues I need to deal with? I will call you again later."

He ended the call. It was not how he hoped the call would go.

The temptation to take her up on her offer to go to the apartment had its appeal, of course it did, but if he had any hope of rebalancing the relationship so that he could keep his marriage intact, he would have to produce a workable strategy. Of course, it would prove to be as elusive as finding a needle in a haystack. Susie would never change, and he knew it. The longer the affair continued, and she had control over his business, the more demanding she would become. Tom sighed. He was tired of scheming, tired of lying to Penny and, indeed, tired of lying to Susie. He desperately wanted to resolve things for the long-term, but he knew he would have to ponder that thought for another day. His whole life was dominated by what Susie might do or what Susie might say, and how he would manage the fallout when it eventually came. He was tired of living a lie.

It was 2.00pm when he received Susie's email. Just as he started to read it, Penny called to say she had arrived safely in Cowes. It had been a choppy crossing, but she had loved the experience. She was making her way to the cottage and had already called friends to arrange for supper that evening. She would stay in touch.

Tom read Susie's email. She had done an excellent job contacting his stakeholders telling them about the fire. Aside from one author who had always been difficult to please, everyone was sympathetic and wished them well. Susie had also received a call from the bank, asking for Tom to call them back. His relationship with the bank had changed for the worse over the years, despite the business prospering and being cash rich.

Like most businesspeople of a certain age, Tom liked to have a bank manager on tap, with whom he could discuss finance at the drop of a hat. But as technology had started to roll out over the last decade, so bank managers had steadily disappeared. They were as elusive as a snowman on a summer's day. It was now almost impossible to speak to anyone, let alone someone with the authority to discuss business finance.

Over the twenty years or so he had been operating the publishing company, there had only been two occasions when he had needed short-term financing and being able to secure it through his branch manager had been a godsend.

The fire had come at a tough time for Tom; not that there was ever a suitable time for a fire. He had invested heavily in infrastructure, inventory, equipment, and technology which had all gone up in flames. His cash reserves were low, and he had further depleted them by paying cash for his Porsche, Susie's Porsche, and Penny's Mercedes in the last two years.

Tom's accountant had advised him to lease cars, but he was old fashioned. He believed in the maxim, 'If you cannot afford to pay cash, you cannot afford it at all.' Added to all that, he had invested heavily in remedial work to their house, bought the yacht, and refurbished part of the island cottage. Overall, it was a considerable outlay, but Tom had thought it affordable as the business was growing rapidly.

What he had not factored in was the fire that would change everything. With the likelihood that the insurer would decline his claim, he needed to secure finance to get over the short to medium term. He also reminded himself that Rod, his loathed brother, now had claim over a huge amount of cash that could have been deployed in the business. That thought alone angered him.

He returned the bank's call. Susie told him he was to contact Wayne Harvey. The first name gave Tom the feeling that he would be speaking to a young person, a junior. Not so. Wayne was a district manager and one of the banks rising stars.

"Hello, Mr. Taylor. Thank you for calling me back. I am the southern regional manager for the bank. I have been looking at your business account, Taylor Publishing, and, having been informed about the fire at your premises, for which I am sorry, I wondered how we could assist you, a loyal customer, during these challenging times?"

Tom was impressed with his tone and professionalism.

"Thank you, Wayne…" Before Tom could say another word, Wayne continued.

"I took the liberty of examining the cash movements in both your business and private accounts over the past year or so, and it would seem the business is seriously exposed, added to which you have a business loan amounting to £180,460, including interest, which is due for settlement in the next sixty days. I wondered how you intended to settle the debt?"

Tom was shocked by the revelation.

"Loan?! I am sorry, Wayne, you must have the wrong client account in front of you!"

Wayne was insistent.

"No, I have your account in front of me, Mr Taylor."

Tom knew his spending the past year or two had been significant, but he had no recollection of taking out the loan Wayne referred to. Ordinarily, it was against his maxim about affordability.

The conversation continued for ten minutes, and Tom was assured a loan had been taken out, and indeed he had signed for it. He ended the call with Wayne and promised he would ring him back later. He immediately called Susie.

"Susie, forgive me, but I need you to go into our banking files and examine the bank statements for the last year to see if we received a loan for a figure in the region of £150,000."

"Hello again, boss. Are you okay?" Tom had no time for chit chat.

"I am sorry… I need you to do this now; I will hold on."

What he wanted to say was, 'If only I had access on my laptop to my business and finances, I would not need to call you.' The exchange with Wayne had reinforced his concerns about Susie having total control over data. It had to change.

"No need to check the bank statement, Tom. I remember it. It was when creepy Roger worked for us. I saw an application for a £150,000 loan on his desk, and out of interest, knowing you prefer to buy everything in cash, I asked him about it. He told me you had asked him to arrange it. I thought no more of it until I saw the bank statement showing it had been credited to the account. Soon after, the money was transferred out to another account, RK Associates, which I assumed you had set up. Is there something wrong?"

He thanked Susie and said he would call her back later.

After he had ended the call, Tom flinched. For a brief period in the previous fiscal year, he had employed a part-time accounts manager to work alongside Susie after she had discovered that accounts were not her strong point.

He decided to recruit someone on a trial basis. The business was expanding and while he tried to keep his employee numbers down to increase profits, it was a worthwhile addition to the team, at least he thought so.

He had been reluctant to hand over all the business finances to his main accountancy firm as they were quite expensive, so he had employed Roger Kemp. Roger was an odd ball, and Susie found him creepy, so his period in office was short-lived. Tom had listened to Susie's views about his creepiness and thought it best to part company with him. It was unfortunate Tom had had to let him go, at least in some respects, because he had been impressed with his grasp of the business finances.

Indeed, Tom made several changes in the accounting processes based upon his recommendations.

Tom was in the office infrequently during that year, as he had undertaken several lengthy overseas trips to see his distributors. When he was office based, Roger would breeze in and present him with various papers for signature. Tom had always been too trusting and rarely checked documents thoroughly, and Roger had obviously picked up on that casualness. Roger had the authority to move funds as he saw fit, and it was obvious that the money transferred to RK Associates was for his personal gain. He had the intention of absconding with the money before the accountants conducted their annual audit and the fraud would be discovered.

The firm of accountants Tom used had also recommended that he invest in monthly management accounts, but Tom did not think it was necessary; he had a grip on things and the business had always been cash rich. If he had taken their advice, Roger's fraud would have been identified much earlier. Eight months had passed since he left when Susie received a call from a friend of Roger's, announcing that he had died on holiday in the Gambia. Both Tom and Susie were shocked at the time but made no further enquiries.

The call from Wayne at the bank was the straw that could break the camel's back. Everything was conspiring against him. Like it or not, he had signed for the loan, that was not in dispute, and he therefore owed the money. What he could not say to Wayne at this point was that he knew nothing of the arrangement and had been conned by a fraudulent accountant. Such a revelation would send shockwaves through Wayne's office, and the bank to protect its position, may well demand immediate settlement of the debt or seek liquidation if it remained outstanding. He had to avoid that at all costs.

He also knew that his discovery of the fraud should, in

normal circumstances, be reported to the police, but these were anything but normal circumstances. A police investigation, especially when he had so much on his plate after the fire, would be inconvenient, to put it mildly. He punched the wall in his study in sheer frustration, and immediately regretted it.

This was becoming a habit. His knuckles were still sore from his altercation with Rod in the driveway.

Having decided it was extremely unwise to tell Wayne about the fraud, and mindful that the loan still had sixty days to run: sixty days for Tom to somehow magic one of his rabbits out of the hat. He phoned Wayne back apologising for his memory lapse and assured him that the loan would be repaid within the next two months. Tom had been a good customer over the years, and the evidence was there to prove his point. Wayne concluded that Tom, in his judgement, would honour his commitment.

The earlier years in the business had not seen the volatility of cash movement that was evident now. Tom had always maintained healthy balances in all his accounts, both business and personal, but this was no longer the case. Ordinarily, Wayne would have probed deeper to better understand precisely how Tom planned to repay the money, but he chose not to do so on this occasion. Wayne also knew from Tom's file that he had assets, especially in his homes, that as far as he could determine were unencumbered. If push came to shove, they could insist they be liquidated.

Tom had endured a run of bad luck that you would only expect to read about in a fictional novel, and he prayed this would be the turning point.

He thought the better of pouring his heart out to Susie telling her about Roger's fraud. She was also unaware of his recent run-in with the police and the likelihood he would be spending time in prison. He knew such confessions would only ignite her desire to bed him, believing that it was the answer to all his problems.

He thought again about calling the police to report the fraud, albeit eight months after it was perpetrated, but with everything else going on in his life, he thought the better of it. No. Somehow, he had to find a way of raising a substantial amount of money to resolve his financial difficulties without panicking anyone, especially Penny.

Selling the house was a possibility as they owned the property outright, and it would certainly help, but Penny would never agree to that. Equally, the island cottage, the yacht, and the cars were all paid for assets that could be used to raise money, but selling such assets meant accepting knock down prices and getting Penny on board would be a marathon job. She liked security and recoiled at the thought of running up debts.

His mind wandered back to Rod. If only he had not been so bloody generous. If only Penny had not transferred the cash after he had torn up the cheque. It was a pointless exercise in self-flagellation that served no useful purpose other than to depress him.

He poured himself a large whisky and necked it in one. He poured another and that, too, disappeared in an instant. He was tempted to repeat the exercise once more but knew it would solve nothing. The only payback would be a hangover in the morning.

Later, he prepared himself a light supper. Despite all the hassle he had endured with Susie as his mistress, there was nothing he wanted more than to spend the night with her. Within the space of two minutes, he could have phoned her and within the hour, his desires would be fulfilled. It was tempting, but he knew it was a bad idea. Instead, he settled for an early night. When Penny was away on rare occasions, he rattled around in the house. It was a substantial space but, oddly, two people seemed to fill it. He thought of phoning Penny before getting into bed to say goodnight but did not want to interrupt her evening. She may be dining with friends. He would call her in the morning.

He woke early as usual, made some tea, and had a light breakfast. He sat on the veranda, soaking up the early morning air and surveying his kingdom. It was a beautiful setting, and he would do everything he could to ensure they did not have to give it up. That said, overnight, he had failed to produce a plan to raise the money he would need to stay afloat. He often had his best and most innovative ideas during the early morning before fully waking, but not that day.

His instinct was to phone Penny. He knew she would be up and certainly pottering about in the cottage garden. They had a gardener and handyman that visited during the summer months to keep the property in good order. Another expense. He was about to call her but put the phone down. He realised he could not contemplate a jolly conversation with her, knowing that she was in the dark about their finances. He knew he had to wait until she returned to discuss the matter and, hopefully, during the interim, he would have found a way to raise enough money to pay what he owed the bank without having to contemplate the sale of personal assets.

With no office to go to, he went into his study, opened his laptop, and began responding to a lengthy list of emails that required attention. It was close to 11.00 am when Susie called. She was missing him and wanted him to go across to the apartment for lunch and extracurricular activities. Again, it was hard refusing her invitation, but he remained firm. He was engrossed in his work and had too much to get through. What about supper? She had no idea Penny was away, and he had no plans to tell her as it would only create a demand for him to spend the week at her apartment. Even worse, she might suggest she spent the week at his house; it would be a way for her to acquaint herself with the property in advance of when she moved in when Tom divorced Penny. The clock was ticking. Susie had already started to count down the 365-day period within which he had promised he would be divorced.

Under pressure, he had said a lot of things just to keep her quiet, but for Susie, every commitment he made, she expected him to deliver on. He knew she was a firework primed to explode in his face.

His will capitulated. How could he refuse supper? He would not have to worry about lying to Penny as to why he planned to be out, and there would certainly be no need to be ultra-imaginative in justifying an overnight stay if it came to it. He agreed to meet her at the apartment at 6.30 pm. She would cook. He would provide the champagne. It was always a celebration for Susie to have Tom to herself.

Early in the afternoon, Penny called. He should have guessed she would do so, not having heard from him.

"Hello, darling. How are you… recovered?"

She told him about her sail across to Cowes and how much she had enjoyed the experience. She suggested that after all the recent dramas they had been through, they deserved a break and should take a month out to sail to Turkey, a journey they had loved doing a few years earlier on a previous sale boat they owned. Their latest yacht, The Storyteller, would be perfect for the voyage and the first lengthy trip they would have made in her.

Tom listened intently and sensed Penny's excitement at the prospect of the adventure. Of course, little did she know about the new challenge he was facing. The last thing he could do, indeed, could afford, was to take a month out on a sailing expedition. She said she had started to think about their itinerary and wanted to discuss it with him when she returned in a week. Tom said little, although not so little as to invite her to ask why he was not sharing her excitement. He desperately wanted to come clean with her about their precarious financial situation, if for no other reason than to unburden his mind onto another human being, a human being he loved deeply.

Worries like this needed to be out in the open, not bottled up, but he knew it would panic her. She would become emotional and that would be counterproductive; it only made sense to tell her when he had a plan of action. Penny paused in the conversation…

"Anyway, darling, I do have a bit of bad news…"

Tom waited to hear what it was. Of course there was unwelcome news! He had not had any for at least an hour, at the current trajectory, he was unquestionably due some.

"What is it?" He held his breath.

"A few problems, in fact. When I arrived at the cottage, I failed to get the hot water to work so I called the plumber.

He said the boiler needed replacing and the system needing flushing and gave me a quote. Overall, it is almost three thousand pounds. I told him to do it this week while I am here. I also spoke to Anthony, the handyman.

He pointed out that the roof had obviously been leaking in two of the bedrooms for some time, and one of the ceilings is about to collapse. He has been on the roof, and it is a mess and needs replacing. He said he could do it all, so I gave him the go ahead.

"How much will it cost?" Tom again held his breath.

"He said he was unable to give me a firm price, but he estimated the total job would be in the region of twenty-five thousand pounds."

Tom swallowed hard. Another bill that would need paying. Penny continued.

"He said he would do it as quickly as possible. I have put buckets in the bedrooms to catch the water and I have moved the antique furniture out. I am sleeping in the sitting room. He asked if he could have ten thousand pounds upfront for materials, so I gave him a cheque. I hope that is okay."

Tom worried it would bounce. They ended their conversation with Penny none the wiser about their true financial difficulties. Tom had fifty-nine days and counting down, to settle the bank loan and just five days until Penny returned home to produce a plan to resolve their financial situation in a way that would win her blessing. It was a tall order.

It was late afternoon. As always, Tom had mixed emotions about visiting Susie at the apartment. He knew his encounters with her just reinforced her desire for him, and further cemented her claim as her husband to be. On the other hand, he knew that his hunger for her would be satisfied. It was always the case unless they got into a row.

With the Range Rover in for repair and Penny's Mercedes parked at Hamble Marina, he would need to drive the Porsche 911 Turbo to her apartment, a journey he was not relishing. After all his recent dramas, the last thing he wanted was to be involved in a collision or, once again, be stopped by the police, for any reason!

He finished his work, showered, dressed, and headed out to the car, champagne in hand. He decided it best to wrap it up and put the bottle in the passenger foot well rather than have it lying on the passenger seat just in case he was stopped again. He was paranoid. Having got into the car, he revved the engine. It was always an exciting feeling, about to drive this monster of a car. Out loud, he said to himself, 'You must drive carefully.' The journey to Susie's, which he knew so well, would take half an hour when adhering to the law. As he headed slowly down the driveway, he looked across at the sculptures on the perfectly manicured lawn and a sense of sadness came over him.

He looked in his rear-view mirror and saw the magnificent home that he was leaving behind, the home of an entrepreneur, a successful publisher, and wondered whether his good fortune was about to run out completely.

He navigated his journey to Susie's apartment without incident. As he pulled up and parked next to her Porsche, he saw the curtains twitch. The two cars from the same stable in identical colours always looked so stunning. She was waiting for him. He took out the champagne. In a flash, she was at the door to greet him. She always looked fabulous, but he could not remember her having looked better, and he said as much. She was thrilled that her man, the man she was desperate to marry and spend the rest of her life with, had paid her a compliment. When Tom was in a relaxed mood, he was the perfect suitor. He knew exactly how to impress the women in his life. He had plenty of practice over the years. Despite his worries, and there were many, he was determined to put them to one side, at least for now, so that the encounter with Susie would go perfectly. He was about to enjoy her food and her flesh in a way he had not done since a few days earlier!

As he had hoped, the meal, the conversation, and the sex were just what the doctor had ordered. He had no hesitation in accepting the invitation to spend the night. Penny was away and his time with Susie was all the therapy he needed. He had drunk a bottle of champagne, but Susie had chosen not to drink at all, which was unusual for her. She was never a big drinker, but she had always enjoyed a glass or two when he visited her at the apartment.

It was just before they retired to bed that she disappeared for a moment. When she returned, she had a big grin on her face. He had never seen her so excited, and it pleased him. She was obviously enjoying their time together. At moments like this, he knew why he was attracted to her and why this affair had lasted for as long as it had. She was an intelligent, albeit highly strung woman, with great beauty and a figure that most women would die for. And for some reason, she wanted him, and only him, in her life. He knew how fortunate he was.

"Come on, why are you so excited?" Tom smiled at her.

"Tom, we are having a baby!"

On that bombshell, she handed him her three-month scan. She had decided to wait before telling him because she wanted to know that everything was okay. There was no question the baby was his. Susie was as loyal and faithful to Tom as Penny was.

In an instant, his emotions had somersaulted. It was too much to take in. With everything going on in his life right now, the very last thing he wanted was to hear this. He was speechless. In the following seconds, his mind was unable to compute a suitable response. Any man hearing the news that he was about to be a father for the first time, which was the case for Tom, would be ecstatic.

Deep down he had wished that he and Penny had made the decision to raise a family. Of course, that was now long past.

Susie waited for a response. He knew that shouting, screaming, and blaming her for getting pregnant and not taking enough precautions would be catastrophic. Such a response would be unintelligent and morally repugnant almost evil, but there was a part of him that wanted to say it anyway. He had been through a period of drama and unwelcome news and while Susie's announcement, under the right circumstances, would mean all his problems melted away, these were absolutely, not the right circumstances. He knew this would only add hugely to his already existing burden. That said, having cartwheeled those thoughts around in his head, he still had to produce a response that would keep Susie on board. She was not thinking of the ramifications of her news vis-a-vis Penny. Why would she? Tom planned to divorce her within the year anyway, so the timing would be perfect for her to claim her man, baby in arms, and move into the family home. Tom had no choice. He had to be joyful, as joyful as he could muster.

"Bloody hell! Pregnant? Wow! And this is the scan?"

"Yes. I waited to make sure everything was okay before I told you. Are you happy, Tom? We are going to be a family!"

"Wow, I cannot believe it…"

"Can you manage a hug and kiss for the new mother-to-be?"

Tom hugged her and she held him tightly. She never wanted to let the man she loved go, the man whose baby she was carrying.

Tom had managed to put on an act that had at least got him over the first hurdle. There was no doubt that Susie would have liked him to be more animated and excited, but she knew it would take time for her news to sink in. He needed to escape to think this through and offered to make some tea.

"Oh, yes please. Could I have peppermint tea? I am told it is good for Mums to be…"

"Of course."

Tom went into the kitchen and screamed silently to himself. The revelation that he was to be a father was just another in a lengthy list of disasters that had been queuing up to assault him. He had years of good fortune in his life, and now it was time to suffer and pay his dues. So many questions flew into his head thick and fast, not least of all… How on earth would he tell Penny?

On the flipside, Susie's announcement was perfect for her.

It was just what she had wanted, as it gave her added power and influence that she craved. No more would she have to play second fiddle to Tom's Penelope, the woman she so despised.

Penny had never given him a child, but she would. With the baby due in six months, she would ramp up the pressure on him to get rid of Penny, and as quickly as possible. He could prevaricate no longer. Why did he have to wait a year to divorce her? No. He would have to start the process in the coming week.

Tom returned to the sitting room with the peppermint tea. His mind had been elsewhere, and he had forgotten to make himself a coffee.

"So, what do you want, Tom?"

His immediate thought in answer to that question was for her to retract her statement and tell him she was only joking about the pregnancy, but that was far more than he could hope for.

"Sorry… want?"

"Boy or girl?"

"I am… I really… I am not sure if I am honest."

This was proving to be so awkward that he knew she would twig sooner rather than later that he was less than pleased with the news. Then, of course, she would get upset and a row would ensue. He had to avoid that at all costs.

"I was offered the chance to find out the sex of the baby when I had the scan, but I decided I did not want to know. I thought we could share the excitement when the baby was born. I think… I would like a boy first. Boys, I am told, are easier to raise than girls and are better at adjusting when the second child is born." The second child? As if the initial announcement had not been enough, now she was planning a whole rugby team?!

"I would like three children, Tom. I am young enough,

there is plenty of time. You will be an older Dad but that does not matter in the least. I cannot tell you how happy I am, Tom! I' have told my parents about the baby. They were slightly taken aback because you told me not to say anything to them about us; they assumed I did not have a boyfriend."

"And… did they ask if you were seeing anyone?"

"We cannot hide our relationship forever, nor should we. Yes, I told them about you. They know you are married, but I told them you were in the process of getting a divorce. They were a little shocked, but they seemed okay. My father asked if he could meet you."

Tom wanted to escape, to disappear… He needed to be alone to take all this in. He could not carry it off if he stayed in the room with her; he knew it would blow up in his face.

"Darling, I know this is not a good moment with such good news to celebrate, but I need to return home I have just remembered I left the house unlocked. I am sorry; will you forgive me?"

Ordinarily, when he asked to leave, Susie would beg him to stay, but she sensed her news had been a surprise for him, but hoped in her heart that he would adjust to the reality that he was to become a father and embrace it. On this occasion, she acceded to his request and within the hour, Tom was at home, pouring himself a large whisky.

As he swallowed his first sip, it dawned on him that he had consumed a full bottle of champagne at Susie's and had just driven the Porsche home. His mind had been so concentrated on the news that he was to be a father; he had completely forgotten how risky it was drinking and driving. It was small comfort that he had got away with it, when compared with the other mounting challenges in his life.

He sat on the sofa. He had reached an all-time low in his life. The news of the baby was a complete shock. He should have been overjoyed that he was to be a father for the first time, but instead he was depressed by the problems it would cause. Earlier in the day, he had believed he had insurmountable problems to contend with, and wondered how on earth he would deal with them. Now, they looked a great deal worse.

He sat staring into space, his mind wandered. His life was in freefall, and it seemed he could do nothing about it. For the first time in a very long time, he truly felt he was on his own, and his fate would be determined by others.

There was no one to talk to, no one to seek advice from, and no one to help him chart a new course in a direction that would free him of his worries.

It was late. He switched on the outside lights and went onto the veranda. The entire garden was illuminated, it was serene. Tom tried to clear his mind hoping for inspiration. There had to be a way of resolving at least some of his crises to give him a fresh start. He thought the unthinkable. Tom and Penny had been married for twenty years and she was still very much in love with him. Their relationship had matured over the years, but that had not diminished their affection and passion for each other. Tom knew she was his soulmate.

In the past, when he had issues going on in his life or in the business, he could talk to her. Her advice was not always what he wanted to hear or appropriate, but the process of sharing with someone close to him was cathartic. He wondered if he was ready to share all his troubles with her, now? Would she have the capacity to cope with the long list of issues he needed to get off his chest, not least of all, the affair with Susie and her pregnancy?

He believed she would cope with the financial situation and the likelihood that they would have to sell assets, including their homes, to pay off their debts and adjust to a more modest lifestyle. What he could not imagine in his wildest dreams, though, was her coming to terms with his adultery and the fact that his mistress, his PA, who she liked, was carrying his baby!

He wondered if he had any other choice but to tell her. She would find out soon enough anyway. As if climbing that mountain was not enough, and even if Penny were somehow accepting, how would he deal with Susie's demand that he divorced Penny, married her, and moved her and the baby into Tom and Penny's home? At a loss, he turned the lights out and went to bed.

He woke with a hangover and took some pills to deal with the pain, but his anguish could not be cured that easily. He dreaded speaking to both Penny and Susie as the day unfolded. He decided to switch off his phone and not answer the landline if it rang. He had no appetite for work.

Overnight, and with little if any sleep, no new ways of overcoming his challenges had emerged. He was trapped in a vacuum of indecision and hopelessness.

A thought occupied his mind. Perhaps the only answer was for him to go away on his own, to disappear and start a new life somewhere else, anywhere that meant he would not have to face up to Penny and Susie. Of course, it was a ridiculous notion, he could not live with himself in the knowledge there were so many loose ends, or with the hurt his actions would inevitably cause. It was not like him to ever contemplate running away from his responsibilities; it was stupid. He made coffee. He had no desire for breakfast.

The landline rang. Having decided not to answer any calls that day, he immediately found himself lifting the receiver. It was Penny. She was missing him. She was due back in two days but decided to sail back on the first tide in the morning. Anthony, the handyman was planning to start work on the cottage roof, and it would be disruptive and noisy, so any form of relaxation was out of the question.

Anthony already had keys to the property so he could come and go as he needed to. He had also agreed to oversee the plumber when he arrived to fit the new boiler, so she was free to leave. Tom agreed to drive down to Hamble to meet her late morning so he could help her de-rig the yacht. In some respects, the thought of working on the yacht raised his spirits. He loved sailing and when he had the time, he would often travel down to the marina and potter around.

He put the phone down on Penny, in an instant, had clarity of mind. He knew he had to be brutally honest with Penny about everything. Telling her half-truths and being selective would not wash.

Upon their return from Hamble, he would sit her down and confess everything about the business, their finances, the affair with Susie, and the baby. Then, he would beg her forgiveness so their marriage could heal.

It was a huge risk, a massive risk, and he knew that by confessing, his marriage was in jeopardy. He loved Penny. Truly, he loved her, and had no desire to see their marriage end, but it was the only way. It was a gamble he must take to maintain his sanity. He could no longer continue with the constant lies about Susie, and indeed everything else. His entire life with Penny and been full of deception and he felt wretched.

He had refined an ability to put aside the guilt that plagued so many people that were unfaithful. Now, he found he could no longer compartmentalise and dismiss those feelings. He was riddled with guilt, and knew he had to cleanse his soul. Doing so was accepting the worst-case scenario: Penny would divorce him and never speak to him again. If she were to find everything out on her own accord, there would be no chance of reconciliation.

As for Susie, he knew would never marry her. He would do

all he could to support her and the baby, but that relationship had to end, irrespective of his confession to Penny and its outcome.

CHAPTER 14 - RECKONING

Tom knew the next day or two would determine his future life. He had set himself an unenviable task, but it was one he had to undertake if he were to avoid the shackles of long-term guilt, and the hurt he was causing to both Penny and Susie.

He had been forced to take this path. It certainly was not one to which he would readily have conceded, but circumstances had led him there. Despite what loomed on the horizon, though, he felt positive of mind. A mental weight had been lifted. The indecision of how to deal with the dramas in his life had subsided. He had a plan, and he had every intention of executing it.

He arrived at Hamble Marina at 9.00 am the following morning. Penny would not arrive at the mooring for a few hours. He had already received a message from her to say she was underway. He had also received two text messages from Susie, asking when she would see him next.

It had been a couple of months since he had last visited the marina. Tom was well known to the tradesmen and the boat owners alike. They all had one thing in common at least: they loved the open sea and were never happier than when talking about boats and, in Tom's case, sailing them.

He went to the café, hoping to meet friends there. It was surprisingly quiet for the time of morning. At 9.00 am, it was usually a hive of activity, but not today. He wandered around looking at the craft moored up. It was always interesting to see if any new boats had taken moorings there, and what they were like.

Hamble boasted some fine craft. Tom's yacht, The Storyteller, a Moody DS 41 with every conceivable extra, was certainly one of them.

With the confession that lay ahead, The Storyteller was

more than an apt name for his boat, testament to the past twenty years of selling other people's stories in paperback while fabricating his own to cover up his infidelities.

It was just after midday when Penny sailed into the marina. The yacht looked magnificent. She saw him at the mooring and waved. Through his binoculars he could see she looked happy. The weather had been unpredictable as she sailed across the Solent and the yacht had tested her competencies. At one point, as she recalled later, she had strayed into the waters of a cross-channel ferry and did her utmost to avoid a collision. She was lucky. As happy as she was sailing solo, it was at such moments that she wished Tom had been with her.

Tom greeted her warmly. She hugged him tightly. They busied themselves de-rigging the boat before they set off for home in separate cars. He was relieved that they would not be sharing a car for the return journey as he did not want to engage in conversation until he was able to sit her down at home and make his confession.

After an uneventful journey, they parked in the driveway and Tom carried Penny's bag into the house. She went upstairs to change while he made some coffee. He was feeling incredibly nervous, but he knew he had to maintain his composure if he was to get through his speech without falling apart.

Penny returned to the drawing room.

"Have you been able to relax while I have been away, Tom? I felt so guilty sailing across to the island leaving you behind."

She sat on the sofa. Tom had to stop her in her tracks. He did not want her feeling guilty; she had nothing to feel bad about. In fact, to the contrary, she had been the perfect wife since they first married. She had been wonderfully supportive with the business, and she did all she could to ensure that he could relax when he took time out. She would do anything to make him happy at the drop of a hat.

Tom sat next to her.

"You have nothing to feel guilty about. I love you, Penny. You do know that."

"Of course, I do, why are you asking?"

"This is the hardest thing I have ever had to do, but I need tell you about a few important things.

But before I do, I want you to know that whatever the outcome, I want to spend the rest of my life with you." Penny looked worried.

"Tom, are you ill?"

"No darling, I am not ill, but I want you to listen to what I have to say."

"You're worrying me, Tom. It sounds like a confession."

He took a deep breath, looked her squarely in the eyes and, maintaining his composure made his confession.

"It is a confession. I want to be totally honest with you and I do not want to leave anything out. First, the business. In the past couple of years, it has grown as you know. I used that growth and increased profitability to invest further in the business, but I also spent a good deal of cash refurbishing the offices, this house, buying the cottage and the yacht and, of course, buying our cars. Added to that, I foolishly gave Rod the money, as you know. Earlier in the week I discovered that Roger, you remember Roger, the accountant who I had to sack, fraudulently took out a loan for one hundred and fifty thousand pound in the business name, which he transferred into his own account."

At this point, Penny was desperate to ask questions, but again, Tom insisted he told her the whole story before she had her say.

"Suffice it to say, Roger got away with it and the bank, who are aware of the fire at the business, have become concerned that we may not have the resources to repay the loan, which is due within the next sixty days. I thought I was on top of things, but the fire and the insurance company refusing to settle the claim has placed us in a precarious position, financially. Everything is conspiring against us, and the only way we can repay our outstanding liabilities is to liquidate assets if we are to avoid losing everything…"

Tom had to stop Penny from speaking…

"I know a few years ago you wanted me to incorporate the business to avoid personal liability, but I thought better of it. I should have heeded your advice. Today, the business debts are, in effect, our personal debts. Unfortunately, even if we sold the cottage, the yacht, and the cars, there would still be a substantial shortfall. Taking out another loan is not an option, I have checked. With the state of our finances, we would be unable to find a willing lender."

Penny was sat ridged. Her eyes were wide open, and she was in shock. She was fixated on Tom. She wanted to ask so many questions but knew Tom wanted to get everything off his chest before she would have an opportunity to interrogate him.

"But darling, for me, what I am about to say is far more important than our finances."

This was the defining moment. Now he had to tell Penny about his affair with Susie and the baby. His bottom lip quivered momentarily as he took his gaze off her.

His mouth dried up. He cleared his throat and looked back at her. She had no idea what was coming. She remained motionless but her jaw had dropped slightly in anticipation of his next words.

"For the past two years, I have been having an affair with Susie."

Penny's eyes popped, and her jaw dropped wide open. A look of horror came over her.

"I cannot tell you how sorry I am. I have been an absolute fool, and obviously I regret what I have done…"

She could wait no longer. His revelations so far had been enough to warrant an outburst, but she had stayed silent, but now she had to speak despite what other admissions might pass his lips.

"…Tom, please tell me it is not true!"

She burst into tears. He tried to console her, but she pushed him away.

"Darling, I know this hurts but you had to know. I have lied for long enough, and I cannot carry the burden of guilt any longer…"

Penny became angry. She stood up.

"…How could you, Tom? How could you deceive me this way, and with Susie? Someone I liked and trusted? She is only a young woman; what were you thinking?" Tom responded immediately.

"I cannot blame her for this. It was me who encouraged the affair. It was just a mid-life crisis…"

"A mid-life crisis?! How pathetic! Have I not been enough for you, Tom? Have I been an uncaring wife? Have I not done everything in my power to make you happy?"

"Darling, you have, you have, you are the perfect wife, and I do want to spend the rest of my life with you!" Tom instantly looked years older. His face was ashen, and his eyes welled up.

"You should have thought about that two years ago! So, why are you telling me now? Has she ditched you and you want to redeem your conscience?"

It was not going well, but it was exactly how Tom had anticipated it would. Penny would naturally be shocked by his confession, and she would be angry that he had betrayed her, and at this point, if that were the end of his story, he could spend the rest of his time trying to persuade her to forgive him.

Of course, though, there was more to come.

"No, she has not ditched me."

He knew he was treading on eggshells. Penny was a woman of principle. She had a moral code. For her, the sanctimony of marriage was a life-long commitment. The thought that she or Tom would ever deceive the other would never have crossed her mind. They were happy. It was only recently that he had bought her expensive jewellery. He constantly told her how much he loved her, so why would he do such a thing? Why would he risk everything they had built over the years for a fling with a younger woman? It made no sense to her, but it hurt deeply, and she felt pained and confused.

"I have been trying to end the affair for some time, but she has been threatening to tell you about it."

"So that is why you have chosen to confess now. Not because you want to end it with her, but because you were fearful, she would tell me!" Tom paused momentarily and lowered his voice.

"No, that is not the reason. Earlier in the week, Susie told me she was three months pregnant…"

It was out. He had told her about the business, their finances, the affair, and the baby. What he was not planning to do was to add all the other affairs he had over the years. That was a bridge too far.

"Pregnant? She is pregnant… with your baby…"

Penny rushed out of the room, beside herself with anger and disbelief. If the affair were not enough to end the marriage the announcement that he would be a father with another woman, certainly was. Tom had hoped that she would hear him out and they would be able to talk about the issues facing them, but he clearly had not considered the degree of emotional reaction she would have upon hearing the news.

Rather than chase after her, he let her go up to the bedroom.

He could hear her crying like a wounded animal and he, too, sobbed. Had he done the right thing in telling her about Susie? Would the situation have resolved itself one way or another if he had not?

He knew it was wishful thinking. The truth had to come out and Penny needed time to allow the revelations to sink in, and importantly, decide what she wanted to happen from here. For once in their marriage, what Tom wanted was of no consequence. It would be Penny that decided their fate as a couple.

Despite having prepared for his confession, he had not turned off his phone. Fortunately for him, if indeed fortunate was the right word, Susie had not messaged or called during his speech. Now, it pinged. Hello, daddy… Tom had read enough. He would read no more. The last thing he could cope with was a conversation or exchange with Susie.

He remained on the sofa, wondering what to do next. Should he wait for Penny to come down and resume the conversation or go upstairs to the bedroom and try to console her? He had no idea what to do. He felt desolate. The last thing he wanted was for Penny to suffer this way, but he knew she would need to go through a grieving process as one would do with the death of a loved one. For her, Tom was her man. He was a part of her. They were an item and everything she did was for them as a couple. Now, she was detached from him, and a part of him was interwoven in the DNA of another woman. How could she come to terms with that?

He wanted to pour a large whisky, so desperate was he for something to ease his mind, but he knew it would only impair his judgement, he had to stay alert and ready to cope with anything Penny was likely to say.

Penny was not the type of woman to resort to violence. She would not lose control and hit out. She would suffer the pain and anguish on her own, and when she was ready to deal with a situation, and only then, would she make her feelings known. He decided that going up to the bedroom was a bad idea. He would wait for her to come down, however long that took. He sat on the veranda and reflected.

He had had a wonderful life with Penny up until now. As he had said to himself many times, she was the perfect wife. There was nothing about their relationship that would cause him to want an affair. His adulterous nature was not something he believed he could control, at least until now. For too many women, he was an attractive man. Younger women latched onto him. He possessed a large ego, and his muses stimulated that ego in a way that was dangerous but exciting; but love, the love he shared with Penny, was never in question. He never fell in love with his mistresses. They were playthings, but of course playthings also have emotions: emotions that demand attention. Susie was a classic case of a mistress who was never satisfied with sex alone; she wanted to transition to be an everyday part of Tom's life, one they would share together without encumbrance. Now, in his current situation, he knew he would trade everything he had, including his need for other women, if he could put right his relationship with Penny.

Hours had passed. It was early evening when Penny eventually came down to the drawing room. Tom was incredibly nervous. She chose not to look at him and he too averted his eyes waiting for her to speak.

She sat on the sofa, and he sat on an easy chair. She looked up at him. Her eyes were sore with the tears she had shed, and her faced was pained, but she was now composed and ready to talk to him.

"It is my turn to talk, Tom, and I would prefer it if you would not interrupt me."

He nodded in anticipation.

"You have no idea how much you have hurt me. I do not know why, but I totally trusted you. I have always believed we had a good marriage, and nothing could come between us, but I was wrong, a fool to think that life was that simple. You have betrayed the trust I placed in you, and I will never forgive you. To think that while I was here, at home, thinking and worrying about you, you were having an affair with Susie, of all people! A physical relationship with another woman that has led to her carrying your child, a child that will be a part of your life until the day you die. What you have chosen to do is trade our marriage and all it represents for casual sex with a younger woman, and if that were not enough, you would no doubt come home and have sex with me afterwards."

Tom was motionless and hanging off her every word, as Penny had been when he gave his speech.

"I am sure it comes as no surprise to you Tom, but I demand a divorce. I do not want to entertain any thoughts you may have of reconciliation. I want a divorce and as quickly as possible. I want you to pack and leave the house today. I will appoint a lawyer to deal with the formalities. Despite my wish, as you mentioned earlier, that you incorporate the business to protect us from debt, you chose not to. I have no choice but to accept that we are jointly liable for your mismanagement of our interests, and like you, I will suffer the consequences. I will not agree to do anything, or sign anything, unless I am instructed to do so by my lawyer. I will ask that they audit the company files and our personal possessions as soon as possible, to determine what is left of our assets. From the moment you leave the house, I do not want you to contact me again for any reason. You need to go through my lawyer, whose details you will get on Monday morning."

It was Tom's turn to be stunned. Penny had been

unequivocal. She would not entertain Tom trying to persuade her to go back on her decision; there was no point, but he felt he had to try anyway. He loved her and, strangely, after her speech, that love was even stronger. She was the woman he wanted to be with. This was the woman with whom he was on a wavelength and shared common interests, not Susie, not anyone else.

"Penny, I know you are angry and rightly so, and I know you are hurting, but we can get through this. I will do anything you ask of me to put things right."

"How do you put right a mistress carrying your baby, Tom?"

"I know how it looks…"

"…How it looks? How it looks has nothing to do with it! You chose to have an affair and get your girlfriend pregnant, knowing that you were risking our marriage. Are you so egotistical to believe that I would want you at any price?"

"No, of course, not. But until I told you about the affair…" Penny's response was immediate…

"…And the baby. Let us not forget the baby, Tom."

"But up until then, you said you loved me. Surely that means something. There must be a chance that we can rebuild what I have destroyed?"

Penny was resolute. There was no way back for them. The marriage was over.

"There is nothing, absolutely nothing you can say or do that will change my mind. I would be grateful if you would pack a bag now and leave as quickly as possible. If you need anything from the house after you have left, let my lawyer know and I will arrange for it to be delivered to Susie's or any other address you choose to live at."

Penny left the room.

To say Tom was deflated would be a monumental

understatement. Within the hour, he had packed a suitcase and his laptop and left in the Porsche. He booked a room at a local hotel – by coincidence, the same one George had booked into when he left Ginny some weeks earlier. The common denominator was, of course, Susie.

He dined late in the hotel restaurant and drank heavily. He had not given up with Penny, not yet. He hoped that she would take a more pragmatic view of the situation over the coming days and change her mind. In his heart, though, he knew that was highly unlikely. He had crossed a moral boundary and there was no way back. Penny was unequivocal, and although deeply hurt and vulnerable, she would rather determine her own future than allow Tom to determine it for her.

Just as he had decided to confess all to Penny, albeit hoping for a better result, he knew he also had to confront Susie and tell her that he had no intention of setting up home with her and the baby. He did not want to hurt her; she had done nothing wrong other than to fall in love with another woman's husband. She was a beautiful woman, and he had more than enjoyed his time with her, but he was not in love with her as he was with Penny. There was no future for them together. He would reassure her that she would not be abandoned. He would make financial provision for her and the child long-term, and as a part of that agreement, he would sign over the apartment to her. In her predicament he could hardly ask her to leave the property or indeed ask her for rent. She would soon be out of a job as the prospect of salvaging the business diminished by the day. Penny's demand to liquidate their assets gave little hope of survival for Taylor Publishing. Penny was totally unaware that they owned the apartment. He had managed to keep that from her. That made it easier for him to sign it over to Susie without causing a fuss. Before he went back to his hotel room, he called Susie and told her he wanted to see her in the morning at 10.00 am. She was thrilled to hear from him and said how much she looked forward to seeing him. She had no inkling of what was in store.

Tom did not sleep a wink all night thinking about Penny and how stupid and self-centred he had been over the years. He knew he had lost the only woman he ever really loved, indeed would ever love. Nothing about the business or his finances really mattered anymore. His future was in the balance.

Tom's hotel was located no more than fifteen minutes away from Susie's apartment. Before pulling into the car park, he stopped in a layby to think through what he planned to say to her. Unlike Penny, who was emotionally measured and did not seek verbal or physical confrontation, Susie might well do. She was highly strung and her way of dealing with things was different.

Turning over in his mind what he planned to say to her proved to be a pointless exercise. He would have to say whatever came into his head and deal with the fallout.

Susie saw him arrive and went out excitedly to greet him. They went inside together, and she immediately attempted to kiss him, but he stepped back.

"Is something the matter?" She looked concerned.

"Look, Susie. I have something to say to you and I want you to wait until I have finished before you say anything, okay?" He used the same approach as he had with Penny hoping it would have a better outcome. If only. Susie responded immediately.

"It depends on what you have to say… have you told Penny you are divorcing her?"

She was hoping that her announcement about the baby had spurred him into action sooner than even she had expected.

"No. But I have told her about our affair and your pregnancy."

"Oh, Tom, that is great! Thank you!"

It was impossible for her to wait for the full story before having her say. Tom was insistent.

"No, please, you must hear me out."

"You seem so serious, Tom. This is good news you want to tell me?"

"I have told Penny about you and the baby, and she wants to divorce me, but I do not want her to."

"Why ever not? Why?"

"Because I love her, Susie, and I do not want our marriage to end."

"But… Am I missing something! You love me, not her! You said so only two days ago… You have said so for the past two years!"

"I know I have said many things to you and made promises I was unable to keep, and I am deeply, deeply sorry." Again, she responded without drawing breath.

"I told my parents after your divorce we would be married! You promised we would be together!"

Tom attempted to hold her, but she pulled away. The reality of what he was telling her began to sink in.

"You cannot leave me Tom… we are having a baby together. Did you really think you could get me pregnant and walk away, just like that?"

"No. Of course not. I am not planning to walk away. I will play my part in the baby's life, and I will support you financially…"

"…Play a part?! What does that mean? Pop in to see the baby every few weeks when you are at a loose end. What about me, Tom? Are you telling me that you have no feelings for me, because I just do not believe it!"

"It will not work Susie. I cannot marry you. I am not in love with you the way I love Penny…"

He did not have time to finish his sentence before she went into a rage, punching and kicking him. He tried to restrain her as she ran into the bathroom, locking herself in. He begged her to come out, but she refused. He slumped back on the sofa and shook his head. How have I got myself into such a mess?

For Susie, Tom and her work were her life, she had dedicated herself to both. Her love for Tom was emphatic. Every waking minute of every day, he was on her mind. She had given up a long-term relationship with a boyfriend to whom she was engaged to be married, believing that she and Tom would one day be together to raise a family and live happily thereafter. There was no doubt in her mind. This was the man she wanted, and she would ensure nothing got in her way. There was no denying he had said he loved her, and on many occasions. He had also told her that he wanted to spend the rest of his life with her, and indeed that they would be married.

He had promised all those things, but he would argue he had done so under duress to avoid confrontation, to avoid her telling Penny about the affair, and to ensure he was able to maintain her services as his mistress. Now, in her mind, he wanted to discard her like an item of old clothing. She came out of the bathroom like a wounded animal, screaming abuse at him.

"Susie… Susie... Listen to me, please listen to me. I am sorry…"

"…You are not leaving me, ever! I will kill you first!" With that, she came at him with a pair of scissors and attempted to stab him in the heart. Tom recoiled and managed to avoid the blade penetrating his body. He knew she was volatile, and that she would not take the news in a cool, calm, and collected way. That was not how she was wired, but he had had no expectation that she would try to kill him.

He was able to take the scissors from her and pushed her onto the sofa. He was worried the stress could bring on a miscarriage and had to calm the situation. He held her tightly to restrain her from striking out.

"Susie, I do not want us to fight like this!"

"You should have thought about that before you…" She broke down in tears.

"If I let you go, will you just listen to me… please?"

She nodded reluctantly. She knew that by talking rather than fighting, she had a chance to change his mind. It made no sense to her. What had his evil wife said to poison him against her? He said she was divorcing him; surely that was what he wanted to hear? She did not believe he had strung her along all this time. No, he loved her, and was not thinking clearly. He had been under a lot of pressure with the office fire recently, and he needed her to comfort him and work with him to resolve their challenges.

"Okay. I am listening." Now, Tom had to think what he was going to say to her.

"I do love you. You are beautiful, funny…"

She started to chuckle thinking he was about to change his mind, "…and we have had a wonderful time together this past two years and I would not change a thing. But I do not love you in the way I love Penny. I am sorry for all the hurt I have caused you."

"But you just said you love me! Of course, I understand you love me differently; you cannot love two people in the same way! We are good together, Tom, we are.?"

She had cooled down, so Tom took the opportunity to sit back more comfortably, thinking a rational, civilised conversation might be possible.

"I know what you are saying, darling…" He knew it was a bad idea calling her darling; it would only fuel her argument about his affection for her…

"…I really do, and under different circumstances, if I was not married, we could make a go of it with the baby, but everything has conspired against us…"

"I fail to understand why. I thought you said Penny wanted a divorce?"

"She does, but that is not what I mean."

"What do you mean then? If you and Penny divorce, we could be together! What could stop us?"

His attempt to end the relationship was falling on deaf ears. He looked at her, struggling to know what to say next.

"Tom. I want you to listen to me. I love you more than you will ever know, and you said you loved me too! I know we can make our relationship work. I know I can be difficult and demanding at times but that is what you really like about me, that I am different from your staid, boring wife. Tom. You have no idea, really… no idea what lengths I have gone to, to make sure you and I can be together.

And now, you do not even have to ask for a divorce! I know you have found that difficult because you are a lovely man, but now she is divorcing you! It is precisely what we wanted…"

Susie paused, her eyes glazed over and her cheeks became ashen. Momentarily, she had lost mental contact. She recovered and continued slowly.

"I have done so much I did not want to do…"

Tom felt an immediate sense of foreboding. Something was deeply wrong.

"What do you mean 'done so much you did not want to do?"

"It does not matter anymore, but believe me, I have sacrificed a lot to get us to where we are."

"I am sorry, what do you mean?"

"Do you really want to know, Tom?" Of course, he did.

Alarm bells were ringing now. He nodded slowly and she went on.

"Do you remember the time we had that flaming row here in the apartment, a week or so before your brother's wife was found dead? It was about you divorcing Penny…"

Tom could not remember it specifically there were so many rows, but he nodded anyway.

"I thought you were going to end our relationship. I was so depressed at the thought of living without you that I thought of a plan that would bring us closer together and get rid of Penny. I thought if I could make her think that you were having an affair with your brother's wife, she would leave you and we would be together."

Tom listened closely eager to understand where she was going with this.

"And…?"

"Well, I prepared a letter from Penny addressed to Mary saying if Mary did not stop her affair with you, Penny would kill her… I assumed your brother would find the letter and all would be out in the open." The revelation hit Tom right between the eyes.

"Letter… from Penny?"

"Yes, Tom. Let me finish. I had to find a way of hiding the letter in the house so it would be found. I knew from what you said that she worked at the library, so I went there and befriended her. She invited me back to her house for coffee a few days later. While she was boiling the kettle, I asked if I could go to the bathroom, and she pointed me upstairs. It was the opportunity I needed to hide the letter and a locket I had bought, which was from you. I had it inscribed 'To Mary, love T.' I hid it in the bedroom next to the letter but then, Mary came upstairs and caught me as I was coming out of the bedroom."

Tom was aghast. It was because of those items that he, Rod and Penny had been arrested and questioned at the police station. He remained silent.

"I went downstairs; she was angry and kept asking what I was doing in her bedroom. I could not think of anything to say. She went berserk and told me to leave and kept shoving me. She grabbed my arm tightly. I flipped. I grabbed one of her scarves that was hanging by the door, and in a moment of rage, I wrapped the scarf around her neck and pulled as tightly as I could, she tried to fight back but it was pointless. Moments later I watched the colour disappear from her cheeks as she struggled to get free. I held my grip determined not to let go."

Tom tried to speak, but it was impossible. His throat was parched. Susie was in a trance. Without another word she got up and casually walked into the kitchen and he followed her.

"Susie…"

She interrupted him. "…That must prove how much I love you, Tom? Who else would go to those lengths?"

She could not have fabricated the story. It had to be true. There were no signs of remorse; in her mind it was a price worth paying to secure their relationship. She had not planned to kill Mary, there was no premeditation, but she had killed her, nonetheless.

Tom struggled mentally to take in her confession. He failed to terms with what she had done. He stared at her trying to fathom what to say next.

"But… you just told me that you murdered Mary. You murdered my brothers' wife… please tell me it is all a lie, some kind of joke?"

"I was not planning to tell you, Tom, but you needed proof of my love for you and now you have it!"

Tom had to call the police as soon as he could. She was clearly mentally unstable and needed help. He knew a nurturing approach was necessary so as not to alarm her. She had already attempted to stab him, and if she thought he was still intransigent, she might try again to kill him again, or even herself. After a short silence Susie turned and walked back into the sitting room and sat on the sofa. Tom followed like a lap dog.

"So, what did your Penny say when you told her I was having your baby?"

Tom was unsure what she wanted him to say. She had just admitted to murder and now wanted to change the subject.

Susie started to laugh. Tom's compassionate approach turned to anger.

"Why are you laughing?"

"I was lying, Tom. I am not pregnant, I never was."

If Tom was shocked by the revelation that Susie had murdered Mary, he was now completely perplexed by this latest admission. Again, he stared at her incapable of saying a word.

"I made it up to get you to confess to Penny. You see the lengths I am prepared to go to… I cannot live without you, Tom."

She threw her arms around him and instantly passed out. As he released her from his arms she fell back onto the sofa. She was unconscious and breathing erratically. Earlier, when she locked herself in the bathroom, she had taken an overdose of sleeping pills wanting to kill herself. Not because she had committed the heinous crime of murdering Mary, no, she was just unable to come to terms with Tom's statement that he loved Penny and not her.

Tom knew he could waste no time. He called an ambulance and twenty minutes later she was rushed to hospital, but he chose not to accompany her, telling the ambulance crew he would follow on later. He needed time to reflect on what Susie had admitted to and decide what course of action he should take.

He was in no doubt she murdered Mary; she could not have made it up. He also had no doubt that she had lied about being pregnant to get Tom to confess to Penny, and of course the ploy worked. Tom spent the next few hours in the flat in his own trance mulling over everything that happened. She was in hospital and would recover, but what next? Her revelations had changed their relationship forever, there was no going back. There was no way time would conceal the truth or allow Tom to wipe clean his knowledge that she had killed Mary.

Susie spent a week in hospital recovering from the overdose.

She knew her plan to plant evidence, suggesting Tom was having an affair with Mary, and that Penny was threatening to kill her if the relationship did not come to an end, seemed crazy to her now. She knew her misguided and ludicrous plan led to Mary's death, and there was no way of undoing the past.

During the week Tom had visited her on several occasions. He witnessed a change in her mindset. She had come to terms with her crime and knew her thinking was consumed by her relationship with Tom, and nothing else mattered. She had brainwashed herself into thinking her life was meaningless unless they were married. Now, she was remorseful. Now she accepted that she had lost all sense of reason and needed to face up to what she had done.

They returned to the apartment. Tom wanted to stay with her knowing she was still vulnerable, but she insisted he returned to the hotel where he was staying after Penny had asked him to leave. This was the first time she had ever turned him away.

During their conversations at the hospital it was Susie, with clarity of mind, who insisted that after returning to the apartment she would call the police and confess to Mary's murder. Tom who previously believed this was the only course of action, changed his mind. He saw a new and different Susie; she was truly remorseful and would carry the burden of what she had done to her grave; surely that was penalty enough? What purpose would be fulfilled if she were incarcerated for years, it would not bring Mary back.

Tom sat in his hotel room and reflected. It was his manipulation of Susie that led to recent events, and the hurt caused to Penny that would end their marriage. The sequence of events in the business, and his private life involving both women could have been avoided, had he not been a self-serving egotist. He believed he was infallible; that he could manipulate people, especially women, to perpetuate his deceitful lifestyle without recourse, but none of us is infallible, eventually our actions and deeds catch up with us, and now it was Tom's turn to suffer.

Two days later as he was finishing lunch in the hotel restaurant with a plan to visit Susie at the apartment, he received a call from Inspector Gale. Susie had voluntarily gone to the police station that morning and admitted killing Mary. Her plea was manslaughter. The following day she was charged with Mary's murder.

Tom arranged for his friend and solicitor Peter, to represent her. She admitted to the crime of manslaughter on the grounds of mental instability, but Inspector Gale had other ideas. He believed she was guilty of murder, and a court would decide her fate.

Four months later, the case went to trial which attracted a great deal of media attention. After a short hearing the jury came down in her favour of manslaughter and was handed down a six-year prison sentence.

Tom sat in court for the duration of the trial. Rod appeared several times and was there when the sentence was handed down. The brothers' never spoke. During the period leading up to Susie's incarceration, Tom had done a great deal of soul searching. He knew his affair and the promises he made to Susie were the catalyst for Mary's murder. He underestimated how vulnerable and needy she was, but not so much she would kill for him. If only he had known. Mary's death had also been the catalyst for his downfall. It triggered a sequence of events with Susie, Rod, Penny, the fire, and his financial liabilities from which he could not recover.

Tom regularly visited Susie in prison. As Tom's financial situation deteriorated, Susie insisted that he check-out of the hotel move into her apartment.

In the following few months, Tom suffered frequent anxiety attacks and was incapable of any attempt to resurrect the business or deal with his liabilities.

As Tom predicted, his insurer refused to settle the claim due to the non-compliant electrical system. All the assets he and Penny owned, including their home, the cottage, the yacht, and the three cars were liquidated to pay off debts. The apartment he now lived in which he bought for Susie to occupy rent free, was transferred into her name for when she was released from prison. Penny never found out about the property. The residue from liquidating Tom's and Penny's assets amounted to thirty-seven thousand, six hundred pounds, which was shared between the two of them. Tom refused to accept his share insisting Penny kept the proceeds.

Penny vowed never to see or speak to Tom again. She was forced to leave the family home she loved and stayed with Ginny and George until the affairs of the business had been reconciled, which took months. Tom did not contest Penny's demand for a divorce. After the divorce she relocated to Australia to be with her sister; she had not seen her for a decade.

In a bizarre twist, in the years that followed, Penny used the experience she had working for Tom in their business years earlier to get a job in a small privately owned publishing firm in Adelaide, owned by Andy Crane, a Canadian who had moved there with his parents when he was five. She proved to be an asset.

Within months of joining the firm, Penny and Andy began a relationship, and three years later they were married.

As Andy enjoyed running the business; the roles and responsibilities that Penny used to undertake for Tom, she discovered a flair for uncovering talented writers and distributors, the job Tom had at Taylor Publishing. She would often attend international book fairs and built a worldwide network of agents. Unlike Tom, she did not abuse her freedoms away from Andy. She was as honest and loyal as the day was long.

When she left for Australia, Penny left behind her closest friend, Ginny.

Once a year, Ginny and George travelled to Australia to spend several weeks with them. The marital rift caused by Angelique was put aside for good. George had repented; he was more than happy to for Ginny to take control of their lives. He had no desire for another affair.

Despite Tom's fears that Rod would drink and gamble away the money he had given him, he was shown to be wrong.

At first, Rod struggled with life. He was imprisoned for twelve months for breaking into the Mini Market and stealing whisky. A part of his sentence took account of his attempt to pervert the course of justice by accusing Tom of Mary's murder.

Being imprisoned was a sanguine lesson for Rod. He underwent a period of reflection, knowing he had to change his perspective on life if he were to have a future worth living after Mary's demise. He enrolled on a positive thinking and small business management course that gave him the confidence and skills he needed to earn a living on the outside.

Rod used Tom's money wisely. He paid off his debts and had enough left over to invest in a small newsagent, which prospered. Within two years he had three outlets, and within five years he had sixteen shops which he eventually sold for several million pounds. During that time, he met and married his second wife three years to the day after leaving prison.

She was an employee in one of the shops he purchased and proved to be the perfect partner, both in marriage and business. She was a steadying influence, giving him the confidence and motivation to make the most of himself. Her name, ironically, was Mary.

After selling the business, they retired to an old country house that required substantial renovation. Rod was not practical enough to undertake the project himself instead hired a team of builders to do the work for him. Just as they had settled into their newly refurbished home, Mary was diagnosed with cancer and six months later, she was dead.

Rod was devastated and alone once more. Two women named Mary had entered and exited his life and he loved them both. After she died, Rod sold the house for a profit and moved to West Wales, where he bought another run-down property waiting to be renovated. Despite struggling with mental health issues, it did not stop him becoming a successful property developer. He focused his attention on renovating old properties in the local area, bringing in teams to undertake the work. A few years later, he sold that business too, for many millions of pounds.

He was now a rich man, just as his brother had been building his businesses with grit and determination, but he had no one to share his life with and his mental health deteriorated further until he met a stranger in a local pub who introduced him to a much younger woman.

Agnesa was from Albania, a beautiful woman who spoke little English. He soon became besotted with her, and within ten weeks they were married. From the outset, she was insistent she should have access to all his bank accounts and other assets in case anything happened to him. Like a lamb to the slaughter, he agreed without hesitation. Now he had someone he loved who he could spend the rest of his life with, his mental health rapidly improved. Unbeknown to him, she started withdrawing large sums of money from the accounts.

She had been trafficked into the country by a ruthless narcotics gang to exploit wealthy widowers. Months later, after Rod discovered the deception, he confronted her, and told her to leave, but it was not that simple.

The gang members' intention was to extort everything he owned before he discovered the crime. Aware he had asked Agnesa to leave, the gang moved into the property and imprisoned Rod in one of the downstairs rooms. To gain complete control over him they drugged him daily with cocaine. It was a sizeable mansion in a rural location the ideal base to administer their elicit business.

Two months later, a gang member, by mistake, left his phone in the room Rod occupied, and in a moment of desperation, Rod called the only persons he knew that might help him. Tom. The brother he vowed he never wanted to see again.

One could be forgiven for thinking that after the trials and tribulations of Tom's recent life had been laid bare his story had been told, but not quite.

As Tom's world was collapsing around him, he was prosecuted for his driving offences and received a twelve-month custodial sentence in an open prison and was banned from driving for three years.

Tom served eight months of that sentence before being released back into society. During his incarceration, he began writing an autobiography.

Leaving prison almost penniless, Tom accepted an offer to join a small publishing firm, where he was able to use his talents to help grow the business. In contrast with his previous earnings, he lived on a modest salary to begin with, but it was enough for him to get by.

The business grew rapidly over the next few years, and Tom was offered a partnership. At that point, his financial prospects changed for the better.

Regularly visiting Susie in prison, and they became close again and upon her release she moved back into the apartment to be with Tom. Of course, it was now her property after Tom had transferred ownership to her.

Tom had fallen in love with her, but this time, it was not predicated on his desire for her as a mistress, but as a wife: the wife she had always wanted to be. Her passion and desire for him had not diminished, but her time in prison had changed her for the better. She was a stronger person and less needy. She had more self-confidence and self-worth and saw herself as Tom's equal, not his plaything.

Within three years, they married and had two young children, a boy, Tom Junior, and Georgia, their daughter. Tom was nearing his sixtieth birthday and Susie her fortieth. They had eventually found peace and contentment together, something that Tom could not have imagined on the day Susie was rushed to hospital after taking an overdose. The new publishing business was doing well, and Tom was earning a good living, enabling them to move out of the apartment and into a large house near to Guildford, near where he had previously lived.

Tom was in the kitchen with Susie when his phone rang. He answered it. Unlike the past, when he had dreaded the phone ringing outside of office hours, knowing it would be Susie or Penny and wondered how to extricate himself from yet another scrape, he was now at ease with himself. He had put aside his days of lust and mistresses. He was content with his life with Susie and the children and had few challenges.

"Hello, Tom Taylor…" In a whispered tone Rod spoke.

"Tom, it is Rod here…"

It had been years since Tom had heard his brother's voice or indeed had thought of him.

"Rod?"

"Yes, your brother…" Tom paused for a moment, unsure of how to approach the conversation.

"Yes, of course, Rod. How are you… why are you calling?"

Rod paused before answering. He was about to have a panic attack and as a result, could only speak with a stutter.

"Tom. You must… must… must help me, please help, help me!"

Tom was shocked. It was obvious Rod was either in serious trouble or a drunken stupor.

"What do you mean, help you? What on earth is the matter?"

There was another pause before Tom heard someone shouting in the background as the call ended.

Susie turned to him.

"Who was on the phone, Tom?" She cuddled up to him.

"Bizarre!"

"Not a mistress, I hope?" She had not lost her sense of humour despite all they had been through.

"It was Rod."

"What, Rod, your brother?"

"The same."

Susie's mood changed.

"What on earth does he want? I thought you were rid of him?"

At that moment, Mary sprung to her mind, and the fact that she had killed her. It all flooded back in an instant. She looked at Tom.

"I cannot bear the thought of seeing him and reliving the past!" Tom hugged her.

"It was definitely him. He seemed frightened or maybe drunk I am not sure. He could barely speak without stuttering." Susie was quick to respond.

"Drunk, more like. That is what he does when he is in trouble; he gets drunk and harasses you." She had forgotten that she had been responsible for him getting drunk and being arrested for Mary's murder. "Promise me you will not speak to him again if he calls; tell him we want nothing to do with him."

Tom was reflective. In the past, what Susie was suggesting would have been his instinct too, but for some unexplained reason, he sensed this was a genuine plea for help. In truth, he had not thought about his brother in years and would have been happy never to hear his name mentioned again, but this was different. Sufficient water had passed under the proverbial bridge to warrant knowing more.

The last thing he wanted to do was cause Susie consternation, but he needed to know why Rod was calling him. Tom and Susie had built a good marriage and were happy and relaxed in family life and wanted for nothing, but he needed to know more. Why had Rod called and ended the conversation so abruptly? He took a moment when Susie left the room to redial his number, but he failed to get through. Susie returned to the kitchen. Tom spoke.

"Look, darling. I have no idea why he called, and he is unlikely to call again so forget it." Later, as Susie was putting the children to bed, Tom's phone rang again. It was Rod. He spoke quietly and again struggled to speak coherently.

"Tom. Please, please help… help me. I cannot talk for long they will hear."

Tom knew this was a genuine call for help.

"Where are you? What is the matter?" Rod struggled.

"I am in West Wales. I live in West Wales. My address, my address is… The Manor House, Borth, Ceredigion…" Before he could complete the instructions, the call ended.

Tom scratched his head and put the phone in his pocket. He heard Susie in the background calling him to read a bedtime story to the children. He went upstairs and wondered if he should tell her about Rod's latest call. He decided it was best not to.

Tom was good at reading the children stories at bedtime. He was a great storyteller and would often dispense with the commercial books and make up his own tales. He thought of writing children's stories but instead decided, one day, to finish his autobiography. He spent twenty minutes with the children before they fell asleep, then went downstairs and joined Susie in the kitchen as she finished off the meal Tom had been preparing earlier.

"Fancy a G & T?"

Susie nodded with a smile but seemed quiet. Tom poured the drinks.

"Tom, I cannot think of anything other than Mary, she is just there in my head…"

With that, she started to cry. She thought she had left that chapter of her life behind her, but now with Rod's call, the past was flooding back to haunt her.

"My darling Susie, I really do not want you to worry or

think about the past. We both did some awful things, and we paid a heavy price for what we did. We must put all that to one side and get on with raising our family."

"But how can we do that, Tom, if your brother knocks on our door one day?"

"That will not happen, I promise you."

"But what if he keeps calling, how can we forget?"

"Seriously, you must not get upset. I love you to bits and nothing, and no one, will undermine what we have. I will not allow it. Please trust me."

Susie finished her G & T in one gulp and demanded another. Tom obliged and served up the meal, taking the plates into the dining room. He had a couple of minutes as he placed the meal on the table to think of a strategy that would hopefully remove her fears about Rod.

"Darling. Let us not talk about Rod again this evening, but before we dispense with the subject entirely, let me just say this. I know he is in trouble.

I have played over the brief exchange I had with him in my head; He was not drunk when he called. I think he is ill. It could be he is dying and needs my help. Despite everything that has happened between us as brothers, he is, whether I like it or not, still my brother. If he calls again, I will deal with it. You need not be involved. Is that okay?" Susie was still visibly upset but she managed a nod.

They spoke no more on the subject for the rest of the evening and eventually went to bed.

Fortuitously, Tom had planned to play golf the following morning with an old publishing pal on a course thirty-five miles away and would be gone all day. As he lay there in bed, he decided he would cancel the golf day and drive to West Wales instead, to the address Rod had given him. He had enough information to get him to the right area at least.

It would be a long journey there and back in a day, but it was doable if he maintained a pace.

The last thing he wanted to do was to deceive or lie to Susie. One of his commitments to her when they married was that he would always be honest, there would be no untruths, and they would tell each other everything, no matter how contentious a subject may be. But on this occasion, knowing how upset she was at the mere mention of his brother's name, he felt justified in keeping his plans secret.

He rose early just before the children stirred, sent a cancellation text to his golf partner, made Susie some tea, and packed his Mercedes four by four with his golf clubs so everything seemed normal. After a quick breakfast, he set off. It was 7.10 am. As he left the driveway, Susie and the children waved affectionately, and he waved back. Once he was out of sight, he programmed his phone sat nav and started the journey. There was no navigation system in the Mercedes, something he had failed to notice when he bought the car and would later regret.

The stresses and strains and the highs and lows of his life had been self-induced. He had allowed his ego to run roughshod over other people's emotions and as a result people had suffered in his wake, chief among them Penny and Susie. Time had allowed him to come to terms with his past, though, and he was now a reformed character in so many ways. He had a family, something he never thought he would have. He had taken his mistress, despite everything he had done to her, and her to him, as his wife, and they were blissfully happy. Mentally, he was in a good place, as he had forgiven himself for his fallibilities and now did everything possible to be a model husband and father.

So, it was inevitable that as he drove away, he experienced a feeling of stress that was familiar from the past. He had set his phone sat nav for Ceredigion, West Wales. It was a journey of just over two-hundred miles that should, with a fair wind, take four and a half hours to complete. If he were to return home without raising suspicion, he could not afford to encounter any delays in either direction.

He tried several times to contact Rod on the number he had but failed. He knew this epic journey could well be a complete waste of time, especially if Rod's call had been a hoax. Despite the odds being against him, and the history he had with his brother, he felt compelled to make the journey all the same.

As he made progress, he felt uneasy and drifted in and out of the memories he had with his brother, his business, Taylor Publishing, and Penny and Susie, right up to the point of Mary's death.

It started to rain heavily, significantly reducing visibility on the road. His journey would take him on the motorway to Bristol and across into Wales, where he would spend most of his time on 'A' and 'B' roads. It was a picturesque route across undulating terrain, woodlands, open farmland, quaint villages, stone walls, and slate roofed cottages. The further he travelled west, the more the pace of life perceptibly slowed. He was three hours into the journey when he stopped for coffee, to stretch his legs, and fill the car with fuel. It suddenly dawned on him that in his haste, he had not picked up the lead to charge his phone. The garage did not sell them. He wondered if there would be enough battery life in his phone to get him there and back.

A few minutes later, he was on his way again. It took him an hour to start his approach to Ceredigion, where he stopped a passer-by to ask for directions to the Manor House in Borth.

Throughout the journey, he wondered how Rod had ended up in rural Wales. Of course, he knew nothing of Rod's business ventures in retailing or property development. He just assumed he had wanted to get as far away as possible from his previous life and had somehow found himself there. He had no idea that Rod owned the Manor House and almost fifty acres of land. He thought he was renting a room somewhere on the grounds.

Tom expected Borth, and the Manor House, to be a few miles away but he was wrong. It was a further twenty-three miles and according to his sat nav, it would take forty-five minutes to get there. He became concerned. This leg would add an extra one and a half hours to the journey time, making it almost impossible to get back home before the children went to bed. Susie would wonder why he was late back from playing golf and would certainly call him. What would he say?

The past was repeating itself. During the days of Taylor Publishing, Susie would call or text him often, invariably at the most inconvenient time, wondering where he was. He became adept at lying or fabricating the truth; it was a part of everyday life. Now though things were different. He did not want to lie to Susie, or worry her unduly, but he knew that later in the afternoon he would receive a call and he would need a plausible story to tell her.

He got stuck behind a tractor; he became agitated. Time was marching on, and he still had another ten minutes to go. The road turned into a country lane and narrowed.

Eventually, he arrived at a T junction, where he saw a sign for 'The Manor House, Borth, pointing straight on. To his considerable relief, the tractor turned left. He then crossed into the lane and the Manor House came into view. It was huge and had obviously been the ancestral home of a very wealthy family long ago. It was nestled in woodland and surrounded by manicured gardens overlooking the sea. Again, Tom wondered what Rod was doing there. Where did he live on the estate? He stopped short of the entrance to collect his thoughts. He had no idea what he would say or do after knocking on the door.

The thought of seeing Rod again, if indeed he was there, did not instil a feeling of joy, but trepidation. He noticed several prestige cars in the driveway, a Range Rover, a Jeep, an Aston Martin DBS, and a BMW.

He parked his car outside the property boundary, as he got out, he mistakenly left the keys in the ignition. He wondered again if the journey would prove to be a waste of time. He walked twenty or so paces to the front entrance and knocked on a solid oak door. The door opened. A short, stocky man wearing sunglasses stared at him, but said nothing. He appeared to be East European. Tom thought he could be Romanian or Albanian. He said only one word.

"Yeah."

"Hi, sorry to trouble you. I am looking for my brother, Rod Taylor. Does he live here?"

"No, mate. No one here with that name." As the man went to shut the door in Tom's face, there was a commotion in the hallway.

"Tom, Tom is that you?" Tom wedged his foot in the door before it was closed and pushed hard. It was Rod's voice. The man responded by opening the door fully and dragged Tom into the hallway. Two other burly men appeared on the scene, one of whom was holding Rod. His face was drawn and pallid and he had aged enormously since Tom had last seen him at Susie's trial.

"What the hell is going on?" Tom shouted at the men.

"Tom, they are… they are holding, holding…" Rod stuttered as he had on the phone the previous evening. He was forcibly dragged into a room and Tom into another.

As Tom was being held tightly by one man, another spoke.

"Why you here? What you want here?"

"Look. I have no idea what is going on, but you are holding my brother against his will. What has he done?"

The man got so close to Tom's face he smelt his breath. His eyes were bloodshot. He stared at Tom.

"You answer my questions, got it?" Why you come here?"

"My brother called me yesterday and said he needed help…"

Tom knew it was not necessarily the best thing he could have said. It would only agitate his captors. His interrogator shouted in Albanian to the men in the room opposite, who were holding Rod captive. Tom was now able to distinguish the accent. A muffled response came back, had no idea what was being said. The man laughed in Tom's face, and as he did, his mouth opened to reveal a set of gold teeth.

"He lying you know… we his friends… his friends that help him…" Keen to know more Tom responded.

"How do you help him? Can you ask your friend to let me go?"

The man snorted and kneed Tom in the groin. As Tom dropped to the floor in pain his aggressor, who was the boss, left the room. Seconds later Tom could hear Rod being ruffed up. Rather than try to get up he decided to remain on the floor, believing that was his best option.

The boss returned and dragged Tom into the room where Rod was face down. Another man grabbed Tom's arm and jabbed a needle into him. Tom looked over and saw Rod's arm outstretched and punctured with needle marks. Rod was drifting in and out of a comatose state.

The men left the two of them on the floor and locked the door behind them. Rod's face was bleeding, he was unable to communicate. Tom attempted to stand but immediately fell to the floor. His mind twisted and turned, and loud noises beat a rhythm in his ears. The drugs were taking effect. Shortly afterwards, he passed out.

When he came to, he had no idea how long he had been unconscious. He was confused and in a heightened state of anxiety. Rod was sitting up, staring at the wall as though he did not have a care in the world. Tom spoke.

"Rod, what is going on here? Who are these people?" Rod looked over to him as a single tear ran down his cheek.

"They… they… are stealing every… everything I have… everything I own…"

Tom was even more confused.

"Do you own this property?"

"Yes… yes… I own everything… its mine… they… they stole…"

He had to draw breath. Tom wanted to ask a hundred questions, not least of all how he had come to own such a large property, but that seemed irrelevant at that very moment. Tom persisted.

"What have they stolen?" Rod tried again.

"I… I wanted a relation… ship. I… I was lone… lonely and met Agnesa… she is from Albania. I… did not know she had been… been trafficked here by them… they used her to… to get everything from me…"

Tom had heard of such things happening on news programmes, but never expected Rod would be a target. Tom tried to open the door, but it was firmly locked. He thought of Susie and the children. He knew in his current predicament, that was unlikely to change anytime soon, that it would be impossible to get home in time before the children went to bed, if indeed he was able to get home at all. He checked to see if he had his phone but remembered he had left it in the car. He needed a plan to escape, but he knew Rod was in a fragile condition and insufficiently mobile to get out without being seen. There was no way he could leave him behind.

A good hour passed, and they remained in the room. Rod had recovered a little, enough to tell Tom more of his story. He stuttered throughout. He told Tom about the success he had in buying and selling a small network of newsagents and the property development company. About his second wife, Mary, and her dying. Tom listened intently. He was astonished that Rod had built himself a mini empire; in fact, his wealth was greater than Tom's had been at the height of Taylor Publishing. Rod was a multi-millionaire several times over until the gang took over, but that was of little consequence in his current predicament.

Tom looked at Rod with a wry smile and said…

"Well done, brother. I can see I have a lot to learn from you!"

Despite Rod's condition, he smiled back, and several tears ran down his cheek. Those few words meant a great deal to him. He had always admired Tom's business acumen, although he would never admit to it, so this acknowledgement was all the recognition he needed.

Rod was in his mid-sixties, but he looked a good ten years older. He was scruffily dressed and had not shaved in some time and was in desperate need of a shower. It reminded Tom of the time Rod turned up at his house, drunk and dishevelled, threatening to break the windows in his Porsche, and the fight that had taken place on the driveway. Little had changed, but everything had changed.

Tom's thoughts returned to their escape, Susie, and the children.

It was late afternoon. He knew Susie would be expecting him home soon, but there was no way of alerting her or anyone else of their predicament. Rod had fallen into a deep drug-induced sleep. It was quiet. There were no audible signs that the men were in the house, at least close by. Tom had heard cars leaving the property but there was no way of knowing if anyone remained.

There were no windows in the room, so it was impossible to get a sense of anything. He assumed the gang would not leave Tom and Rod alone for any length of time.

Late afternoon led to evening and nothing had changed. Rod remained comatose. Tom knocked on the door and called out, there was no response. He knocked louder but again, no response. This might well be the only opportunity for them to escape if he could only get the door open. He had left his car in the lane opposite the house with the keys in the ignition. It was likely the gang would have taken or removed the car, but he had to believe it was possible that it would still be there, waiting for them to make their escape.

Tom banged his fist on the door. It reminded him of the time he found out from Penny that she had transferred the money into Rod's bank account, and in a moment of anger, he punched the wall in his study and grazed his knuckles. Looking around the room he saw a dining chair amongst a pile of rubbish. He picked it up and smashed it against the door. If anyone were in the house, they would surely be alerted? He repeated the exercise several times. It was a solid door and not about to fall apart. He smashed the splintered chair against the door handle and to his surprise, the handle broke off leaving the spindle exposed.

Rod was beginning to come round and encouraged Tom to find a pair of pliers, which he knew were in a toolbox somewhere in the room. A few moments later, Tom was turning the rusty spindle. He was in luck; the door opened. Tentatively, he looked out to see if anyone was visible, the coast was clear. It was the opportunity they needed to escape.

Rod could not travel on foot unaided, and Tom knew it. He decided he would go first, leaving Rod in the room. He would attempt to get to the front door, open it, and see if his car were still there. If his luck held out, he would check to see if the doors were unlocked, and whether the keys were in the ignition. Then, he would return for Rod and somehow get him into the car and drive off. At least, that was the theory.

He crept out and headed toward the front door. Once there, he turned the latch slowly. It squeaked and rattled as he did. Gradually, the door opened. The Aston Martin was still in the driveway, but the other cars had gone.

He saw his Mercedes in the lane, but were the keys still in the ignition? He ran to the car to avoid being noticed. The car was unlocked as he had left it, but the keys were missing. The gang must have removed them, but fortunately his phone and wallet had not been touched; he put them in his pocket and headed back to the house, taking the opportunity to glance through the window of the Aston Martin and to his surprise saw its ignition keys on the passenger seat. He quietly opened the passenger door and grabbed them, leaving the door open. It was this car they would use to escape.

Rod was standing shakily when he arrived back in the room. Tom said nothing there was no time to explain his strategy. He put his arm around his brother to support him, and partially dragged him to the door. At any moment he expected someone to see them. He tentatively looked out and when he was satisfied it was clear, he helped Rod into the Aston Martin, gently closed the door, and got into the driver's seat.

Within a minute, he had started the engine and pulled out of the driveway. At that moment, A BMW came into view with lights flashing. The gang had returned. Tom made a sharp left turn onto a dirt track, hoping, praying, it led them to freedom. He looked in the rear-view mirror and saw the BMW in pursuit. Rod was more animated than before and kept pointing forward. He obviously knew the direction they were heading.

The almost new Aston Martin was getting a rough ride. The dirt track narrowed, making it difficult to move at speed. Eventually, as the track widened slightly, they entered an area of woodland. It was less than ideal terrain for any car let alone a sports car. The BMW suddenly took a detour. Tom wondered if they knew a better route that would cut them off. Rod again insisted Tom continued in the direction he was travelling.

They lost sight of their pursuers altogether as they picked up another dirt track that took them to a swing gate. Tom hurriedly got out and opened it. The BMW's engine was revving somewhere behind them. With the gate fully open, he got back in the car and drove onto the lane in front of him and stopped dead. He had to try and call the police, but his phone battery was flat. Driving to the next village to seek help seemed the best option. He put his foot down and sped away.

Within a couple of minutes, the road had narrowed once again, and they found themselves behind a tractor. It was a single-track lane with no passing places. Tom checked his rear-view mirror and saw the BMW racing up behind him. Rod, it seemed had slipped back into a comatose state just when Tom needed directions. The lane widened and became a 'B' road giving Tom the opportunity to drive at speed and put distance between him and the BMW, but he lost control of the car and careered off to the left hitting a cluster of small trees.

Immediately, he put the car in reverse gear and revved the engine. They were back on the road; the car was drivable but severely damaged. As they sped away the BMW disappeared; Tom assumed they had taken another detour to get in front of them. The fuel gauge indicated the tank was almost empty.

It was almost dark, and it started to rain heavily. Minutes passed, the fuel gauge, as if Tom needed confirmation showed they were out of petrol. A signpost for Llandre, on the road to

Aberystwyth, was lit up in his main beam. Tom turned to Rod to tell him the news, but he was slumped forward in his seat.

There was no sign of the BMW. Finally, as they limped into the village of Llandre a petrol station magically appeared on the left-hand side. Tom pulled into a parking space and seconds later the engine stopped. Every drop of fuel had been consumed. Immediately, he turned to Rod and attempted to wake him up, but he was unconscious. By now, Tom was exhausted, and his heart was pumping. Magically, a police car drew up to re-fuel. Tom rushed over to the officers and explained the ordeal they had been through. Within minutes all local police forces had been alerted to look for the BMW.

Tom returned to the Aston Martin with a policeman who opened the passenger door to discover Rod was dead. Since arriving at Rod's house, Tom had feared for his and his brother's life. Of course, Rod had endured far worse and over a longer period. Twenty-four hours earlier Tom did not have a care in the world, and the last person on his mind was his brother, someone he had rarely if ever thought of since Susie's trial. Now, Tom was distraught and shed tears like a child. He was inconsolable. His only brother was dead, and that reality would stay with him for the rest of his life. Within twenty minutes, several police cars arrived on site including members of the serious drug squad. Later, Tom was interviewed and was able to call Susie.

At Rod's inquest, it was revealed he died of a cocaine overdose. His heart had failed. The gang were known to the authorities and had been under surveillance for some months, although they were unaware that Rod's Manor House was being used for drug and money laundering. The men were eventually tracked down; prosecuted and given life sentences. The police were also able to link them to several high-profile murders.

The drug and trafficking rings were disbanded, and tens of millions of pounds worth of drugs, as well as a manufacturing lab, were discovered at the Manor House. A network of dealers and couriers were also detained and served lengthy prison sentences. It was a major coup for the Welsh constabulary.

The inquest also discovered that Rod had changed his will after his second wife Mary had died, leaving everything to Tom.

From a handwritten note attached to the Will it was clear that Rod had always wanted to reconcile his relationship with his younger brother. He had always admired him, and it was Tom's gift of over six hundred thousand pounds that had allowed him to pay off his debts and start afresh with his first business venture, a humble newsagents shop.

Once the case had been closed, and probate was completed on Rod's estate, Tom received a legacy amounting to almost nine million pounds. With Susie's agreement, they decided to share Tom's newfound wealth with Penny. She was reluctant to accept Tom's gift, but Tom and Susie insisted. After everything that had transpired following Mary's death, Tom and Penny were able to mend fences and established a friendship between the couples that endured.

Rod's life had been a roller coaster ride. During his marriage to his first wife, Mary, he had been unable to motivate himself to work, let alone develop a career like his younger brother. He lacked self-confidence and found solace in blaming Tom for his problems. After Rod's death Tom took time to mourn his brother's passing and wondered what he could have done differently to bring the two of them closer. He knew it was a pointless exercise knowing the past can never change, we can only influence the future.

Tom took time to finish the autobiography he had always

promised to write.

His life was laid bare. He wrote about his marriage to Penny, his affair and eventual marriage to Susie. Mary's death, Susie's court case and imprisonment, Tom's imprisonment, the fiasco at Mary's funeral, Tom's business success and eventual failure, and finally Rod's remarkable business achievements and sad death at the hands of the drug gang.

A good deal of Tom's life had attracted local, national, and international coverage at the time. It was no surprise that following publication of his autobiography the book became an international top ten best seller, with royalties from book sales swelling his already substantial fortune. He was wealthier than he had ever been.

CHAPTER 15 – SIX YEARS LATER

It was a warm summers day, and the sun was shining brightly. Susie was in the kitchen, looking through the window watching Tom play cricket with the children. Tom was batting. He took a swing and hit the ball some distance as the children ran off to fetch it. In that moment, Tom clutched his chest, bent forward, and fell to the ground. Susie knew it was serious and rushed into the garden to save the man she had always loved, but her attempts were in vain. She was unable to resuscitate him. The children heard Susie crying out and returned with the ball to find their father dead. They were quickly inconsolable.

The results of the autopsy showed Tom had suffered major heart failure and died instantly.

At the age of sixty-nine, having just retired fully from the publishing business he had helped to build in recent years, Tom's death had come too soon. He had been doing what he loved, playing with the children in the garden. It was an uncomplicated end for a man who had lived a complicated, and in many respects, a flawed life.

Susie was devastated. She had lost the only man she had truly, deeply loved. A man for whom she had killed another human being.

Penny loved him too despite all that had happened between them. Even Rod, regardless of the chasm that existed between the brothers, had always held Tom in high esteem; although he would never have admitted it, until that fateful twenty-four hours they finally spent together. Rod's will, leaving everything to Tom was testament to the long-held admiration he had for his younger brother despite everything that had gone between them.

Tom's children adored their father. He could never be replaced. His sense of fun, his love of life, his generosity of spirit, his patience, and his love for them was unquestioned.

At Tom's funeral, several hundred people gathered for his final farewell. He had lived life to the full. He had more than demonstrated his talent as a publisher and, latterly, an author in his own right. His memory would never leave them.

The intensity of feeling Susie had for Tom remained within her until her dying day. She never remarried and lived to be ninety-two.

Throughout his life, Tom had lied, cheated, and wreaked havoc on the lives of those that mattered most, but they still loved him even though, like every human being, he was flawed; he was fallible.

THE END